W9-CDH-536

Brothers
Keepers

DONALD E. WESTLAKE

Brothers Keepers

M. EVANS AND COMPANY, INC.
New York, N.Y. 10017

M. Evans and Company titles are distributed in
the United States by the J. B. Lippincott Company,
East Washington Square, Philadelphia, Pa. 19105;
and in Canada by McClelland & Stewart Ltd.,
25 Hollinger Road, Toronto M4B 3G2, Ontario

LIBRARY OF CONGRESS CATALOGING IN PUBLICATION DATA

Westlake, Donald E
Brothers keepers.

I. Title.
PZ4.W53Br   [PS3573.E9]   813'.5'4   75-11831
ISBN 0-87131-193-3

Copyright © 1975 by Donald E. Westlake
All rights reserved under International and
Pan-American Copyright Conventions

Design by Joel Schick

Manufactured in the United States of America

9 8 7 6 5 4 3 2

AND THIS ONE IS FOR
BYRNE and GEORGE
FELLOW FIREMEN

Brothers
Keepers

ONE

BLESS ME, Father, for I have sinned. It has been four days since my last confession."

"Yes, yes. Go on."

Why does he always sound so impatient? Rush rush rush; that's not the proper attitude. "Well," I said, "let's see." I tried not to be rattled. "I had an impure thought," I said, "on Thursday evening, during a shaving commercial on television."

"A shaving commercial?" Now he sounded exasperated; it was bad enough, apparently, that I bored him, without bewildering him as well.

"It's a commercial," I said, "in which a blonde lady with a Swedish accent applies shaving cream to the face of a young man with a rather prognathous jaw."

"Prognathous?" More bewildered than exasperated this time; I'd caught his attention for fair.

1

"That means, uh, prominent. A large jaw, that sort of sticks out."

"Does that have anything to do with the sin?"

"No, no. I just thought, uh, I thought you wanted to know, uh . . ."

"This impure thought," he said, chopping off my unfinished sentence. "Did it concern the woman or the man?"

"The woman, of course! What do you think?" I was shocked; you don't expect to hear that sort of thing in confession.

"All right," he said. "Anything else?" His name is Father Banzolini, and he comes here twice a week to hear our confessions. We give him a nice dinner before and a nightcap after, but he's surly all the time, a very surly priest. I imagine he finds us dull, and would rather be hearing confessions over in the theater district or down in Greenwich Village. After all, how far can a lamb stray in a monastery?

"Um," I said, trying to think. I'd had all my sins organized in my mind before coming in here, but as usual Father Banzolini's asperity had thrown me off course. I'd once thought I might jot down all my sins in advance and simply read them from the paper in the confessional, but somehow that lacked the proper tone for contrition and so on. Also, what if the paper were to fall into the wrong hands?

Father Banzolini cleared his throat.

"Um," I said hurriedly. "I, uh, I stole an orange Flair pen from Brother Valerian."

"You *stole* it? Or you borrowed it?"

"I stole it," I said, somewhat proudly. "On purpose."

"Why?"

"Because he did the puzzle in last Sunday's *Times*, and he knows that's my prerogative. He claims he forgot. I imagine you'll be hearing the story from his side a little later tonight."

"Never mind anyone else's sins," Father Banzolini said. "Did you make restitution?"

"Beg pardon?"

A long artificial sigh. "Did you give it back?"

"No, I lost it. You didn't see it, did you? It's an ordinary orange—"

"No, I did not see it!"

"Oh. Well, I know it's around here somewhere, and when I find it I'll give it right back."

"Good," he said. "Of course, if you don't find it you'll have to replace it."

Forty-nine cents. I sighed, but said, "Yes, I know. I will."

"Anything else?"

I wished I could say no, but it seemed to me there had been something more than the Flair pen and the impure thought. Now, what was it? I cast my mind back.

"Brother Benedict?"

"I'm thinking," I said. "Yes!"

He gave a sudden little jump, the other side of the small screened window. "Sorry," I said. "I didn't mean to startle you. But I remembered the other one."

"There's more," he said, without joy.

"Just one. I took the Lord's name in vain."

He rested his chin on his hand. It was hard to see his face in the semidark, but his eyes appeared hooded, perhaps entirely closed. "Tell me about it," he said.

"I was in the courtyard," I told him, "and Brother Jerome was washing windows on the second floor when he dropped the cloth. It landed on my head, wet and cold and utterly without warning, and I instinctively shouted, '*Jesus Christ!*' "

He jumped again.

"Woops," I whispered. "Did I say that too loud?"

He coughed a bit. "Perhaps more than was absolutely necessary," he said. "Is *that* all of it?"

"Yes," I said. "Definitely."

"And do you have contrition and a firm purpose of amendment?"

"Oh, positively," I said.

"Good." He roused himself a bit, lifting his chin from his propped hand and shifting around on his chair. "For your penance, say two Our Fathers and, oh, seven Hail Marys."

That seemed a bit steep for three little sins, but penances are non-negotiable. "Yes, Father," I said.

"And it might be a good idea to close your eyes during television commercials."

"Yes, Father."

"Now say a good act of contrition."

I closed my eyes and said the prayer, hearing him mumble the absolution in slurred Latin at the same time, and then my turn was finished and I left the confessional, my place being taken at once by old Brother Zebulon, tiny, bent, wrinkled and white-haired. He nodded at me and slipped behind the curtain, out of sight but not out of hearing; the cracking of his joints as he knelt down in there sounded through the chapel like a pair of rifle shots.

I knelt at the altar rail to zip through my penance, all the time trying to think where that blasted Flair could be. I'd taken it Thursday afternoon, and when I'd changed my mind the next morning—felt remorseful, in fact—the pen was absolutely nowhere to be found. This was Saturday night, and I had now spent the last day and a half looking for it, with so far not the slightest trace. What on earth had I done with it?

Finishing my penance without having solved the mystery of the missing Flair, I left the chapel and looked at the big clock in the hall. Ten-forty. The Sunday *Times* would be at the newsstand by now. I hurried along toward the office to get the necessary sixty cents and official permission to leave the premises.

Brother Leo was on duty at the desk, reading one of his aviation magazines. He was the exception to the rule, Brother Leo, an extremely stout man who wasn't the slightest bit jolly. He was named for the lion, but he looked and acted more like a bear, or a bull, though fatter than either. All he cared about in this world was private aviation, the Lord knows why. Relatives from outside subscribed him to aviation magazines, which he read at all hours of the day and night. When a plane would pass over the monastery while Brother Leo was in the courtyard, he would shade his eyes with a massive pudgy hand and gaze up at the sky as though Christ Himself were up there on a cloud. And then, like as not, tell you what sort of plane it had been. "Boeing," he'd say. "Seven oh seven." What sort of response can you make to a thing like that?

4

Now Brother Leo put down his magazine on the reception desk and peered at me through the top half of his bifocals. "The Sunday *Times*," he said.

"That's right," I agreed. My weekly journey on Saturday evening to get the Sunday *Times* afforded me a pleasure even Brother Leo's sour disposition couldn't spoil. It—along with Sunday Mass, of course—was the highlight of my week.

"Brother Benedict," he said, "there's something worldly about you."

I looked pointedly at his magazine, but said nothing. Having just come from confession, my soul as clean and well scrubbed as a sheet on a line, I had no desire to get into an altercation in which I might become uncharitable.

Brother Leo opened the side drawer of the desk, took out the petty cash box, and placed it atop his magazine. Opening it, he scrunched among the crumpled dollar bills toward the change at the bottom, and finally came up with two quarters and a dime. He extended his hand to me, the quarters looking like nickels in his huge palm, the dime a mere dot, and I took them, saying, "Thank you, Brother. See you in a very few minutes."

He grunted and returned to his magazine, and I went off for my weekly adventure in the outside world.

✛

I have not always, of course, been Brother Benedict of the Crispinite Order of the Novum Mundum. In point of fact, for most of my life I wasn't even a Roman Catholic.

I was born, thirty-four years ago, to a family named Rowbottom, and was christened Charles, after a maternal grandfather. My parents having divorced in my youth, my mother next married a gentleman called Finchworthy, whose name I then used for a while. Mr. Finchworthy died in an automobile crash while I was still in high school, and my mother for some reason I never entirely understood reverted to her maiden name, Swellingsburg, taking me with her. She and I had a falling out while I was in college, so I switched back to Rowbottom, under which name I was drafted into the Army. It was simplest to keep that name even after my mother and I settled our differences, so Charles

5

Rowbottom I remained from then until I entered the monastery. So much for my name. (They never leave enough room on application blanks.) As to my becoming Brother Benedict, that all began in my twenty-fourth year, when I met a young lady named Anne Wilmer, a devout Roman Catholic. We fell in love, I proposed marriage and was accepted, and at her urging I undertook instruction to enter her faith. I found Roman Catholicism endlessly fascinating, as arcane and tricky and at times unfathomable as the crossword puzzle in the Sunday *Times;* and when my mother passed on shortly before I was to be baptized, my new religion was a great source of solace and comfort to me.

It was also a great source of solace and comfort a short while later, when Anne Wilmer up and ran off with a Lebanese. A practicing Mohammedan. "As a jewel of gold in a swine's snout, so is a fair woman which is without discretion." Proverbs, XI, 22. Or, as Freud put it, "What does a woman want?"

I suppose it would be fair to say I entered the monastery on the rebound from Anne Wilmer, but that wasn't the reason I stayed. I had always found the world contradictory and annoying, with no coherent place in it for me. Politically I disagreed equally with Left, Right and Center. I had no strong career goals, and my slight build and college education had left me little to look forward to but a lifetime spent somehow in the service of pieces of paper: a clerk or examiner, an administrator or counselor or staff member. Money was unimportant to me, so long as I was adequately fed and clothed and housed, and I saw no way that I was likely to attain fame or honor or any of the other talismans of worldly success. I was merely Charles Rowbottom, adrift on a white-collar sea of mundane purposelessness, and if Anne Wilmer had ditched me at any other time in my life I would surely have reacted like any of my ten million look-alikes; I would have been unhappy for a month or two, and then found an Anne Wilmer look-alike, and gone ahead with the marriage as originally planned.

But the timing was perfect. I had just completed my instructions in Catholicism, and my mind was full of religious repose. Father Dilray, the priest who had been my instructor, was connected with the Crispinite Order, so I already knew something about it, and when I investigated further it began to seem more and more that the Order of St. Crispin was the perfect solution to the problem of my existence.

St. Crispin and his brother St. Crispinian are the patron saints of shoemakers. In the third century the two brothers, members of a noble Roman family, traveled to Soissons where they supported themselves as shoemakers while converting many heathens to Mother Church. The emperor Maximianus (also known as Herculius) had their heads cut off around the year 286, and they were buried at Soissons. Six centuries later they were dug up again—or at any rate *somebody* was dug up—and transferred partly to Osnabruck and partly to Rome. Whether all the parts of each brother are in the same place or not is anybody's guess.

The Crispinite Order of the Novum Mundum was begun in New York City in 1777 by Israel Zapatero, a half-Moorish Spanish Jew who had converted to Catholicism solely to get himself and his worldly goods safely out of Spain so he could emigrate to America, but who then underwent a miracle in midocean, a vision in which Saints Crispin and Crispinian appeared to him and told him the Church had saved his life and goods so that both could be turned to the greater glory of God. His name meaning "shoemaker" in Spanish, it was the shoemaker brothers who had been dispatched to give him his instructions. He was to found a monastic order on Manhattan Island, devoted to contemplation and good works and meditation on the meaning of Earthly travel. (Crispin and Crispinian had traveled to the scene of their missionary work, and their remains had traveled again several centuries after their deaths; Israel Zapatero was at the moment of his miracle traveling; and the very concept of shoes implies travel.)

Thus, upon arrival in New York, Zapatero took a ninety-nine-year lease on a bit of land north of the main part of Manhattan, assembled some monks from somewhere, and built a monastery. The Order sputtered along, supported by Zapatero and by begging, but never had more than half a dozen monks in residence until the Civil War, when a sudden upsurge in vocation occurred. Just after the turn of the century there was a schism, and a dissident faction went off to found the Crispinianite Order in South Brooklyn, but that by-blow faded away long since, while the original Order has continued to prosper, within its limitations.

The limitations are many. We are still within the confines of the one original monastery, with no intention or hope of ever expanding. We are neither a teaching nor a missionary Order, and so are little heard of in the outside world. We are a contemplative Order, concerning ourselves with thoughts of God and Travel. There are at the moment sixteen of us, housed in the original Spanish-Moorish-Colonial-Greek-Hebraic building put up by Israel Zapatero nearly two centuries ago, which has room for only twenty residents at the most. Our meditations on Travel have so far produced the one firm conclusion that Travel should never be undertaken lightly, and only when absolutely necessary to the furthering of the glory of God among men—which means we rarely go anywhere.

All of which suits me admirably. I prefer not to be part of a large sprawling hierarchical organization, some monkish Pentagon somewhere, but feel more comfortable with the casual comradeship possible among sixteen mild-mannered men sharing the same roof. I also like the monastery building itself, its tumbled-together conglomeration of styles, the dark warmth of the chestnut woodwork everywhere within, the intricate carving in the chapel and refectory and offices, the tile mosaic floors, the arched ceilings, the gray stone block exterior: the whole giving the effect of a California Spanish mission and a medieval English monastery intermingled in the mind of Cecil B. DeMille.

As to Travel, I never did care much for that. I am perfectly willing to spend the rest of my life within the monastery walls as Brother Benedict, now and forever.

Except, of course, for my weekly sally to Lexington Avenue for the Sunday *Times*.

✢

I strode briskly down Lex toward the newsstand, brown robe whishling around my legs, cross dangling at my side from the white cord that encircled my waist, sandals slapping the pavement

8

with a double te-*thwack*. It was a beautiful crisp late autumn evening, the first weekend in December, perfect for a walk. The air was clean and chill, the sky was clear, and a few of the brightest stars could actually be seen through New York's aureole.

The sidewalks were crowded with Saturday night revelers; couples strolling hand in hand, cheerful groups in loud happy conversation. I returned the occasional surprised look with a smile and a nod, and strode on. Some evenings I was treated to passing witticisms from people misunderstanding my garb and thinking me merely an isolated nut, but those were mostly out-of-towners who did that; New Yorkers are used to weirdos on their streets.

There were no remarks tonight, though a sidewalk Santa ringing a bell over a charity pot did give me a wave, as to a colleague. I was dubious, but I smiled back, and walked on to the newsstand, where the newsy said, as usual, "Evening, Father."

"Evening," I said. Years ago I gave up trying to explain to him that I was not a Father but a Brother, not a priest but a monk. I cannot say Mass or hear confessions or give extreme unction or perform marriages or do any of the other priestly duties. I am the male equivalent of a nun: a Brother, as she is a Sister. But it was too fine a distinction for the newsvendor, who from his accent I took to be Jewish, out of Russia via Brooklyn. After a year or so of gentle corrections, week in and week out, I had finally given up and now acknowledged the greeting for what it was—a friendly salutation between merchant and customer—and let it go at that.

The Sunday *Times* is never a particularly small newspaper, but in the two months before Christmas it becomes positively engorged, reaching at times to a thousand pages. It has been my practice for years to stop at the trash basket just north of the newsstand and lighten my load by depositing therein those sections of the paper we have no use for in the monastery. (There was some discussion several years ago, led mostly by Brother Flavian, a true firebrand, that this habit of mine was actually a form of censorship, but that storm long since abated, mostly because it simply wasn't true.) The Classified sections go, of course, and all advertising Supplements, and Real Estate. Travel

9

And Resorts goes, since the *Times's* philosophy *in re* Travel is so utterly at variance with our own. (Brother Flavian's chief weapon of attack that was, till he admitted he himself wouldn't read Travel And Resorts if I did bring it home.) At the request of various Brothers, however, I do keep News, Sports, Book Review, Magazine, Week In Review and Arts And Leisure. Which, prior to Christmas, is armload enough for anyone.

And so I headed home, slightly lightened. As I walked tonight I reflected on how totally this neighborhood had changed since Israel Zapatero and his tiny band had first put up our building on a leased bit of barren land surrounded by farms and woods and small—but growing—communities. Zapatero would hardly recognize the place now, nestled amid the hotels and office buildings of midtown Manhattan. We are on Park Avenue between 51st and 52nd Streets, and the city has rather grown up around us. The Waldorf Astoria is two blocks to the south, the Manufacturers Hanover Trust Building is across the way, the House of Seagram is one block to the north, the Racquet and Tennis Club is diagonally opposite, and our other near neighbors include the International Telephone & Telegraph Building, the Colgate-Palmolive Building, and Lever House. We have been called an anachronism, our little monastery squatting amid all those high-priced high rises, and I suppose we are. But we don't mind; we rather enjoy the bustle and scurry of the world around us. It gives more meaning to our own silences and meditations.

I must say, however, that I am yet to become reconciled to the PanAm Building, jutting up out of Grand Central Station like the hilt of a bayonet out of some beautiful creature that has been stabbed in the back. Much construction has been undertaken on Park Avenue in the past decade or so, and while beauty rarely has seemed to have been a part of the overall intention, most of the buildings are at least clean and neat and inoffensive, like a bleached bone on the desert. Only PanAm rouses me to an un-Christlike irritation; but then, they have the wrong idea about Travel, too.

I returned home tonight without looking directly at PanAm— it is less garish yet more sinister after dark—and carried the paper to the calefactory, where the usual cluster of Brothers awaited its arrival. Brother Mallory, a former boxer and onetime ranking welterweight, had first call on Sports. Brother Flavian, the firebrand, was as ever pacing by the doorway awaiting the editorial page in the Week In Review. Brother Oliver, our Abbot, has priority on the News section, and Brother Peregrine, whose checkered career in the theater included both set design Off Broadway and summer theater ownership somewhere in the Midwest, kept up with his former vocation through Arts And Leisure. The Book Review was for Brother Silas, who had once had published a nonfiction book describing his career as pickpocket-burglar (all prior to his joining our Order, of course), and I myself kept the Magazine, with its crossword puzzle; my one vice.

Which meant that I didn't read Ada Louise Huxtable's column on architecture in Arts And Leisure until the following afternoon. The instant I did, of course, I went directly to the Abbot.

✛

"Brother Oliver," I said.

He lowered his brush and looked at me reluctantly. "Is it important?" he asked.

"I'm afraid it is." I nodded at his latest Madonna and Child —a bit darker in feeling than his usual mode, though Mary did have some sort of unfortunate smirk on her face that left the impression she'd just kidnapped the child in her arms—and said, "I wouldn't disturb you otherwise."

He sighed, and put down palette and brush. "Very well," he said. Stocky and white-haired and as gentle as any dishwashing product on the market, Brother Oliver was now sixty-two and had been Abbot since he was fifty-six. He'd taken up painting only four years ago, and had already filled most of our corridors with his Madonnae and Children, done in a number of recognizable styles and with a great deal of meticulous craftsmanship, but not very much talent.

Still, it was better than all those lumpishly leaded stained glass windows the previous Abbot, Brother Jacob, had constructed during his tenure and had caused to be placed in all the bedroom windows, eliminating at one stroke light and air and the view. (Those windows were now stacked in the attic, along with Abbot Ardward's matchstick mangers, Abbot Delfast's photo albums of the changing seasons in our courtyard, and Abbot Wesley's fourteen-volume novel on the life of St. Jude the Obscure. Space had been left up there for Madonnae and Children, though no one ever said so out loud.)

Even after putting down his palette and brush, Brother Oliver gazed wistfully at his painting a few seconds longer, studying it as though he would have liked to enter it, climb in and go for a stroll amid the broken stone columns in the murky background. But then he shook his head, turned to me, and said, "What is it, Brother Benedict?"

"This," I said, and handed him the paper, folded to the right part of the right page.

He took the paper from me, frowning, and I watched his lips move as he read the headline: SOME DISASTERS WHICH MAY NOT HAPPEN. His frown intensified. "What is this?"

"Ada Louise Huxtable's column," I explained. "She writes on architecture for the *Times*."

"Architecture?" He gave the paper a puzzled look, his painting a forlorn look, and me an almost-annoyed look. "You want me to read a column about architecture?"

"Yes, please."

He sighed again. Then, slowly and with much reluctance, he began to read.

I myself had only gone through the article twice, but the relevant paragraphs were already so fixed in my brain that I could almost quote them word for word. Paragraph one: "The struggle to retain the best of our heritage in the teeth of real estate interests motivated exclusively by short-term considerations of profit is an unending one. For each battle won or lost, three more battlegrounds appear, and the forces of tradition and good taste must hurriedly regroup themselves and hare off yet again. Today, we'll mention a few of the most recent combat zones where the issue still remains in doubt, and some others looming just over the horizon."

The succeeding paragraphs then dealt with a hotel in Baltimore, a Post Office in Andover, Massachusetts, a church in St. Louis, an office building in Charlotte, North Carolina, and a onetime dentists' college in Akron, Ohio, each of these buildings being architecturally or historically valuable for one reason or another, and each of them in current danger of demolition. Then, three paragraphs from the end, there came this:

"Right here in New York, yet another pair of landmarks are threatened by the trolls of mindless office-space expansion. According to Dwarfmann Investment Management Partners, this very active Manhattan-based realty firm is completing negotiations to purchase a parcel of land and structures on Park Avenue, in an area already saturated with available office space. The structures on the tract include the lovely old Alpenstock Hotel, with its interesting Teutonic treetrunk sculptured columns in the lobby, and the unique Crispinite Monastery, with its echoes of Spanish and Greek religious motifs. A DIMP spokesman has announced that these two buildings, each distinctive and in its own way irreplaceable, will be torn down in favor of a sixty-seven-story office building. There's still much that has to be done before the bulldozers start moving, and it's far too early to tell if this particular battle will be won or lost, but on the basis of recent real estate history, and DIMP's track record generally, the prognosis here is gloomy."

I watched Brother Oliver as he read, and I saw his face change when he suddenly understood what was being said. When he looked up from the paper at last, his face was nearly as white as his hair. "Dear sweet Jesus," he said, "they mean to tear us down."

"That's what it says. Are we really selling?"

"We?" He frowned at the newspaper again, then shook his head. "It's not us," he said. "It's not up to us."

"Why not?"

"We don't own the land," he explained. "We own the building, but not the land. We have a lease on the land."

"When is the lease up?"

He was looking more and more pained, as though a toothache

were coming on him. "I'm not sure," he said. "I suppose I ought to go check."

"Yes," I said. "Yes, indeed." The fact that Israel Zapatero had put up this building on leased land was mentioned in the small biography of our Founder given to each new entrant to the Order, but it had never occurred to me that we were *still* in a leasing arrangement. When I'd read that item about the sale, I'd assumed it was either an error or possibly some plan of Brother Oliver's that he hadn't yet decided to mention to the community at large. Now it was apparently something much worse; we didn't own the land we stood on, and our lovely old monstrosity of a monastery—our home—was perhaps to be torn down around our ears.

Brother Oliver was, if possible, even more flustered and dismayed than I. "I'll," he said, and dithered, and finished the sentence, "look into it right away." He started off, clutching the paper, then stopped and held the paper up, saying, "May I borrow this?"

"Of course," I said, and as I did so my eye was caught by a streak of orange on Brother Oliver's easel. That object in the tray, was it not an orange Flair?

Brother Oliver turned away again, hurrying toward the door. With sudden urgency, I called, "Brother Oliver?"

He stopped. "Yes? Yes?"

"Where did you get that pen?"

Bewildered, he frowned in the direction I was pointing. "Where did I what?"

"This pen." I picked it up.

"Oh. I found it, in the library."

"It belongs to Brother Valerian," I said.

"I was using it for the infant's cheeks. Are you sure?"

"Oh, yes. I, uh, I borrowed it from him, and then lost it."

"Ah."

"May I give it back?"

"Yes, of course."

"Thank you," I said, and we hurried off on our separate missions. I felt a great relief at having found the Flair after all—I would have been hard pressed to come up with the forty-nine cents to replace it—but my joy was tempered by my realization that at the very moment of discovering the Flair I had committed yet another sin; I had lied to the Abbot in saying I'd "borrowed" the pen.

Ah, well. Father Banzolini would be back to hear confessions again on Tuesday.

TWO

I'M GETTING SICK of that orange Flair pen," Father Banzolini told me.

So was I, but I said nothing. The confessional seemed
the wrong place for chit-chat.

Father Banzolini sighed. He was capable of the least
realistic performance of long-suffering I'd ever witnessed. "Is
there anything *else*, Brother?"

"Not this time," I said.

"Very well. For your penance," he said, and paused, and I
thought, *I'm going to get it now,* and he said, "four Our Fathers
and—*twenty* Hail Marys."

Oo. "Yes, Father," I said.

He trotted us through the Act of Contrition and the absolution,
and out of the confessional I went, to go kneel awhile at the
altar.

Two thoughts occupied my attention as I knelt there, plowing interminably through my penance: *"Hail,* Mary, full of *grace,* the Lord is with *thee,"* etc. Thought number one was my sense of relief that the incident of the orange Flair was at last behind me. Thought number two was curiosity as to whether the spiteful laying-on of excess penance was not itself a sin, which Father Banzolini would have to confess in his turn and then do his own penance for; and what penance would be considered excessive in *his* case?

"—pray for us sinners, now and at the hour of our death, a-*men."* Twenty. I stood at last, my knees cracking like old Brother Zebulon's, and I found Brother Oliver waiting for me at the rear of the chapel. "That was a very *long* penance, Brother Benedict," he said.

"I was meditating," I said. And oh, dear—was that a lie? Would I have to confess it Saturday, receive another excessive penance, on and on, world without end, amen? But I *had* in fact been meditating, hadn't I? It struck me as a gray area, and I suspected that, come Saturday, I'd be giving myself the benefit of the doubt.

In any event, the answer satisfied Brother Oliver. "Do come along now," he said. "I want you at the meeting."

"Meeting?" But he was already hurrying away, like Alice's White Rabbit, so all I could do was hurry after him.

We went to his office, a low-ceilinged wood-lined irregular room like something built inside a tree trunk. The diamond-pattern leaded windows looking out on the unkempt grape arbor in our courtyard—our grapes were scanty, sour and useless—bolstered this elves'-forest image, and so did the brown-robed monks already there, seated at the refectory table in the middle of the room. Three of them: Brothers Clemence, Dexter and Hilarius.

Brother Oliver took his usual seat in the carved-oak chair at the head of the table, and gestured me to the seat at his left, saying to the others, "Brother Benedict told me something yesterday that I want him to repeat to you. Brother?"

"Oh," I said. Public speaking is not my strong suit; I would never have done well in a preaching order. I looked around at

17

the curious and expectant faces, cleared my throat two or three times, and said, "Well."

The faces remained curious and expectant.

There was nothing to do but blurt. So I blurted: "They're going to tear down the monastery!"

All three Brothers jumped, as though their chairs had been electrified. Brother Clemence said, "What!" Brother Dexter said, "No!" Brother Hilarius said, "Impossible!"

But Brother Oliver, at the head of the table, was sadly nodding. "I'm afraid it's true," he said.

Brother Clemence said, "*Who* is going to tear it down?"

"Certainly not the Flatterys," said Brother Hilarius.

Brother Oliver told them, "Someone named Dwarfmann."

"That's absurd," said Brother Dexter, and Brother Hilarius said, "No one named Dwarfmann owns this monastery. It's the property of the Flatterys."

"No longer," said Brother Oliver.

Brother Clemence, who used to be a Wall Street lawyer before his conversion from the things of Caesar, said, "Flattery? Dwarfmann? Who are these people?"

Brother Oliver said, "Perhaps Brother Hilarius should give us the historical background."

"Excellent idea," said Brother Clemence, and now we all turned our curious and expectant faces toward Brother Hilarius.

Who was not at all daunted by public speaking. "Of course," he said. A humorless stolid phlegmatic man with a heavy flat-footed way of standing and walking, he was utterly unlike his name, but then so was the saint he'd been called after, who had been Pope from 461 to 468. Brother Hilarius, a onetime department store clerk, was our monastery historian.

Speaking now in a methodical monotone, Brother Hilarius told us, "Our Founder, the Blessed Zapatero, established this monastery in 1777, taking a ninety-nine-year lease on the land, which was then owned by one Colton Van deWitt. The Van deWitts daughtered out during the Civil War, and the—"

Brother Oliver said, "Daughtered out?" He looked helpless, the way he had the time Brother Mallory had suggested he do a painting which was *not* of a Madonna and Child.

"The line eventually produced no sons," Brother Hilarius explained, "and therefore the name ceased to exist. During the Civil War, ownership of our land passed to a good Irish Catholic family named Flattery, who have retained title to this day."

Brother Clemence asked, "Do we pay any rent?" A heavyset roguish man with a great unmowed field of white hair all over his head, Brother Clemence still looked like the expensive attorney he used to be, and he still took huge delight in argument for its own sake, the more nit-picking and the less substantive the better. He had been on my side in the great censorship controversy, more than once in the course of it reducing firebrand Brother Flavian to sputtering speechlessness. From the glint in his eye when he asked now about rent, I suspected he had some sort of legal trickery up his sleeve.

Brother Hilarius answered, "I wouldn't know. Does it matter?"

"In law," Brother Clemence told him, "unchallenged occupancy for a period of fifteen years endows the tenant with title."

Brother Oliver, echoing again the word he didn't understand, said, "Title?"

"Ownership," Brother Clemence explained.

"Ownership?" Brother Oliver's face lit with startled hope. "You mean we *own* our monastery?"

"If we've paid no rent for fifteen years," Brother Clemence said, "and if there has been no challenge in that time from whoever holds title, then it's ours. The question is, *do* we pay rent?"

"Not exactly," said Brother Dexter, entering the conversation for the first time. A narrow-bodied narrow-headed man with a permanent air about him of scrubbed cleanliness, Brother Dexter was generally believed to be next in line for the abbotcy, once Brother Oliver had been taken to his reward. In the meantime he was Brother Oliver's assistant, where his background—he came from a Maryland banking family—was a continual blessing in the balancing of our meager but messy books.

Brother Clemence frowned at him. "What does 'not exactly' mean, Brother?"

"We are required," Brother Dexter told him, "to pay an annual rental, every February first, of an amount equal to one percent of the entire monastery income for the preceding year. The Blessed Zapatero invested his remaining capital when the monastery was founded, and other residents have also turned over income which has been invested in the general behalf. Also, for the first hundred years or so a certain amount of begging was undertaken, but the investment program was a sound one from the beginning and mendicancy has been unnecessary since well before the turn of the century."

Brother Clemence, disguising his impatience very well I thought, gently said, "Brother, have we been fulfilling our obligations vis-à-vis the rent?"

"Yes, we have. We've been relieved of the necessity of actually paying over the rent, but in effect the rental situation remains intact."

Brother Oliver said, "I'm not understanding one word in ten. We don't pay the rent but the rental situation remains intact? Is that even *possible*?"

I was glad he'd asked that question, since I wasn't understanding one word in twenty-five, but I hadn't felt I should interrupt the flow of expertise. Now I squinted my eyes at Brother Dexter, the better to hear his answer.

He began with a sentence I had no trouble comprehending. "The Flatterys are rich." Then he went on, "They've never needed our rent money, so they used to return it as a contribution. But for the last sixty-odd years they haven't taken it at all."

"That's the part I don't follow," Brother Clemence said, and the rest of us all nodded; even Brother Hilarius.

"I was *trying* to explain," Brother Dexter said. Experts always get snappish when laymen are slow to understand. "Sometime before the First World War," he said, "the Flatterys sent us a letter saying we should *not* send the rent money any more, but should consider it a charitable contribution."

"Ah," Brother Clemence said. "I see. They don't forgive us the rent. We still have to determine the amount and collect it, but then instead of paying it to them we give it to ourselves."

Brother Dexter nodded. "That's right. And we send them a memo telling them how much they gave. Last year, for instance, their contribution turned out to be four hundred eighty-two dollars and twenty-seven cents."

Even in grade school I had trouble with decimal points. But I'd lived in this monastery for ten years and this was the first hint I'd ever been given as to how we managed to make ends meet, so I was determined to work it out no matter what. Our communal property was in "investments," and last year's income from those investments had been four hundred eighty-two dollars and twenty-seven cents times one hundred. Add two zeros—move the decimal point to the left—no, the right—forty-eight million dollars?

Thousand! Forty-eight thousand, two hundred twenty-seven dollars. Split among sixteen men, that gave us an average annual income of three thousand dollars. Not very much. Of course we did live here rent free—sort of—and we were exempt from property taxes, and our mode of life didn't encourage us toward very expensive tastes.

Brother Dexter, ever the banker, now added, "Our income, by the way, represented nearly nine point four percent return on capital investment."

No. That one was beyond me. Some people—Albert Einstein, say—might be able to figure out from that clue how much money we had in these mysterious investments, but not me. Casting all numbers from my brain, I returned my attention to the conversation.

Which Brother Hilarius had reentered, saying, "I'm no attorney, but if we aren't in arrears in our rent they can't throw us out, can they?"

"Not until the lease is up," Brother Clemence said, and looked around the table hopefully, saying, "Does anybody know when that is?"

"I can't find it," Brother Oliver said. He gestured helplessly toward our filing cabinet in the darkest corner, a cabinet I myself knew to be every bit as neat and organized as our attic and those grape vines out there. "I spent hours last night looking for it."

"Well, let's work it out," Brother Clemence said. Turning to Brother Hilarius he said, "You told us it was a ninety-nine-year lease. Starting when?"

21

"It was signed with Colton Van deWitt in April of 1777," Brother Hilarius told him, and through his normal stolid manner the pride of the historian briefly peeked.

Sounding startled, Brother Oliver said, "Then it expired a hundred years ago!"

"Ninety-nine," Brother Clemence said, and something in his voice sounded ominous. "The lease would have been up in 1876, and would have been renewed as of then."

"With the Flatterys," Brother Dexter said.

"And would have run out again this year," Brother Clemence said. "In April."

No one had anything to add. We sat there in a growing silence, looking around at one another's pale faces as we absorbed what was happening. Our monastery. Our home.

Brother Clemence at last broke the silence, if not the mood, by saying to Brother Oliver, "Well, I see now why you wanted a meeting." He glanced around at the rest of us, and I thought a slight puzzlement clouded his expression when his eyes met mine.

Brother Oliver must have seen that, too, because he said, "Brother Benedict was the first one to know about this. I wanted to keep this meeting small, just those who had to know or already knew. I don't want to tell the other Brothers just yet. I don't want to alarm them until we know for certain there's no possible solution."

Brother Dexter turned to Brother Clemence, asking, "Who owns the building? The Flatterys own the land, but who owns the monastery?"

"The owner of the land," Brother Clemence said heavily, "owns any improvements thereon. So the Flatterys own the building."

"Not any more," Brother Oliver said. "I called Dan Flattery today. It was very difficult to get through to him, but when I finally did he told me he'd sold the land to this fellow Dwarf-mann."

Brother Clemence said, "Then Dwarfmann owns our monastery."

"Dwarfmann owns our monastery," echoed Brother Hilarius. He said it with a kind of morose awe.

22

Brother Clemence said, "I'd like to see that lease, see the exact wording."

"I just can't find it," Brother Oliver said. "I know I've seen it in the past, but last night and today I searched and searched, and it has just disappeared."

"Then, with your permission, Brother Oliver," said Brother Clemence, "I should like to Travel downtown to the County Clerk's office. There'll be a copy recorded there."

"Certainly," Brother Oliver said. "You could do that tomorrow. Brother Dexter will arrange subway fare for you. How much is the fare now, do you know, Brother Dexter?"

"I'll find out in the morning," Brother Dexter said. "I could also call this man Dwarfmann and sound him out. He might be interested in selling the land back to us."

Now I had a contribution of my own to make, though not a very cheery one. "I doubt that," I said. "Even if Dwarfmann was willing to sell, this is prime midtown office-space property here and I'm afraid the cost would be far more than we could afford. We must have at least a hundred feet of sidewalk frontage."

Brother Dexter looked grim. "You're probably right, Brother Benedict," he said, "but we might as well find out the worst."

"And I," Brother Hilarius said, "will look through every scrap of history we have, to see if I can find anything at all that might be helpful."

"I knew I could count on you all," Brother Oliver said. "With you at work, and with the Lord's help, we might yet save our monastery."

I said, "And I? Is there anything I can do, Brother Oliver?"

"Yes, there is," he said.

Startled, I said, "There is? What?"

"You," he told me, "can write to that architecture woman at the New York Times."

✠

December 10, 1975

Miss Ada Louise Huxtable
The New York Times
229 West 43rd St.
New York, NY 10036

Dear Miss Huxtable:
I am writing to you in reference to the column of yours that you wrote in the Arts and Leisure section of the *Sunday New York Times* last Sunday, December 7th, 1975, to tell you that I am a monk in the monastery about which you wrote in that column, and to ask you if there is anything

December 10, 1975

Miss Ada Louise Huxtable
The New York Times
229 West 43rd St.
New York, NY 10036

Dear Miss Huxtable:
I am a monk. I am a resident in the unique Crispinite Monastery. You say that we are going to be torn down. We wonder if

December 10, 1975

Miss Ada Louise Huxtable
The New York Times
229 West

24

December 10, 1975

Ms Ada Louise Huxtable
The New York Times
229 West 43rd St.
New York, NY 10036

Dear Ms Huxtable:
   I am a monk in

December 10, 1975

Miss Ada Louise Huxtable
The New York Times
229 West 43rd St.
New York, NY 10036

Dear Miss Huxtable:
   I am a monk in the Crispinite Monastery on Park Avenue.
We did not know we were going to be torn down until we
read about it in your column. Is there anything you can
suggest that would help us from being torn down? If you

December 10, 1975

Miss Ada Louise Huxtable
The New York Times
229 West 43rd St.
New York, NY 10036

Dear Miss Huxtable:
   I am a monk in the Crispinite Monastery on Park Avenue.
We did not know our monastery was going to be torn down
until we read about it in your column. Is there anything you
can suggest that would help us to keep our monastery, which
is also our home?

We feel urgent about this because we just found out our ninety-nine-year lease is up.

Yours in Christ,
Brother Benedict, C.O.N.M.

Our monastery:

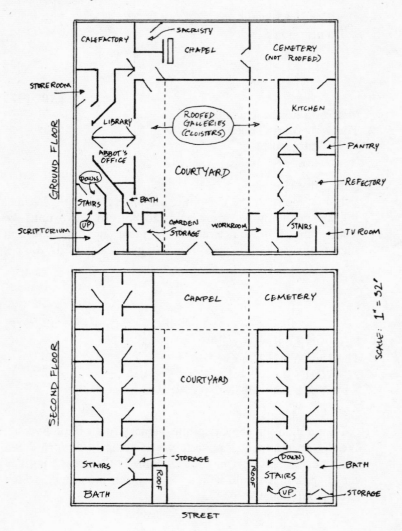

Wednesday's meeting was grimmer than Tuesday's. Outside the leaded windows, a gray December rain was raining. One of the other Brothers—I couldn't tell which, because his cowl was up against the rain—puttered at our grapes. Within, I was still twitching and exhausted from my hours at the community typewriter, and none of the others had anything pleasant to report.

Brother Clemence spoke first. "There's no record of the lease with the County Clerk," he told us. "I swear to you that when I expressed surprise at that, an ancient clerk there snapped at me, 'Don't you know there was a war on?' Meaning the Revolution. Most of New York City was held by the British under martial law throughout the Revolution, and many deeds and leases and other legal papers just didn't get properly recorded. A transfer of property would eventually have found its way into the records, but a simple rental doesn't create as many legal necessities."

Brother Dexter said, "But the lease is still binding, isn't it, even if it isn't recorded?"

"So long as one party retains a copy of it and wishes to enforce it," Brother Clemence said, "it's still binding. But I just wish I could get a look at the wording of the thing. Brother Oliver, still no luck with our copy?"

"I spent all *day* searching for it," Brother Oliver said mournfully, and the dust smudges on his cheeks and the tip of his nose bore silent witness. "I've searched everywhere, I was even in the attic. I went through every page of VEILED FOR THE LORD, just in case it had been put in there by mistake."

Brother Clemence squinted. "VEILED FOR THE LORD?"

"Brother Wesley's fourteen-volume novel," Brother Oliver explained, "based on the life of Saint Jude the Obscure."

"I've never actually read that," Brother Hilarius commented. "Do you recommend it?"

"Not wholeheartedly," Brother Oliver told him.

Brother Clemence, who was usually a jovial galumphing St. Bernard sort of man, could become a bulldog when his attention was caught, and this time his attention had been caught for fair. "I need that lease," he said, his heavy white-haired head thrusting forward over the refectory table as though he would chomp the

27

missing lease in his jaws. "I need to *look* at it, I need to see the *wording*."

"I can't *think* where it is," Brother Oliver said. He was looking the way I'd felt at that awful typewriter.

Brother Hilarius said, "Wouldn't the Flatterys have a copy? Why don't we ask to look at theirs?"

"I don't think so," Brother Clemence said. "I don't think it would be a good idea to let the other side know we can't find our own copy of the principal document."

Brother Hilarius said, "But the Flatterys don't own us any more, so what difference does it make?"

"That's not exactly the case," Brother Dexter said, raising a finger for our attention, and never in his life had he looked so neat and clean and controlled, though not particularly joyful.

Brother Oliver, who seemed to be getting closer and closer to some sort of distractive fit, said, "Not *exactly* the case? Not *exactly* the case? Do they own the land or not? Dan Flattery told me they'd sold it. Did he lie to me?"

"I'm sorry, Brother Oliver," Brother Dexter said, "but the only short answer I can give you is, 'Not exactly.'"

"Then give me a long answer," Brother Oliver said, and pressed both palms flat on the table as though our ship had entered heavy seas.

"I spoke to a Dwarfmann assistant this afternoon," Brother Dexter said. "Actually I spoke to several people in the Dwarfmann organization all day long, but finally this afternoon I got through to someone at an executive level. Snopes, his name is."

"This is a longer answer than I'd anticipated," Brother Oliver said.

"I am getting to it," Brother Dexter told him, exhibiting just a touch of that expert's peevishness again. "According to Snopes, they have taken an option on this land and on several other parcels of land around here."

"Option," said Brother Oliver. "Option means choice. You mean they're going to choose one bit of land and let the rest go?"

Brother Clemence said to Brother Dexter, "May I?"

"By all means," Brother Dexter said to Brother Clemence.

28

Brother Clemence said to Brother Oliver, "In law, an option is a binding agreement to make a purchase. For instance, I might say to you that I want to buy your, um . . ." Frowning massively, Brother Clemence ground to a halt. "You don't own anything," he said. He looked around at the rest of us. "None of us own anything."

"Perhaps I ought to try it," Brother Dexter said.

"You're welcome to," Brother Clemence told him.

Brother Dexter said to Brother Oliver, "Suppose you owned the chair you're sitting in."

Brother Oliver looked doubtful but willing. "Very well," he said.

"Suppose," Brother Dexter went on, elaborating his fantasy, "suppose we *all* owned the chairs we were sitting in."

Brother Oliver looked at us. I looked steadfastly back, trying to fix about my face the gaze of a man who owns the chair he's sitting in. Even more doubtfully, but just as willingly, Brother Oliver said again, "Very well."

"Now suppose further," Brother Dexter said, risking all at every step, "that I wish to own *all* the chairs."

Brother Oliver gave him an astounded look. "What for?"

Brother Dexter was patently stymied for just a second, but then he leaned forward and said, clearly and distinctly, "For purposes of my own."

"Yes!" cried Brother Clemence. He had obviously caught Brother Dexter's drift and was pleased with the structure under formation. Leaning forward to stare intently at Brother Oliver while waggling a finger at Brother Dexter, Brother Clemence cried out, "For reasons of his own! Personal private reasons! He has to own *all* the chairs!"

"That's the point," Brother Dexter said.

Brother Oliver, apparently at the point of despair, looked at him and said. "It is?"

"I have to have *all* the chairs," Brother Dexter said. "Just some of them won't do, not for, uhh, those purposes of mine. I need them all. So I come to you," he rushed forward, "and I tell you I'll pay you, oh, fifty dollars for your chair."

29

Brother Oliver twisted about to look at his chair, which was in fact a very handsome carved-oak antique. "You will?"

Brother Dexter was not about to get sidetracked into a discussion of furniture. Racing along, he said, "However, I explain to you that I can't use your chair *unless* I can also buy all the other chairs. So we sign an agreement."

"An option agreement," put in Brother Clemence.

"Yes," said Brother Dexter. "An option agreement. The agreement says that I will buy your chair for fifty dollars next Monday, *if* I have managed to conclude similar agreements with the owners of all the other chairs. And I will pay you five dollars now as an earnest of my intentions. With that agreement, and once you accept the five dollars, you can no longer sell your chair to anyone else, even if someone were to make you a better offer. If Brother Benedict, for instance, were to come along tomorrow and offer you a thousand dollars for that chair, you couldn't sell it to him."

Brother Oliver studied me in bemused astonishment. "A thousand dollars?"

For some reason I remembered yesterday's very long penance, which Brother Oliver had noticed, and I became very very guilty. I think, in fact, I blushed, and I know I averted my gaze.

But Brother Dexter wasn't going to permit that digression either. "The point is," he said, "once we sign that option agreement we are committed to the sale of the chair *if* the other conditions are met by the deadline. Being next Monday."

"I think," said Brother Oliver cautiously, "that some parts of this are beginning to make sense."

"Good," said Brother Dexter.

"Peripheral parts," Brother Oliver added. "But now, if you would expand your parable from chairs to monasteries, I just might be able to follow you."

"I'm sure you will," Brother Dexter said. "The Dwarfmann people—by the way, they seem to refer to themselves as Dimp, which would stand for Dwarfmann Investment Management Partners—so the Dimp people—"

30

Brother Hilarius, incredulity ringing in his voice, said, "The *Dimp* people?"

"That is what they call themselves," Brother Dexter said.

"Quickly," Brother Oliver said. "I feel it all slipping away."

"Certainly," Brother Dexter said. "The Dimp people have acquired options on several pieces of land in this area. The Alpenstock Hotel, for instance, and this monastery, and that building on the corner with the silver-fronted store. You know the one."

"I'm afraid I do," Brother Oliver said. The store in question, very Bauhaus in its facade, was called the Buttock Boutique and it featured ladies' slacks. When a member of our community did find it necessary to Travel, he almost always set off in the opposite direction from that shop, no matter what the destination.

"Well, these options," Brother Dexter said, "come due on January first. At that time, if all the necessary parcels of land have been acquired, the sales will go through."

"I don't understand about necessary parcels," Brother Oliver said. "If they buy one piece of land—or one chair, come to that— why do they have to have another one as well?"

"Because of the building they intend to put up." Brother Dexter did some crisp but unintelligible things with his hands on the table top, the while saying, "If they were to buy the land on either side of this monastery, for instance, but then didn't buy the monastery, they wouldn't be able to put up one large office building spreading over all their land."

"I don't like large office buildings anyway," Brother Oliver said.

"Nobody *likes* them," Brother Dexter said, "but they do intend to build one, and unfortunately we are on part of the land they intend to use."

Usually I preferred to keep my own two cents' worth out of these discussions, but an issue had been raised a minute ago and I wanted to explore it a little further, so I said, "Brother Dexter, are you saying that if they *don't* get options on every piece of land the deal is off? They won't buy the monastery after all, and they won't put up their office building?"

The light of hope shone in several faces around the table, but

31

not for long. Smiling sadly at me and shaking his head, Brother Dexter said, "I'm afraid it's too late, Brother Benedict. They already have all the options they need. They don't intend to close before January, but unless something unforeseen happens there's no chance that the deal won't go through." Turning back to Brother Oliver, he said, "Now you see why I said *not exactly* when you asked me if the Flatterys still owned the land. In a sense, they do, but the Dimp people have taken an option and will complete the purchase in January."

"I understand enough of it now," Brother Oliver said, "to know there's little comfort in it. The more I understand, in fact, the more depressing it becomes. It might be best not to explain anything to me from now on."

"There are a *few* thin rays of sunshine," Brother Dexter said. "When I told the Dimp man, Snopes, that Brother Benedict here was in communication with Ada Louise Huxtable, he assured—"

"Brother *Dexter!*" I said. I was truly shocked.

Brother Dexter gave me the crystal-clear glance of the true sophist and said, "You do read her column, don't you? You've written to her, haven't you? If that isn't being in communication I'd like to know what is."

Patting the table impatiently, Brother Clemence said, "We'll leave that to you and Father Banzolini to work out, Brother Dexter. What did this Dimp person assure you, after you'd name-dropped at him?"

"That the Dwarfmann organization," Brother Dexter said, "would make every effort to help us find satisfactory new quarters, and would also help to allay the expense of our moving."

"Sunshine?" Brother Oliver's voice was nearly a squeak. "You call that a ray of *sunshine*? How can there *be* satisfactory new quarters? If the quarters are new, they won't be satisfactory! Look around you, look around just simply this one room—where on the face of God's Earth would we find its counterpart?"

"Nowhere," Brother Dexter said promptly.

Brother Hilarius said, "And you forget the question of Travel. The process of Moving, the permanent relocation of not only one's self but also all of one's possessions from point A to point B, is the *profoundest* form of Travel."

"It's just impossible," Brother Oliver said. "The more one thinks about it, the more one sees we simply can't leave this monastery."

Brother Hilarius said, "But if they tear it down?"

"They must not, that's all there is to it." Brother Oliver had clearly brought himself back from the edge of despair and helplessness, and had determined to fight back. "Through the forest of your *not exactlys*," he said to Brother Dexter, "I seem to discern one tree. The land is promised to Dwarfmann or Dimp or whatever those tools of Satan call themselves, but until January first the *owner* of the land is Daniel Flattery."

"Technically," Brother Dexter said, "yes."

"Technically is good enough for me," Brother Oliver said. "Tonight I will continue to look for that missing lease, though I can't think what corners there are left to search in, and tomorrow I shall Travel."

We all looked at him. Brother Hilarius said, "Travel? You, Brother?"

"To Long Island," Brother Oliver said. "To the Flattery estate. Daniel Flattery was embarrassed to tell me the truth on the telephone. In person, perhaps I can turn that embarrassment to honest shame and put an end to this sale."

Brother Clemence said, "If there's already a signed option agreement, I don't see what we can do."

"I know very little about rich men," Brother Oliver said, "but one of the few things I believe about them is that they became rich by knowing how to renege on their promises. If Daniel Flattery *wants* to void that option agreement, he'll void it."

Smiling slightly, Brother Clemence said, "Remembering my days on the Street, Brother Oliver, I must say I think you have something there."

Brother Dexter said, "Would you want us to go with you? You wouldn't want to Travel alone."

"I would prefer a companion," Brother Oliver admitted, but then he looked around doubtfully and said, "But if I were to

33

arrive with an ex-banker or an ex-lawyer we might very well degrade ourselves to a business level, when the effect I intend to strive for is one of good strong Catholic guilt." He mused aloud, saying, "On the other hand, we five are the only ones in the monastery who know about this, and I still don't want to alarm the others." His eye lit on me. "Ah," he said.

THREE

RAVEL. The world is insane, it really is. I'd forgotten, during my ten years inside our monastery walls, just how lunatic they all are out there, and my weekly stroll to the Lexington Avenue newsstand had not been exposure enough to remind me. I had come to think of the world as colorful, exciting, variegated and even dangerous, but I had forgotten about the craziness.

Brother Oliver and I, our cowls up protectively about our heads, left the monastery at eight-fifteen Thursday morning, after Mass and breakfast and morning prayer, and turned our faces south. And the city struck us head on, with noise and color and motion and confusion beyond description. Large ramshackle delivery trucks rounded corners continuously, always too fast, always jouncing a rear tire against the curb, always changing gears with terrifying clash-grind-snarls in the middle of the operation. Taxis, all of them as yellow and speedy as a school of demented fish, were incessantly either honking their horns or squealing their brakes, the meantime jockeying for position like children hoping for the largest piece of birthday cake. Pedestrians of all sizes and shapes and sexes (including the dubious), but of one uniform facial expression—scowling urgency—elbowed along the sidewalks and raced in front of speeding cabs and shook their fists at any driver who had the temerity to sound his horn.

Why was everybody Traveling so much? Where was the need? Was it even remotely possible that so very many people had just discovered they were in the wrong place? What if everyone in the world were to call up everyone else in the world some morning and say, "Look, instead of you coming here and me going there why don't I stay here and you stay there," wouldn't that be saner? Not to speak of quieter.

Like babes in a boiler factory, Brother Oliver and I huddled close to another as we set off, Traveling south along Park Avenue. Scrupulously we obeyed the intersection signs that alternately said WALK and DON'T WALK, though no one else did. Slowly we made progress.

Park Avenue stretched half a dozen blocks ahead of us, as far as Grand Central Station, with the hilt of the PanAm Building sticking out of its back. We would be taking a train eventually, but not from that terminal; the Long Island Railroad connects in Manhattan with Pennsylvania Station, quite some distance away. Eighteen blocks south and four blocks west, slightly over a mile from the monastery, the farthest I had been in ten years.

We crossed 51st Street, jostled by hurrying louts, and I gestured to an impressive church structure on our left, saying, "Well, that's reassuring, anyway."

Brother Oliver gave me the tiniest of headshakes, then leaned his cowl close to mine so I could hear him over the surrounding din. "That's Saint Bartholomew," he said. "Not one of ours."

"Oh?" It *looked* like one of ours.

"Anglican," he explained.

"Ah," I said. The sanctum simulacrum; that explained it.

In the next block we passed the Waldorf Astoria, a veritable cathedral of Travel; not one of ours at all. At 49th Street the WALK–DON'T WALK signs were so displaced that we chose to cross to the far side of Park Avenue, a very great distance in it-self, the endless lanes of traffic separated in the middle by a grass-covered mall, as scruffy as but narrower than our courtyard. On the far side I looked back and could barely make out our monas-tery in the distance, huddled there like some ancient wood-and-stone flying saucer among the technological barbarians.

"Come, come," Brother Oliver said to me. "It'll be over soon."

✠

It wasn't. The walk to Penn Station was both interminable and terrifying. Madison and Fifth Avenue were even more crowded and bustling than Park Avenue—and narrower as well—and west of Fifth Avenue we were in Babel. The citizens had become shorter and stouter and swarthier, and they spoke such a con-fusion of tongues we might as well have been in Baghdad or an evangelist's tent. Spanish, Yiddish, Italian, Chinese, and God alone knows what else. Urdu and Kurd, I don't doubt. Pashto and Persian.

Pennsylvania Station was a different sort of nightmare. The Penn Central and Long Island railroads both terminate there, and the resulting furor was too blurred with frenzy for me to see it clearly, much less describe it. One rode an escalator down to the floor of the main terminal building, and as I descended into it the whole panorama looked to me like nothing more nor less than a fistful of ants scrambling in the bottom of an amber bottle.

Then we couldn't find the railroad. We found the other one with no difficulty, we found it over and over again: Penn Central to the left of us, Penn Central to the right of us, but where oh where was the blessed Long Island Railroad?

In the bowels of the earth. We commandeered a bustling main-tenance man long enough to be given hurried grudging directions, and learned we had to descend more stairs to a different kind of station. The transition was very like that from the east side of Fifth Avenue to the west; we had descended not only physically but also in caste. It was very obvious.

"Now I understand," I told Brother Oliver, "why Hell is always depicted as being beneath the surface of the earth."

"Strength, Brother Benedict," he advised me, and pressed onward to an Information booth, where we were given rapid-fire instructions *in re* ticket purchasing and train catching. There would be a train to be caught in the direction of Sayville in twenty-five minutes. "Change at Jamaica," the Information man rattled off, "no change at Babylon."

Brother Oliver leaned toward him, pushing his cowl back the better to hear what was being said. "I beg your pardon?"

"Change at Jamaica, no change at Babylon." And the Information man pointedly looked at the inquirer next in line behind us.

"I'm not at all surprised to hear that," Brother Oliver said, and I was pleased to see the Information man frown in bewilderment after us as we went away to buy our tickets. So it *was* possible to attract the attention of one of these dervishes after all.

✠

"In 1971," Brother Oliver told me as our train rolled through the industrial squalor of Queens, "Nelson Rockefeller, then Governor of the State of New York, declared the Long Island Railroad to be the finest railroad anywhere in the world. As of the first of November that year."

"Then I am all the more amazed," I said, "that anyone ever Travels at all."

The car in which we found ourselves was a sort of two-tiered slave quarters. One entered upon an incredibly narrow central corridor, lined with metal walls broken by open entrances to the cubicles on both sides. These cubicles were alternately two awkward steps up or two awkward steps down from the corridor, so that someone sitting in a lower cubicle was directly beneath the rump of the passenger in the next upper cubicle. We had chosen a lower, and huddled there like mice in an egg carton while the train rolled first through a tunnel and then through neighborhoods as grim as the imagination of Hieronymus Bosch. The knees and ankles occasionally passing in the corridor seemed calm enough, inured to this harsh environment, but I couldn't have felt more dislocated if I'd awakened on the planet Jupiter.

The train slowed. Brother Oliver, peering out the window, said, "Jamaica."

"What?"

"We change here."

Into swine? Into stones?

Into another train, across a concrete platform, where we found a more ordinary railroad car, with pairs of seats on both sides and no metal-walled cubicles. It was about half full, mainly with people smoking in violation of the posted sign, and it lurched forward almost before we'd found seats. More visions of Hell went by outside, but at least we were sitting in a space designed for human beings. That other car had affected me like an overly tight hat.

Neither Brother Oliver nor I had done much talking so far, both of us intimidated by the enormity of our excursion, but now Brother Oliver said, "I might as well tell you what I know about the Flatterys before we get there, little as it is."

I looked attentive.

"The one I knew best," Brother Oliver went on, "was old Francis X. Flattery. He would visit once a year or so to demand a blessing and some whiskey. He firmly believed we were all alcoholics, and wanted to take part in our binges. Would you remember him?"

"A skinny old man? With a mean mouth?"

Brother Oliver looked slightly pained. "My own description," he said, "might have been somewhat more charitable, but I believe you have the right man."

"I saw him twice, I think," I said. "In the first year or so that I was there."

"The family is in the construction business," Brother Oliver said, "and old Francis started coming around after his sons forced him to retire. Daniel's the oldest son, so he inherited us when Francis died—that would have been five or six years ago."

"Do you know Daniel?"

"We've met," Brother Oliver said, though not with much enthusiasm. "Two or three times I had to telephone him to come take Francis away. Then he did visit the monastery after his father's death, asking us to remember the old man in our prayers. He's a very religious man, Daniel, in a gruff blaspheming sort of Gaelic way."

"What about the rest of the family?"

39

"Daniel's the only one that matters," he said. "The rest don't count."

As it turned out, he could not have been more wrong.

✠

The cabdriver at the Sayville railroad station became much less effusive when he learned we merely wanted directions and not to hire his services. "Bayview Drive?" He shook his head, curling his lip like a meat inspector rejecting a bad roast. "It's too far," he said, "you can't walk it."

"Oh, I'm sure we can," Brother Oliver said.

The driver gestured almost angrily at his ramshackle cab. "A buck and a half," he said, "and you're there in five minutes, in comfort and convenience."

"Then we can walk it in twenty," Brother Oliver said gently. "If you could just point the way?"

The driver looked around the empty station. Our train had departed, there were no other potential customers, and a cold wind was gusting across the blacktop parking lot. Yesterday's rain had transformed to today's clammy air and heavy clouds. The driver shook his head in disgust. "Okay, *Father*," he said, and flung out one arm to point in a direction I took to be south. "You just walk that way till your ass gets wet," he said, "and then you turn right."

"Thank you," Brother Oliver said, and I had to admire his dignity.

The driver grumbled and muttered and lunged himself into the cab, slamming the door. Brother Oliver and I started walking.

The weather wasn't particularly pleasant, but our surroundings had improved tremendously since first we had committed ourselves to the Long Island Railroad. We had Traveled fifty or sixty miles through a seamless quilt of small Long Island towns until eventually there came to be bits of green, actual lawns and parks and fields and at last even some pocket parcels of woodland. This quiet town of Sayville was such an utter contrast with the frenzy of Manhattan and the industrial grime of Queens that I felt almost giddy. Those who Travel more frequently become

40

used to constant wrenching changes in their environment, but for me these swift changes—it was not yet noon—were like wine, too much of it drunk too quickly.

Our route now took us to a neat but very busy main business thoroughfare where a polite overweight policeman gave us more comprehensive and less offensive directions. He also assured us it was too long a walk, but he was obviously mistaken. A grown man in reasonably good health can cover perhaps twenty-five miles in a day, and the directions we were given led me to believe the Flattery house was less than two miles from the railroad station.

Which is a strange thing about Travel. People who do it all the time become enslaved to many false gods and absurd dogmas. The cabdriver and the policeman—and undoubtedly nearly anyone else in that town we might have asked—have grown so used to the idea of driving an automobile when engaged in the process of Travel that they have come to disbelieve in the very existence of other modes. Did that policeman live two miles from his place of duty? If he did, and if he walked to work every day rather than drive, he would be less overweight.

We are not capricious, you see, in thinking Travel too serious to be undertaken lightly. Overindulgence in Travel, as in other questionable activities, leads to weaknesses that are moral, physical, mental and emotional. Imagine a healthy adult thinking two miles too far to walk! And yet he would laugh at someone who claimed, say, that the earth was flat.

South of the business district we came on grander houses, set well back amid lawns and old trees and curving driveways. Occasional large loping dogs, dalmations and Irish setters and suchlike, romped out to study us, and one German shepherd trotted along at our heels until Brother Oliver had to stop and tell him firmly that he should go home, that we were not prepared to accept responsibility for him. He smiled at us, and went back.

Occasional cars rustled past us and we did meet one pedestrian, a tiny old woman who was talking to herself. She reminded me so much of old Brother Zebulon that I felt a sudden deep stab of homesickness. "Ahhh," I said.

41

Brother Oliver raised an eyebrow at me. "What is it?"

"Nothing," I said.

"We're nearly there," he assured me, demonstrating just how rapidly Travel can make even someone like Brother Oliver fall into error. I didn't want to be nearly there; I wanted to be nearly home.

Bayview Drive was aptly named. As we walked along it, we caught glimpses to our left of the Great South Bay which separates Long Island from Fire Island. The houses along here were estates, undoubtedly very expensive, and the ones on the bay side tended to have docking facilities at the farther end of the back lawn. Gleaming clapboard and weathered shingles combined here to create an aura of rustic wealth.

The Flattery property was enclosed by a spike-tipped iron fence, but the driveway gate stood open and we walked up the gravel drive to the house. No dog came out to welcome us, which was something of a surprise, but Brother Oliver's ringing of the door-bell produced almost at once a short stocky woman in orange pants and a woolly blue sweater who opened the door, took one look at us, and said, "Ah. Just one minute." And then, before Brother Oliver could say a word, she shut the door again.

Brother Oliver and I looked at one another. I said, "Maybe she went to get Daniel."

"It's very strange," Brother Oliver said, and the door snapped open again.

She was back. This time she had a large black patent-leather purse in one hand and a five dollar bill in the other. Pressing the bill into Brother Oliver's hand she said, "There you are, Father. Bless you." And reclosed the door.

Brother Oliver stared at the closed door. He stared at the bill in his hand. He stared at me, and a red flush began to creep up his cheeks from his neck, but whether it was a flush of embarrassment or annoyance I couldn't entirely tell. Shaking his head, he firmly pushed the doorbell again.

The woman, when she reopened the door, was very clearly annoyed. "Well, *now* what?" she said.

"First, madam," Brother Oliver said, "you can have your money back. Mine has not been a mendicant order for at least a hundred years, and I doubt we *ever* begged from door to door."

The woman frowned as Brother Oliver forced the crumpling bill into her fist. "Well, what on earth—?"

"We are here," Brother Oliver said, with a dignity that was becoming just the slightest bit frosty, "to see Daniel Flattery. *If we may.*"

"Dan?" The idea that anyone might want to see the man who lived in this house seemed to bewilder her utterly. "I'm Mrs. Flattery," she said. "Can I be of help?"

"I am Brother Oliver, Abbot of the Crispinite Order, and this is Brother Benedict. We would like to see your husband in connection with our monastery."

"Your monastery? *Dan?*" She gave a disbelieving laugh and said, "Put the thought right out of your mind. Dan in a monastery? I don't know who gave you his name, but they were pulling your leg. Dan!" And she laughed again, in an earthy beery manner I found rather unattractive.

"Daniel Flattery," Brother Oliver said, his voice trembling somewhat, "*owns* our monastery. We are here to talk with him about its sale."

"What? Oh, *that* place! The place in New York!"

"That's right."

"Why, I haven't thought about that place in *years*! Come in, come in!"

So at last we crossed the threshold of the Flattery house.

We had entered upon a rather bare front hallway, with a sweeping flight of white stairs leading away upward and a narrow wood-floored hall pointing straight ahead to a glass-paneled door with white curtains on its farther side. Two awkward paintings of weeping clowns hung on the side walls flanking the front door, with a nice antique writing desk under the one and a graceless grouping of brass hatrack, wooden chair and elephant-foot umbrella stand under the other. Past all this, archways on left and right led to rather dark and cluttered rooms, one of which appeared to be mostly living room and the other mostly library.

It was toward the library that Mrs. Flattery gestured, saying,

"Come in. Sit down. I *am* sorry I didn't know who you were, but Dan never told me he was expecting you."

Brother Oliver said, "He hasn't told you about the sale?"

"Sale?"

"Of the monastery."

"Oh, Dan never talks business with me." Having ushered us into the library, she now shooed us into matching tan leatherette armchairs. "Sit down, sit down."

We sat. Brother Oliver said, "I'm hoping to convince him not to sell."

That struck me as a cleverly oblique opening—attract first her curiosity, then her sympathy—but I saw at once it just wasn't to be. "Oh, I'm sure Dan will do the right thing," she said comfortably. "He has a fine business head."

Brother Oliver did not easily give up the ship. "Sometimes," he said, "a business head can make us lose sight of more important values."

"Well, I know you'll keep Dan on the straight and narrow," she said, smiling at the both of us. "I'll just radio him that you're here."

Brother Oliver, distracted from his doomed campaign, said, "Radio?"

"He's out on his boat, with some friends. I suppose he simply forgot you were coming." She sounded as though being indulgent of her husband's willfulness or waywardness was her sole occupation and greatest pleasure in life.

"Well, in fact," Brother Oliver said, treading delicately, "your husband *doesn't* know we're coming."

She looked surprised. "You didn't call?"

"I spoke with him on the phone, yes. But then I felt there was more to say and the phone wasn't the best way to say it, so I took the chance on coming out."

Mrs. Flattery frowned and pondered; I could see the movement on the side of her face where she was gnawing her cheek. Then she raised her eyebrows and shook her head and skeptically said, "Well, I don't know. If you think that's the way to handle him . . ."

44

"Handling" Daniel Flattery was obviously this woman's career. She was speaking as a professional now, and she was dubious of our method. Still, there was nothing for us but to go through with it, and Brother Oliver said, "I'm just hoping that in a face-to-face meeting your husband and I will be better able to see one another's point of view."

"You may be right," she said, without conviction. "I'll radio," she said, and departed.

"Brother Oliver," I said, when we were alone, "I am losing faith in this journey."

"Never lose faith, Brother Benedict," he told me. "We may lose battles, but we never lose faith and we never lose the war."

That sounded good but I doubted it meant anything, so rather than answer I spent the next few minutes looking at the Flatterys' books. The far wall, which one saw most prominently on entering the room, was filled with Good Books obviously bought by the yard: a set of Dickens, a set of Twain, a set of Greek playwrights, another set of Dickens, a set of James Branch Cabell, a set of George Washington's letters, another set of Dickens, and so on. The wall to the right was a veritable museum of recent trashy novels, all in book club edition but all with their dust jackets removed in the apparent hope that naked they would look older and more respectable. And the wall to the left was the no-nonsense bastion of a purposeful man: books on business accounting, on taxation, on real estate, books on inflation, on devaluation, on depression, books on politics, on economics, on sociology—and a biography of John Wayne.

I was looking at the fourth wall—religion, auto repair, gardening and physical fitness—when Mrs. Flattery came back, looking disheveled but undaunted. "So you'll stay for lunch," she said, rather more forcefully than necessary, and I guessed her radio contact with her husband had been less than totally serene. He had more than likely objected to his wife's having let us into his house, and she had more than likely informed him it was up to him to come back and do his own dirty work. At least, that was the little drama I invented for her current appearance and invitation.

45

Brother Oliver bowed politely and gave her our warm thanks and told her we would be delighted to stay for lunch. She nodded briskly and said, "That's settled, then. Dan won't get back for an hour or so, you'll have plenty of time. Come along now, I'm sure you'll want to wash up."

✠

Her name was Eileen. She was Daniel Flattery's daughter, she was at the most thirty years of age, and she had a black-haired delicate-boned cool-eyed slender beauty that would undoubtedly keep on improving until she was well into her forties.

She was introduced to us at lunch. So were her brothers, two stick figures named Frank and Hugh, and Hugh's stick-figure wife Peggy. And so was a callow, shifty-eyed, weak-chinned, silly-moustached fop named Alfred Broyle who was introduced as "Eileen's young man." I wasn't surprised to note the girl's lips tighten with annoyance at that description; of *course* he wasn't her young man.

These five, with Mrs. Flattery and Brother Oliver and myself, made up the luncheon party on the glass-enclosed slate-floored back porch. I had expected servants, but Mrs. Flattery and Eileen served the meal, while the unmarried son, Frank, was dispatched later for extra or forgotten items.

Mrs. Flattery asked Brother Oliver to say grace, which he did; I rather liked the way Eileen's full black hair lay across her cheek-bone when she bowed her head. Brother Oliver prayed:

"Almighty God, bless we pray this repast that has been prepared for the stranger as well as for family and friends. Bless the householder who has made it possible and keep him safe upon the bosom of Your ocean. Bless, we supplicate Thee, those who dwell in this house and safeguard them always, that they may never be forced naked from their shelter into the coldness of the outer world. Protect all Your children, we beseech Thee, and provide them with the food and shelter they must have. For this feast before us, we are grateful to Thee."

I thought all that a bit heavy-handed, but Brother Oliver had apparently decided to batter away at Mrs. Flattery's indifference no matter how Herculean the task. As to the lunch being a feast, that was hardly any overstatement at all. There were cold roast beef, cold ham and cold chicken, potato salad, macaroni salad and cole slaw, white bread and pumpernickel, coffee, tea, milk and beer. We sat at a long glass-topped table with chrome legs—wasn't Eileen's skirt rather short for this time of year?—and spent the first five minutes or so in happy confusion, passing trays and condiments back and forth. The sons and Brother Oliver and Mrs. Flattery all constructed great tottering sandwiches while the rest of us eschewed bread—well, I did chew some pumpernickel—and ate mostly with knife and fork.

I do drink wine and beer sometimes in the monastery, but I thought it better today, so far from home and so surrounded by new experiences—eating at a table with women for the first time in ten years, for instance—to limit myself to tea. Brother Oliver, however, drained his beer glass several times with obvious enjoyment.

I was on the side of the table facing the windows and the short-cropped lawn with its few large old trees and the gray waters of the Bay beyond. That wind-ruffled water looked cold, and I found myself wondering what might happen if, despite Brother Oliver's recently expressed wishes on the subject, something of a fatal nature were to happen out there to Daniel Flattery. Would his wife or these sons be easier to deal with?

I was skating close to the precincts of sin all at once, coming very near to desiring the death of another human being. I averted my gaze from the Bay, trying to distract my thoughts. Glancing obliquely through the glass top of the table I spied again Eileen Flattery's gleaming knees and the shadowed slopes curving away from them. I quickly looked at the remains of the cold ham.

Conversations proceeded around me. Brother Oliver was giving the history and physical description of our monastery to Mrs. Flattery, who kept interrupting him to urge bread or mustard or cole slaw on this or that guest. The sons discussed professional football. I'm a fan of the Jets myself, and thanks to Brother Mallory I know more than I might have about professional football, but the sons seemed uninterested in expanding their discussion group and so I remained silent, as did Peggy, the wife of Hugh. And Eileen was having a bitter argument with Alfred Broyle.

I might have noticed it earlier, except that I was sedulously keeping my gaze away from that end of the table. None of the others noticed it, being involved respectively in monastery-depiction, hostessing and professional football, except Peggy, who had neither a conversation of her own nor any reason to avoid looking at anyone. It was her interest in the proceeding that attracted my attention, and when I glanced toward the two at the end of the table she was looking coldly furious and he was looking mulish and sullen.

How her eyes glistened when she was in a rage. Her heavy hair seemed more full, her sculptured face more slender, her expressive hands more long-fingered. And as for him, he was looking so loutish I half expected acne suddenly to begin popping out on his cheeks like bubbles on cooking fudge. They *called* him Alfred, so what sort of man could he be? If he had any gumption at all he'd be called Fred, or even better Al, and he would *still* not be good enough for her. And as an Alfred?

As I watched—I know I should have looked away, but I didn't —the argument heated up. They had been exchanging tight angry remarks in low voices, inaudible to anyone else, but now he distinctly said, "You *would* say something like that."

She became audible too, but still more controlled than he. "That's exactly the way you were in Flynn's," she said.

"And whose fault was *that*?" His voice had risen sufficiently now to attract the attention of everyone else at the table with the exception of Brother Oliver, whose proselytizing for the monastery would brook no interruption. His narration, as though for an educational film, rolled on in the form of harmony while Eileen and Alfred provided the angry tune. "It was your fault, Alfred," she told him, "and if you had the brains God gave a gnat you'd know it was your fault."

"Well, I'm just not going to put up with it any more," he announced, and flung his napkin onto his place. "I don't know why you call me at all, you never like me when I'm here."

48

"Indeed I don't," she said.

He leaped to his feet, and it seemed for a second as though he might raise a hand to her, but one of her brothers growled—it was exactly that, a low warning growl—and the gesture died. "I suppose," he said nastily, "that was the way you talked to Kenny, and that's why you're here at all."

Her face pinched in, as though he had indeed slapped her. Neither of them said anything for two or three seconds—even Brother Oliver had trailed away to silence by now—and then Alfred Broyle ran from the room, going not like someone in triumph following a smashing exit line but like someone who has shocked and embarrassed himself.

Frank Flattery got to his feet, his intention clear, and his mother said with quick loud cheeriness, "Oh, Frank, while you're up, would you get the dessert? There's ice cream, dear, and Eileen made that pound cake."

It was a simple stratagem, but it deflected Frank. While he stood there, trying to make up his mind what to do, Eileen looked out the windows and said, with something very like sarcasm in her voice, "Well, just in time. Here comes Daddy."

✛

An enclosed motorboat, gleaming white and with green curtains on its small windows, had arrived at the small dock at the end of the lawn. It bobbed there in the churning water while a man came up out of the cabin, clambered onto the nose of the boat, picked up a coiled rope there, and jumped heavily ashore. He was stocky and meaty, with a big balding head and a heavy thrusting way of moving his body. He was wearing dark trousers and a black-and-white checked jacket, and as I watched he lashed the front of the boat to a metal projection on the dock.

So that was Daniel Flattery: he looked strong-minded. But even as I was thinking that another man appeared at the back of the boat, tossing another rope to the first man. This new one was dressed in a ratty green sweater and baggy khaki trousers, but physically he was identical with the first: heavy, powerful, fifty-ish, truculent.

49

And after the second rope had also been made fast yet a third example of the type put in an appearance, this one wearing a sheepskin coat and dark green slacks. They all got out of the boat, with a lot of apparent hilarity and comradeship among them, and then the trio strode in this direction across the lawn. Tweedledee, Tweedledoh and Tweedledum—and which one was Daniel Flattery?

✝

Number two, in the green sweater and khaki pants. The other two walked on around the outside of the house, with a great deal of hallooing and arm-waving as they went, and the real Daniel Flattery entered through a door somewhere away to our left. Banging doors marked his approach, as the sound of falling trees would indicate the approach of a bull elephant, and then he came into the room with the rest of us. Frank had seated himself again by now, both Broyle and dessert forgotten, and the family members greeted their patriarch with respectful if not overly warm hellos. Ignoring the lot of them, Flattery brooded first at me and then at Brother Oliver. "Well, here I am," he told Brother Oliver at last. "Come along, we might as well get it over with."

Brother Oliver and I both rose, but Flattery gave me a bloodshot glare—I suspected he'd been doing some drinking on that boat—and said, "Two against one?" Pointing at Brother Oliver, he said, "You're the Abbot. I'll talk to you. Come along."

Flattery turned and stomped out of the room. Brother Oliver gestured to me to stay where I was, and off he went in Flattery's wake. I stood at my place, feeling awkward, knowing that the family members were all feeling even more awkward than I, and then Eileen Flattery stood up and said, "Well, I'm finished anyway. Come on, Brother, I'll give you the grand tour."

✝

"No, no and no!"

Eileen and I had done the house and were out on the side lawn now when we heard that bellow in Daniel Flattery's voice. I said,

"Brother Oliver doesn't seem to be getting very far with your father."

"No one gets very far with my father," she said.

I hunted around for a response. "I guess not," I said, and yet again the conversation died.

It had been dying with regularity for the last twenty minutes. This was a social situation so foreign to my experience of the last decade that I could barely walk, much less talk. Strolling through a strange house with a beautiful woman—if riding a train through Queens had been for me as alien as being dropped onto the planet Jupiter, this new experience was outside the known universe entirely.

But my own cumbersomeness wasn't the only reason for our silences. Eileen was obviously still upset about the scene with Alfred Broyle at lunch, so much so that the tiny vertical frown lines in her forehead seemed almost permanent. All through the house, we would enter a room and she would tell me what room we had entered—"This is the kitchen," in a room featuring sink, stove and refrigerator—and I would describe it as very nice, and the silence would fall again, and we would walk on to the next room. Now we were outside on the lawn and she was pointing to trees and I was saying *they* were very nice.

I had made a few faltering attempts at general conversation but they had all, like this last one concerning Brother Oliver and her father, barely survived one exchange. If I did get a response from her on my first statement I had no idea what to do next, how to follow through. Thud. Silence again.

We were moving around toward the rear of the house. She pointed at a clump of tall slender white birches. "We planted those when I was ten," she said. "Those birches there."

"You've both grown up to be very beautiful," I said, and was so astounded and delighted by myself that I didn't even care that I was immediately blushing.

Eileen didn't notice the blush anyway; in fact, she hardly noticed the compliment. "Thank you," she said, with the thinnest of smiles, and pointed at a weeping willow. "That's a weeping willow. It was here when we bought the house."

51

"It's very nice."

We moved on, and eventually were at the very end of the lawn, where the water lapped at a retaining wall of gray vertical wooden planks. "That's my father's boat."

I took a deep breath. "You ought to stay away from Alfred Broyle," I said.

She looked at me with amused astonishment. "I what?"

"I'm sorry. I wasn't going to say anything, and then I . . ." I waved my arms around and looked out at the Bay. "That's the Bay, isn't it?"

"What's the matter with Alfred?"

"Well, for one thing he's called Alfred."

Peripheral vision can be a cruel thing; even though I wasn't looking directly at her I could see her condescending smile. "Should I call him Al?"

"Nobody can call him Al," I said. "If they could, he'd be a different man."

Did peripheral vision lie, or did her expression change to one of surprised recognition? No, peripheral vision did not lie. She said, "How right you are."

"And I don't like his moustache."

"Neither do I."

I looked fully at her, and she was smiling, but the smile was friendly now and not patronizing. "It's a very weak moustache," I said.

"It suits him," she said.

"That's the problem."

"So it is."

"Brother *Behnnn*-edict!"

I turned, and Brother Oliver was just outside the back door of the house, waving at me. "Oh," I said. "I have to go."

She touched my arm, a cool but friendly touch. "Thank you," she said, "for taking an interest."

"It was hard not to," I said, returning her smile, "under the circumstances."

"Brother *Behnnn*-edict!"

"You've made up my mind for me," she said. "From this moment, Alfred is out of my life."

52

"Good," I said. "It was a pleasure to meet you, Miss Flattery."

"Mrs. Bone," she said.

I stared at her. "What?"

She leaned close to me, deviltry in her eyes, and with unholy glee she whispered, *"I'm divorced!"*

"Oh." And I was so astounded that I couldn't think of another word to say. The "Kenny" mentioned by Alfred as his closing remark, that must have been the husband. Kenneth Bone. Another stupid name. I decided I didn't like him. If this girl, a good and beautiful Irish Catholic girl from a good Catholic home, had found it necessary to divorce him, there had to be something really drastically wrong with him.

"Brother Benedict!"

"I have to go. Good-bye, Muh-Mi-Mi—"

"Eileen," she suggested.

"Eileen. Good-bye, Eileen."

"Good-bye, Brother Benedict."

I could feel her smiling eyes on me as I hurried back across the lawn to Brother Oliver, who was in a foul mood. "That took long enough," he said. "Ready to give up your vows, Brother?"

"Oh, Brother Oliver," I said. "Flattery wouldn't change his mind?"

Almost at once his manner thawed. "You're right," he said. "I'm upset at Flattery, not at you. But do come along now."

We walked around the house, rather than through it. I said, "Is there no hope at all?"

"We'll see," he said, though without much confidence. "There's always Dwarfmann."

FOUR

ROTHER OLIVER," I asked the next day, as we were preparing to leave the monastery, "can a dream be a sin?"

He was brooding deeply on problems of his own—mostly, I suppose, his failure yesterday with Daniel Flattery and the anticipated meeting this afternoon at the Dwarfmann offices—and he frowned at me for some time in complete incomprehension before saying, "What? *What?*"

"What I mean is," I explained, "say there's an action that's a sin if you were to do it in real life. And it would be a sin of intent if you did it in a purposeful fantasy. But if it happens in a dream? Is that a sin? And if it is, what kind of sin is it?"

"Brother Benedict," he said, "I haven't the vaguest idea what you think you're talking about."

"I do have the vaguest idea," I said. "That's all I have, the vaguest idea."

"I think you ought to ask that question, whatever it was, of Father Banzolini when he comes to hear confessions tomorrow night."

"I suppose so," I said. And what a sigh Father Banzolini would produce when I asked him—I could hear it already. Or was that me sighing?

"Are you ready to go, Brother Benedict?"

"Not really," I said. "But as much as I'll ever be."

"Brother Benedict," he said, with a kind of paternal impatience, "don't you think I know how you feel? Don't you think I myself would rather be back to my painting, and not have to Travel Travel Travel all the time?"

No, I did not. My own personal feeling was that Brother Oliver was getting a secret thrill out of all this Travel, that he had adjusted very quickly yesterday to the outside world, that he had enjoyed the journey back from Long Island even more than the journey out—despite the failure of our mission—and that he was positively looking forward to the Travel aspect of today's expedition. I had seen him yesterday slip that Long Island Railroad timetable inside his robe. The retaining of souvenirs is the surest sign of a luxuriating relationship with Travel. In my opinion, that incomplete Madonna and Child figured in Brother Oliver's current thoughts not at all.

None of which I said aloud, just as I had not made any mention yesterday of my having noticed the timetable disappear. I contented myself with an ambiguous but not actually rebellious shrug, and I said, "Well, I suppose we might as well get going."

And so we went. Out to the courtyard, where Brother Leo was frowning upward at a passing airplane as though uncertain whether or not it was one of ours, and then through the great oak door and once again into the rapids of the teeming world.

But though I went quietly, inside I was mutinous. It was bad enough that Brother Oliver was secretly enjoying all this Travel, and it was certainly bad enough that my first experience with Travel since joining the Order should have presented my mind with so many utterly indigestible experiences. What made it all so much worse was the knowledge that I shouldn't be going through all this in the first place. I wasn't one of Brother Oliver's close associates, one of that small group who actually ran things here— Brothers Dexter and Clement and Hilarius filled those roles—and the only reason I was involved in this at all was that I'd been the one to notice our monastery's name in the newspaper. That was the *only* reason.

Now, that could have happened to anybody. Brother Peregrine, our former Off Broadway set designer and summer theater owner, had been the first to read Arts And Leisure. If his interests had only expanded to include arts other than those involved with the stage he might have read the architecture column himself and now *he* would be the one Traipsing around the world and giving love-life advice to beautiful women. Brother Hilarius, whose historical interests had led him by capillary action into the areas of coins and stamps, both of which are also covered in Arts And Leisure, had been another to read that section of the paper before it reached me, and *he* might have been the one to see the item. In fact Brother Valerian, he of the infamous orange Flair pen, one of whose great pleasures in life was reading panning reviews of gallery openings, had himself seen that section ahead of me. If any one of them had looked at the architecture column, any *one* of them, I would not be on my way out of the monastery today, I would not have taken those train rides yesterday, and I would not have had Eileen Flattery introduced into my calm and contented life.

I couldn't help thinking, as we closed the monastery door behind us once again, of Proverbs XXVII, 8: "As a bird that wandereth from her nest, so is a man that wandereth from his place." Or, as Shakespeare put it in *As You Like It*, "When I was at home, I was in a better place."

Well. At least the weather today was better than it had been recently. The clouds and clamminess had gone, leaving a royal blue sky and crisp sunlit air, the kind of weather still just possible now in mid-December. If one *had* to Travel, this was certainly the weather for it.

And the time of day. Yesterday we had started out during the morning rush hour, and so had been immersed from the outset

56

in a whirlpool of rushing men and women. Today we were leaving at two in the afternoon, and the slackening in urgent energy was very noticeable. There were still far too many people and cars and cabs and buses and trucks, and most of them were still going too fast, but the desperate and terrifying edge was gone. The driver of a florist's delivery truck parked in front of the monastery was actually nodding over a newspaper propped on his steering wheel, as though he were napping beside some rural stream, and the majority of his fellow citizens seemed to be rushing now out of habit rather than need.

Our journey today would be entirely on foot. We crossed Park Avenue at the corner and walked west on 51st Street. In the block between Madison and Fifth Avenues we walked with St. Patrick's Cathedral on our left—definitely one of ours. Though in fact it is really more brave front than working church, since its parishioners total less than three hundred souls. No one lives in midtown Manhattan, you see; the people have all been driven away to make space for office buildings.

After Fifth Avenue we moved through Rockefeller Center, a cathedral to money containing many little chapels to Travel. At Sixth Avenue we turned left past the American Metal Climax Building—I'm not sure whether my finding that name funny is an offense against the Sixth Commandment or not—then walked three blocks past Radio City Music Hall, the Time-Life Building, the RCA Building, the Standard Oil Building and the U S Rubber Building to the Solinex Building. "What a lot of Buildings there are," I said. "And yet they want more."

"It's an edifice complex," Brother Oliver explained.

I pretended I hadn't heard him.

✠

The Solinex Building was one rectangle repeated seven million times. In glass, in chrome, and in what might have been but probably was not stone. It was set back from the public sidewalk, leaving space for a fountain with a statue in it. The statue was an abstract, but seemed to represent a one-winged airplane with measles which had just missed its landing on an aircraft carrier and was diving nose-first into the ocean. At least that's the way it looked to me.

Apparently it looked otherwise to Brother Oliver. "Lot's wife," he commented as we went by.

Inside the building, different banks of elevators went to different groups of floors. "We want the fifty-seventh floor," Brother Oliver said, and pointed. "One of those elevators over there."

"That sounds very high," I said, following him.

He frowned at me. "Do you get nosebleeds?"

"I have no idea."

Bland music played in the elevator, which had imitation wood-grained walls and which we shared with several other people. The three chattering gum-chewing girls got off at 51, the bent old man carrying a manila envelope almost as big as himself got off at 54, and the two neat wind-up Japanese gentlemen got off at 56. At 57, Brother Oliver and I stepped out onto pale green carpeting defining a large space containing a receptionist's desk and a waiting area with red leatherette sofas. Great red letters on the wall behind and above the receptionist spelled out DIMP.

Brother Oliver gave our names to the receptionist, who had a reserved manner and an English accent, and she did some things with a very complicated telephone console before telling us, "Have a seat over there. Mr. Snopes' secretary will be right out."

The red sofas were Danish in style, minimal in construction and uncomfortable to sit upon. White formica tables amid them contained copies of *Forbes* magazine and *Business Week* and several real estate trade journals and something called *Travel And Leisure,* which turned out to be a magazine for American Express credit card users. The enjoyment and personal satisfaction to be found in such places as Bangkok was described. Brother Oliver chose that to leaf through—I made no comment—and I glanced at *Business Week,* a magazine I'd never seen before. I soon noticed they had a tendency to use the word "aggressive" to describe activity of which they approved. Another form of behavior they felt positive about was belt-tightening. As I continued to read, it seemed to me that all American business was divided into two camps, those who were aggressive and those

58

who tightened their belts, and that *Business Week,* unable to choose the better from the worse, had given its unqualified blessing to both.

"Brother Oliver?" It was the same English accent as that of the receptionist, but here combined with a softer voice and a more friendly-seeming girl. At her call, we set aside our magazines, got to our feet, and followed her through a door, down a long cream corridor decorated with poster-size black-and-white photographs of tall buildings, and into a very large room dominated by two sweeping walls of windows. Outside the windows were the fifty-seventh floors of other buildings. Inside was a wood-veneered desk the size of a backyard swimming pool and the shape of a lima bean, along with a forest of potted plants ranging from one to four feet in height, two large building models on their own tables, and a thin swarthy hawk-faced man who came around the end of the desk and approached us with a facile smile and an outstretched hand. "Brother Oliver! And Brother Benedict!"

Brother Oliver shook hands for both of us. In the division of American business, this was clearly not a belt-tightener. Aggression poured from him in a gleaming oily river. "I'm Elroy Snopes," he announced, still pumping Brother Oliver's hand. "We've only met on the phone before this. Sit down, Brothers." He released Brother Oliver in order to make a sweeping gesture at a pair of wooden-armed chairs with black leather seats and backs. "Coffee? A coke? Anything at all?"

We both demurred.

"I'm having coffee myself," Snopes insisted. We were all still standing, and he was leaning toward us, smiling, expectant, pushing his personality on us like a magician at a children's party.

"Then I'll have coffee with you," Brother Oliver said. "Milk, no sugar."

I understood his reasoning there. It was important to get into some sort of friendly relationship with this man, and throughout history the easiest way to do that kind of thing has been to break bread together. Or, in this case, to break coffee together. So I said, "Me, too. Regular, please."

Snopes aimed his personality like a floodlight at the girl who had brought us in here. "Miss Flinter?"

"Yes, sir," she said. "Right away." And off she went, closing the door behind her.

Brother Oliver sat down, while Snopes strode away to the far side of his desk. Brother Oliver gave me a fast down-patting gesture, so I quickly sat in the other chair next to him, while Snopes settled himself behind his desk like a concert pianist at his Baldwin. He slapped his elbows onto the desktop, rubbed his hands together beneath his chin, beamed a smile at us, and said, "I'm glad you contacted us, Brother Oliver. We'd scheduled to contact you after the first of the year, but you can never have too much lead time in a situation like this."

"I agree," said Brother Oliver.

"Now as I understand it," Snopes said, "you have a monastery population of sixteen."

"That's right."

"Including Brother Benedict here." He flicked the light of his personality at me, and returned to Brother Oliver, saying, "Plus of course you have specialized requirements, chapels and whatever, spatial necessities of a distinctive nature."

"Yes, we have."

"On the *other* hand, several of the more usual factors *don't* get cranked into the mix."

Brother Oliver leaned forward. "I beg pardon?"

"There's no co-ed problem, for instance," Snopes said. "And no children."

"That's true," Brother Oliver said, and he sounded as puzzled as I felt. What was the purpose of this endless recital of the obvious?

Snopes, offering no clues, rattled onward. "Children create," he told us, "an entire spectrum of housing needs all their own, believe me. So to that extent, we're working with a simplified problem. Then there's garaging. Do you have vehicles?"

"No," Brother Oliver said. "We rarely Travel."

"Another simplification." The Snopes beam of friendly approval became broad enough to include Brother Oliver, myself

60

and a good third of the hovering plants. "The job at hand looks complex at first blush," he told us, "but only because the problem is new, it's different, it isn't run of the mill. But once we look more closely, define our areas and our terminology, we can see that it doesn't complex itself at all."

This man's use of the English language, his apparent belief that any word could be turned into a verb by a simple effort of will, was starting to make me squint. "Contact," "schedule," "garage," and "complex" all had become verbs at his hands so far, and who knew what else he might say before we got safely out of his office and back to our monastery?

The other problem, aside from his form, was his content. What in fact was he talking about? *What* job wasn't as complex as it at first appeared? Brother Oliver now asked this very question: "Exactly what job are we talking about, Mr. Snopes?"

"Why, relocation, of course."

Brother Oliver stiffened. "Relocation?"

"Not that there's any hurry," Snopes said smoothly. "The way it looks now, we won't be at the demolish stage with your facility at least until next September and possibly not till the following spring."

Demolish stage: so now he had begun to redress the imbalance in the language by taking a verb and turning it into . . . what? An adjective, modifying "stage"? Or its own noun?

But it was the gist that Brother Oliver concentrated on. He said, "But we don't want you to demolish us. We don't want to be relocated."

The Snopes personality wound itself up another forty watts, to include sympathy and human understanding. "Boy, I know just how you feel, Brother Oliver." Flash: "You, too, Brother Benedict." End of flash. "You people have been living there for years, haven't you? You kind of get attached to a place."

"Precisely," said Brother Oliver.

"But we've got ourselves almost a year lead time," Snopes told us, and his flashing eyes told us how happy that made him. "We'll come up with just the right relocate long before we get deadlined."

"Un," I said.

Snopes raised a gleaming eyebrow at me. "Brother Benedict?"

"It's nothing," I said. "I was just gastricked there for a second."

"Miss Flinter has Alka Seltzer," he offered.

"No. No, thank you."

Brother Oliver gave me a quick shut-up glance and returned to Snopes. "Mr. Snopes," he said, "you don't understand."

"I think I do, Brother Oliver," Snopes said. He paused to emanate sympathy, then went on. "I do understand your special needs, and believe me we're not placing you in the position where you either move into some fleabag or wind up out on the street."

"Those are not the options—"

"For instance," Snopes said, interrupting more with his smiles and gestures than with his words, "we're already doing a potentiality survey on a little place up in New Paltz."

"New Paltz?"

"Upstate," Snopes said. "Up the Hudson. A former two-year community college. It got phased out, the facilities are there and in good shape, and it's a very handsome little campus."

"But—"

"Brick buildings, in what you might call your Ivy League style, only more modern, if you know what I mean."

"I'm afraid I do, but—"

"They did a lot of tree planting, too," Snopes went on, "and in years to come those trees are going to be beautiful. Gorgeous. When they get a little taller, you know."

"Mr. Snopes, we—"

"Listen, on that subject." Leaning across his desk, turning the wattage way down to indicate confidentiality, Snopes said, "You don't do any drug work there, do you? In the monastery? Drug rehabilitation, any of that?"

"No, of course not, we're a contempla—"

"Well, that's fine." Snopes leaned back, smiling, but with the wattage still down. "That would have been a problem with the community," he said. "It might have been, I think it might have been. I think they'll sit still for a religious situation, but drugs or anything like that, it might have been a problem."

62

"Mr. Snopes," Brother Oliver said firmly, "we have no intention of going to New Paltz."

Snopes was amused by that. "I'm going to be honest with you, Brother Oliver," he said. "We're not going to get you anything on Park Avenue."

"We're *on* Park Avenue."

"Yes, but you can't expect—"

"And," Brother Oliver said, doing some of his own interrupting, without benefit of personality, "we're going to *stay* on Park Avenue."

Mr. Snopes frowned, with many many muscles. "Well, I don't see—"

"In our present building," Brother Oliver told him. "In our monastery. We are not going to move."

Mr. Snopes came to a stop. He brooded at Brother Oliver, thinking things over. With his personality turned off he looked like a desert bandit or a Mafia lawyer's clerk. He also looked very difficult, much more difficult than Daniel Flattery. I glanced at Brother Oliver, and I saw that his brave front was held together with chewing gum and matchsticks, but that it was holding.

Mr. Snopes, speaking softly, almost gently, said, "Brother Oliver, I don't think you understand what's going on here."

"Oh, yes, I do."

"Let me recap you anyway, just in case. What's happened here, Dwarfmann Investment Management Partners, Incorporated, has bought some land. There are structures on that land. The structures will be removed and a new building will be put in their place. You and your other monks are tenants in one of those structures and you will be relocated. That's what's going on, Brother Oliver, and it has gone on in this city for the last thirty years, and you just have to look out the window to see it. And when the process starts, it goes through to the finish. Now, most of the time everything is calm, everybody is happy, and there's no problem, but sometimes you get a situation where a tenant refuses to vacate. Does that desist the process? No, it does not, Brother Oliver. What happens, Federal marshals and New York City policemen enter the premises and remove the tenant and remove the tenant's possessions and then the structure is knocked down per schedule and the new building is erected per schedule and the tenant makes a fool of himself on the sidewalk with his possessions for maybe three hours. Now, that's what happens, Brother Oliver."

"Not this time," Brother Oliver said.

"Every time," Mr. Snopes said.

Brother Oliver shook his head. "No. I'm sure you would have called us after the first of the year to talk about relocation, because by then you'd own the land. But we found out ahead of time, *before* you own the land, and that means we have the chance to stop you."

"We have an option, Brother Oliver, and that's just as good as ownership."

"No, it isn't," Brother Oliver insisted. "We have time now, and we'll *use* that time, and we'll *stop* this from happening."

Scornfully, Mr. Snopes said, "By doing what? You'll go talk to Dan Flattery?"

There was no way Brother Oliver could admit we'd already been turned down by Flattery, but on the other hand how could he tell a direct lie? I admired his way out. He said, "Why not?"

"Flattery will get you nowhere," Mr. Snopes said. "He wants this sale just as much as we do. In fact, more."

"There are other ways," Brother Oliver said. "We can get ourselves designated a landmark."

Mr. Snopes shook his head. "You're wasting your time," he said.

"We can mobilize public opinion. Don't you think public opinion will rally behind sixteen monks driven from their two-hundred-year-old monastery?"

"I'm sure it will," Mr. Snopes said. "And if Mr. Dwarfmann or I were running for public office we'd probably be pretty scared. But we're not, Brother Oliver. The public has nothing to do with us. The law is all we're concerned with."

Brother Oliver took a deep breath. I figured he was counting to ten, so I counted also, and when I got to seven he said, "I didn't come here to argue with you, Mr. Snopes, or to trade challenges with you. I came here to find out what solution we could come to together that would enable us to keep our monastery."

Mr. Snopes had never become impassioned below the surface, and so had no need to count rapidly and angrily to ten. He clicked on his personality once more, now that the air raid was over, and flashed us some rueful comradeship. "I'm really sorry, Brother Oliver," he said. "I wish there was a way, and I know Mr. Dwarfmann wishes the same thing, because your monastery could up the esthetic values on the whole site. Better than a Picasso. Now, if you were on a corner we could probably work something out, but you're right in the middle of the parcel, and there's just no— Comere, take a look at this."

He popped up from his chair, bounded around the desk, and gestured us to come to one of the building models at the side of the room. "Here, this'll explain the whole thing."

Brother Oliver got to his feet, so I did too, and we both walked over to look at this thing. On a more or less square surface stood two featureless white slabs. They looked like tombstones on a macrobiotic diet. Tiny trees and people and automobiles disported themselves around the base of the slabs. The slabs were united at the bottom, and then were united again briefly about halfway up, like Siamese twins joined at the hip.

Pointing, Mr. Snopes said, "Now, that's where your monastery is right now. You see the situation. Site logistics give us no alternative placement."

Brother Oliver waggled a finger at the slabs. "Is *that* what you intend to put up instead of our monastery?"

"I suppose you're more comfortable with an older style of architecture."

"I'm comfortable with style," Brother Oliver told him, "and I'm comfortable with architecture. And now, more than ever, I am determined to save our monastery."

"Don't make grief for yourself, Brother Oliver," Mr. Snopes said, demonstrating true concern and fellow feeling. "Remember, it's an old saying but it's true, you can't make an omelet without breaking eggs."

Brother Oliver glanced again at the slabs. "I see the broken eggs, Mr. Snopes," he said, "but I see no sign of the omelet."

Mr. Snopes shrugged. His manner showed that he was giving up on us at the moment, but that he still was prepared to think of us as nice guys. He said, "I do sympathize, Brother Oliver. I said that before, and I meant it. But there's nothing to be done." He shifted to a brisker gear. "Now, what I suggest, you and Brother Benedict here, you go back to the monastery and talk it over, discuss it among yourselves, maybe consult an attorney, that's always a good idea. Brother Benedict, I understand you're friends with Miss Huxtable from the *Times*, you might want to sound her out, let her give you the real estate facts of life, and find out for yourselves what the situation is."

I said, "She won't be in favor of what you're doing. She already said so in the paper."

"Brother Benedict," Mr. Snopes said, "so far as I know Ada Louise Huxtable has never liked *anything* that Dimp has done. All I'm saying is, she knows her way around in the real world, she'll tell you what your chances are."

"She'll be on our side."

Mr. Snopes shrugged. "Fine." Turning back to Brother Oliver, he said, "When you've had a chance to think it over, give me a call. This New Paltz site isn't the only potentiality, and like I said before we've got almost a year. Plenty of time."

Brother Oliver said, "I want to speak to Mr. Dwarfmann."

"He won't tell you anything different from me, Brother Oliver."

"I want to speak to him."

"I'm sorry, that's impossible."

"If he's alive and conscious, it isn't impossible."

"He's in Rome," Mr. Snopes said. "All week."

"Then I wish to make an appointment for Monday."

"It won't do you any good, Brother Oliver, I wish you'd take my word on that."

"I want a meeting with him."

Mr. Snopes shrugged again, giving up on us once more and this time indicating less assurance in our nice-guyness. "I'll speak to Mr. Dwarfmann when he returns to the office," he said, "and then I'll phone you."

"I don't want to talk to you any more, I want to talk to Dwarfmann."

66

"That's what I'll phone you about, a meeting with Mr. Dwarf-mann."

"When?"

"I'll be in touch no later than Monday afternoon."

"Good. Come, Brother."

"Right," I said, and with one last backward glance at those slabs I followed Brother Oliver toward the door.

Which opened, just before we got to it, and Miss Flinter backed in with a tray containing three plastic coffee cups. "Oh," she said, when she saw we were leaving, and she just stood there holding the cups.

"It's the thought that counts," Brother Oliver assured her, and he stopped in the doorway to look back at Snopes and say, "Mr. Dwarfmann is in Rome?"

"That's right."

"You people have no designs on St. Peter's, do you, or the Vatican?"

Snopes laughed, as though it were all a friendly joke. "No, Brother Oliver, we don't. And not on the Coliseum, either."

"Well, you wouldn't," Brother Oliver said. "That's already a ruin."

FIVE

EVER HAD my little room looked so good to me. These patched and repatched plaster walls, white with paint that I had brushed on myself, this uneven wideplanked floor that I kept waxed and polished to the gleaming hue of honey, these two rough ax-hewn ceiling beams that gave me splinters every time I swept away the cobwebs, that heavy oak door with its filigreed iron hinges and handworn iron latch, the small diamond-paned window deeply inset in the exterior wall with its view—no, its glimpse—of the courtyard down below and the other arm of the monastery across the way, all enclosed me in the comfort and warmth of the familiar. There was not an inch of this room that I had not cleaned, touched, looked at, concerned myself with. It was mine in a way that Dwarfmann's twin slabs would never be Dwarfmann's.

Brother Oliver was right; Dimp *had* to be stopped. Should a wrecking ball be permitted to come crashing through that wall, by that window? Should a bulldozer be permitted to crumple and splinter and bury the planks of this floor?

And the furniture. It belonged to me, naturally, but it also belonged to this room. The bed, a four inch foam rubber pad (four dollars and fifty cents, downtown) on a small plywood platform with legs made of stubby two-by-fours, had been constructed by me, with the help of Brother Jerome, and its dimensions had been planned with this room in mind. Along *this* wall, with a specific relationship to the window and a specific relationship to the door. And the box beneath the window, in which I kept my changes of clothing and my personal possessions, that I had built myself from pieces of packing crates, oiling the wood when I made the box and now waxing it every time I did the floor, that box had been designed for the dimensions of the window above it and for its second purpose of being a seat whenever I had anyone else in the room. (I sat, of course, on the bed.) The two pieces of furniture filled this room because they had been fitted to it and fulfilled all the room's functions, but take them out of here and put them in some anonymous smooth-walled cube and you would make a room that could only be empty and barren and uncomfortable.

I sat for quite a while on my bed, once we returned from our journey to Dimp, watching the slowly changing trapezoid of afternoon sunlight on my floor and thinking about my recent experiences of Travel. How complex the world is, once one leaves the familiar and the known. It contains—and has for years contained, without my knowing it—both Eileen Flattery Bone and Elroy Snopes. If one were to Travel every day, would one go on meeting such richly intrusive personalities? How could the ordinary brain survive such an onslaught?

I was meditating on the possibility that perhaps ordinary brains did *not* survive such onslaughts, and that the coming of the Age of Travel produced by the end of feudalism and the social changes of the industrial revolution had in fact created mass psychosis (a theory that would explain much of the world's history over the last few hundred years), when Brother Quillon, our

69

resident homosexual, knocked on my open door and said, "Pardon my interrupting your meditation, Brother Benedict, but Brother Oliver would like to see you in his office."

"Mm? Oh. Thank you, Brother Quillon, thank you." I blinked and nodded and moved my limbs about in a disorganized fashion, readjusting myself to the world outside my head.

Brother Quillon gave me a shy smile and went away down the corridor, trying to walk like a man. What a difficult life he had set for himself, poor man. We were all celibates in these walls, of course, but the rest of us had removed ourselves from the arena of temptation, while Brother Quillon was smack in the middle of it. If a girl on a television commercial—not to mention the physical presence of Eileen Bone—could strain the dam of my sexuality, think what Brother Quillon had to go through, every day of his life. His success was a continuing inspiration to us all.

Well. I left my room and hurried downstairs to see what Brother Oliver wanted.

✣

It was another meeting, but this time there were six of us gathered around the refectory table. In addition to Brothers Clemence (attorney), Dexter (banker), Hilarius (historian), Oliver (Abbot) and myself (innocent bystander), there was also Brother Jerome. A stocky heavy-armed man with bushy eyebrows, Brother Jerome was our handyman and general fixit master. He understood carpentry, plumbing, home wiring and the insides of small appliances. He it was who had helped me construct my bed, and he it also was who had become an accidental occasion of sin for me when he'd dropped a wet cloth on my head a few days ago, resulting in my taking the Lord's name in vain.

He had been brought here by Brother Clemence, who explained that Brother Jerome "has something of interest to tell us. But it's only a footnote, it can wait. We should hear the main text first."

So we did. Brother Oliver began by giving a summary of his meeting with Daniel Flattery yesterday—a much less emotional summary than the one he had delivered to me in the railroad car

70

on our way back from the Flattery house—and then he gave a rather detailed account of our meeting with Mr. Snopes, including a description of the structures Dimp intended to put in our place. "Although I intend to do my best with Mr. Dwarfmann when eventually I meet him," Brother Oliver concluded, "I must say I don't feel much optimism in that quarter. The sum of our efforts so far, I would say, Brother Benedict's and mine, is that we have met the enemy. We know somewhat more than we did about the kind of people with which we must deal, but I wouldn't say we know as yet very much about *how* to deal with them."

"It sounds," Brother Hilarius said, "as though aesthetic appeals would have very little effect on such people."

"About as much effect," Brother Oliver said, "as an appeal to conscience."

Brother Hilarius said, "What about an appeal in terms of money? Wouldn't that be the sort of thing they might understand?"

"In terms of money? What does that mean, Brother Hilarius?"

"What if we offered to buy the monastery ourselves?"

Brother Dexter entered the conversation, saying, "We couldn't possibly afford it."

"But couldn't we," Brother Hilarius asked him, "mount some sort of fund drive?"

Brother Dexter shrugged. "For the kind of money we'd need? An obscure order like ours? I really doubt it."

"Well, how much money are we talking about?"

"I made some calls today," Brother Dexter said, "to relatives down in Maryland. They talked to banking people they know in New York, and then they called me back. Now, they couldn't find out *exactly* how much Dwarfmann's paying Flattery for this land, but given the general range of current land prices in this area they came up with a ballpark figure of around two million dollars."

"Oh," said Brother Hilarius.

Brother Oliver said, "Ballpark figure? What's a ballpark figure?"

"An approximation," Brother Dexter explained. "It means we

may not exactly be at home plate, but we're inside the ballpark."

"Everybody knows phrases that I don't know," Brother Oliver said. He sounded forlorn.

Brother Hilarius said, "Maybe we could interest a movie star. Someone to do a telethon for us or something."

It seemed time for me to speak. I rarely had anything to say at these meetings, but occasionally it did fall to me to pass along some depressing fact, and one of those occasions was now upon me. "They wouldn't sell to us," I said.

They all looked at me. Brother Hilarius said, "Why not?"

"Because they want to put their building up," I told them. "We're not the only thing they're buying. They're taking everything on this whole block. If they don't buy this monastery they won't be able to put up their building."

Brother Hilarius wouldn't give up easily. He said, "What if we offered them a profit?"

"There's still the other parcels," I said. "They're buying the hotel next door, and the buildings on the other side of us, and as I understand it they have options on those too. So they'll have to pay the money for them. The only thing we could possibly try to buy from them would be the whole block."

Brother Dexter said, "I wouldn't even mention the dollar figure for something like that."

Brother Oliver, with the hopeful expression of a man trying out a new bicycle, said, "It's not in the ballpark?"

"It's a different ballgame entirely," Brother Dexter told him.

The new bicycle fell over.

Brother Hilarius said, "Well, what about these other buildings? Maybe *they* don't want to be torn down either."

"Now," said Brother Clemence, "we get to Brother Jerome. Go ahead, Jerome, tell them what you told me."

Brother Jerome had a habit of pushing his sleeves up to his elbows before speaking, as though speech were a difficult physical activity that required strength, determination and a lot of forethought. Because the sleeves of our robes are very loose, his usually flopped right down to his wrists again, as they did this time. "They want to sell," he said. He had a gruff, under-utilized kind of voice, and he always crammed his eyebrows down hard over his eyes when using it.

Brother Oliver, still distressed at the failure of that bicycle, frowned back at him and said, "*Who* wants to sell?"

"All of them," Brother Jerome said. He wasn't one for wasting words.

Brother Clemence, urging him along as gently as a prospector with a favorite mule, said, "Give them the details, Jerome." Then, before that could happen, Brother Clemence turned to the rest of us himself and explained, "Jerome knows the maintenance people around here, the janitors and superintendents and all that. They tell him what's going on in the neighborhood."

Brother Oliver said, "And what *is* going on?"

Brother Clemence said, "Well, let's take the other buildings one at a time. On our left here, going down to the corner, we've got the Alpenstock Hotel. Tell them about that, Jerome."

"They want to sell," Brother Jerome said.

"Well, yes," said Brother Clemence. "But tell them why."

"On account of the Nazis."

Brother Oliver was on the verge of incoherence. He said, "*Nazis?*"

"Maybe I'd better," Brother Clemence decided. And none too soon, either. "You check me on this, Jerome," he said, and then told the rest of us, "The history of that hotel is a little odd. Local German-American citizens built it before the turn of the century, planning to present it to the homeland for their New York Consulate. But Germany didn't want it, and the builders couldn't find a buyer for it, so finally they converted it to a hotel, just to pay it off. During the thirties the place got taken over by the German-American Bund, pro-Nazis, and they set it up to be Nazi Headquarters for after the invasion."

Brother Oliver said, "What invasion?"

"The invasion of the United States. By Nazi Germany." Brother Clemence reassuringly patted the air, saying, "It never happened."

"*I* know that," said Brother Oliver. "What has this got to do with tearing the building down?"

"We're getting there," Brother Clemence promised. "Now, there *wasn't* an invasion, so the—"

"We all *know* that, Brother!"

"Yes, that's right," Brother Clemence said. "I'm just getting to the point."

"Good," said Brother Oliver.

"The point is," Brother Clemence said, retaining his attorney's calm in the face of the hysterical layman, "that the Bund was disbanded during the war, and the group that owned the Alpenstock Hotel simply disappeared. Eventually the bank took over, for nonpayment of mortgage. Two banks, actually, they'd had the building very heavily financed. The banks have operated the hotel themselves for the last thirty years, and they don't like any part of it. It's been continuously on the market for all that time, but this is not the city in which to sell a Nazi hotel. The place has generally earned out its expenses, the property taxes and staff and so on, but very little dent has been made in the principal of the indebtedness. So the banks are delighted to have a buyer after all these years."

Brother Dexter said, "What banks are they, do you know?"

"One of them is Capitalists and Immigrants Trust." Brother Clemence turned to Brother Jerome. "Do you remember the other one?"

Brother Jerome hiked up his sleeves and lowered his brows. "Um," he said. "Douchery."

Brother Oliver said, "*What?*"

"That's it," said Brother Clemence. "Fiduciary Federal Trust."

"Ah," said Brother Dexter. He nodded with fatalistic satisfaction. "Dimp does business with both of those banks," he said. "According to the people I've talked to, they're the principal paper holders on this very project."

Brother Oliver closed his eyes. Faintly he said, "Paper holders?"

"They're putting up the money," Brother Dexter explained.

Brother Hilarius said, "They're all entwined with one another, aren't they? Dwarfmann buys the hotel from the two banks, and the two banks loan him the money to make the purchase."

"There's another tie-in," Brother Clemence said. "At least

potentially. For myself, I'll be very surprised if the Flattery Construction Company doesn't do some of the work on the new building."

Brother Oliver opened his eyes. "I've said it before," he said, "and I'll say it again. If one is very patient, if one listens very carefully, if one just keeps asking questions, sooner or later *everything* begins to make sense."

"I'm becoming interested in those buildings on the other side of us," Brother Dexter said. "Just how do they tie in?"

"Not quite as neatly," Brother Clemence said. "But there are still connections. For instance, Capitalists and Immigrants Trust also holds the mortgage on the building on our other side."

"You mean the Boffin Club," Brother Oliver said.

"Right." Brother Clemence nodded. "The building is owned by the club. It's a nonprofit corporation, like the Lambs Club or the Players Club."

Brother Hilarius said, "Those are actors' clubs, aren't they?"

"Mostly," said Brother Clemence. "But the Boffin Club is primarily for writers."

"Nicodemus Boffin," Brother Oliver said, rather unexpectedly, "was a character in Dickens' *Our Mutual Friend*. He was so in love with books that he kept buying wagonloads of them, even though he didn't know how to read."

"Now, *there's* a friend of writers," said Brother Dexter. "I can see why they named their club after him."

"But the founders of the Boffin Club," Brother Clemence said, "were mostly radio writers. This was back in the twenties. They've had some playwrights and television writers over the years, but very few novelists. And in fact the membership has declined very badly in the last ten years or so."

Brother Dexter said, "I believe that's the case with all clubs of that sort. Society changed after the Second World War, something happened, people aren't as interested in social clubs as they once were."

Brother Clemence said, "I don't know about any other clubs, but the Boffin Club is in very bad shape. Most of the founders are gone, the remaining members are generally older men who

75

don't do that much writing any more and don't have as much money as they used to. The club's been on the brink of bankruptcy for years. Brother Jerome has a friend over there who's told him the situation."

Brother Jerome lifted his sleeves and lowered his eyebrows. "Tim," he said.

"That's right," said Brother Clemence.

Sleeves up, eyebrows down. "Action writer."

Brother Clemence nodded. "Yes. It seems this fellow Tim used to make a very good living as a writer. He wrote radio shows like *The Shadow* and a lot of short stories for the old pulp magazines. Had an estate out on Long Island."

Sleeves, eyebrows. "Hindenburg."

"That's right," Brother Clemence said. "He was a passenger on the zeppelin Hindenburg. Not the time it blew up, of course."

Sleeves, eyebrows. "Himalayas."

"I think," Brother Oliver said firmly, "we've heard all we need to hear about the adventures of Brother Jerome's friend Tim."

"Well, you get the picture," Brother Clemence said. "These days, Tim lives at the club. He's sort of a janitor-watchman, in return for room and board, and *he* tells Jerome the membership is delighted at the thought of selling the place. They'll make a nice profit on it, pay off their mortgages and other debts and still have some cash left over to distribute to the remaining members. They had a private meeting several months ago, and Tim was the only member to vote against making the sale."

Sleeves and eyebrows. "Granddaughter."

"Yes. If the club is torn down, Tim will have to go live with his granddaughter in Racine, Wisconsin."

S & E. "Women's Lib."

"Thank you, Brothers," Brother Oliver said, raising his hand to halt the flow of information. "I think that's all we need to know about the Boffin Club."

Brother Dexter said, "You say Capitalists and Immigrants Trust holds the mortgage on the club?"

Brother Clemence nodded. "That's what Tim told Jerome, yes."

76

"So the bank," said Brother Dexter, "has yet another reason to want this construction project to go forward. If the club is sold, the bank gets a full return on the mortgage. If it isn't sold, but goes into bankruptcy, the bank gets only a percentage return on the dollar. Possibly only twenty or twenty-five percent."

Brother Oliver said, "I'm beginning to lose sight of the enemy here. At first I thought we were struggling against Dan Flattery. Then I thought it was Dwarfmann, or at least Dwarfmann's company, or at least this man Snopes. Now you say the true villain in the piece is this bank."

"Not villain," said Brother Dexter. "The bank isn't doing anything illegal, or even morally wrong. The bank has investments, and is both legally and ethically required to safeguard those investments and bring in the best possible return for the shareholders. This is a perfectly ordinary business proposition, in which a new commercial building is put up. The bank's interests are affected in several different ways, but there's no conflict of interest."

"I wish I shared your objectivity, Brother," Brother Oliver said. "But I keep feeling the weight of those slabs pressing down on the top of my head."

Brother Dexter offered us his thin cool smile. "I'll grant you it's unfortunate," he said, "that we're the toad beneath the harrow this time. But if we're going to prevail in this situation, and I hope we are, I think it imperative we have the clearest possible picture of what's going on."

I expected Brother Oliver to stumble on that toad-harrow thing, but apparently he knew his Kipling as well as his Dickens, because he simply nodded and said, "The clearest possible picture. How I've been looking forward to seeing it." Turning back to Brother Clemence he said, "You and Brother Jerome have one building to go, don't you? The one on the corner with the, uh, shop in it."

We all knew he meant the Buttock Boutique. There was a general clearing of throats, and then Brother Clemence said, "Well, yes. The tenant in there, the, uh, shop, they don't want to be evicted any more than we do, but the landlord is once again very very happy to get out from under a financial headache."

77

Brother Jerome geared himself up toward speech in the usual way, and said, "Tell them about the rear end."

"Uhh, yes," Brother Clemence said. "Jerome," he quickly told us, "is referring to the back of the building. The situation is, once again, a little complex. The building was moved to that site in the eighteen-fifties."

"Moved there?" Brother Oliver expressed our general surprise. "That's a very large building."

"That's right. In fact, it was too large to move. As this place would be, for instance. Even if we were to find another site, the monastery wouldn't survive being moved."

"Disassemble," said Brother Jerome. His sleeves slid back down.

Brother Clemence shook his head. "If this building were taken apart," he said, "two-hundred-year-old stone walls, two-hundred-year-old beams, wooden floors, all the rest of it, there'd be so much crumbling and decay and destruction we'd never get it back together again."

"Please," said Brother Oliver. "We were talking about the building with the, uh, shop in it."

"Yes." Brother Clemence got back on the track, saying, "That building was originally northwest of here, in the area that became Central Park. It was one of the few buildings in that rectangle worth saving. A retired slave ship captain named Brinley Chansberger bought it from its original owner and had it moved on great log rollers over to its present location. But in the process, the rear wall was severely weakened, and several times in the latter half of the nineteenth century portions of floors collapsed, or windows abruptly fell out into the back garden, or half a dozen bricks would suddenly spurt out into the air for no reason. Chansberger spent much of his slave-trading fortune trying to repair the place, and when he died his heirs sold it to the city, who turned it into a firehouse."

Brother Oliver rested his elbow on the table and his forehead on his cupped hand. "I do believe," he said, "these histories of yours are getting longer."

"There's not much more to this one," Brother Clemence

promised. "The building was never very good as a firehouse. The city spent a lot of money trying to fix it up, adding their own municipal architecture gloss to Chansberger's nautical alterations to a sort of basic townhouse original structure. Then, when in the late twenties a hook and ladder about to race out in response to a fire alarm suddenly fell through the floor into the basement instead, the city put the place up for auction. A combine consisting mostly of uncles and cousins of City Council members bought the place on the cheap, and there've been any number of tenants in the fifty years since. But the building *still* isn't structurally sound, and hasn't been for a hundred and twenty-five years. Inside it now, Jerome tells me, it's a mish-mash of styles and architectural monstrosities, with support walls all over the place and bricked-up doorways here and there, and the general feeling is that political influence is the only thing keeping the building from simply falling down and dying. Reputable tenants won't go near the place, so it winds up renting to tenants like the, uh, shop. Which lowers the tone of the entire area, of course. So that not only do the owners want to sell, but many *other* owners in this neighborhood favor the Dwarfmann plan if only because it will rid the section of that eyesore."

"And of us," Brother Oliver pointed out.

Brother Clemence spread his hands, saying, "The people around here say, you can't make omelets without breaking eggs."

"I believe I've heard that," Brother Oliver said. "Does that finish Brother Jerome's presentation?"

"Yes, it does," Brother Clemence said.

"I have something," Brother Hilarius said. "Nothing definite, just a sort of preliminary report."

We all looked at him. Brother Oliver said, "Yes?"

"It's about this question of getting ourselves designated a landmark," Brother Hilarius said. "I've done some phoning, but there's nothing conclusive yet."

Brother Oliver said, "Just what's the advantage of becoming a landmark?"

"If we can get the designation," Brother Hilarius said, "that would effectively stop the bulldozer."

We all perked up at that. Brother Oliver said, "Is *that* what they mean by a landmark? We couldn't be torn down?"

"That's right."

Brother Clemence made an impatient gesture, saying, "Well, what do you think? Is there a chance?"

"I don't really have that much to report yet," Brother Hilarius said. "It takes time to find the right person in the city bureaucracy. But I think I have the right one now, and I'm supposed to call back on Monday."

Brother Oliver said, "Well, why shouldn't we be a landmark? We're two hundred years old, we're certainly unique from an architectural point of view, and we're a religious order."

"I'd love it to be that easy," Brother Dexter said, "but somehow I don't believe it."

Brother Hilarius nodded. "The people I've talked to so far haven't been very encouraging," he said. "A building's use, for a monastery or a hospital or whatever, has nothing to do with whether or not it gets designated a landmark. And I'm told the Landmarks Commission shies away from designating any building that's already scheduled to be demolished. Apparently there are legal problems involved."

"But you don't know for sure yet," Brother Oliver said. "You'll find out on Monday."

"I'll make more phone calls on Monday," Brother Hilarius said. "And I'll let you know what happens."

"Fine. I think that's very encouraging." Brother Oliver looked around. "Is there anything else?"

There was silence. We all looked at one another, and then back at Brother Oliver, who said, "In that case, I'll—"

Brother Jerome cleared his throat, with window-rattling force. He hiked his sleeves up three or four times, he stamped his feet under the table to be absolutely certain they were flat on the floor, he lowered his eyebrows halfway down his cheeks, he gave himself a side-swiping punch across the nose, and he said, "I don't want to move."

We had all become geared up for a rather more apocalyptic statement. As the rest of us gazed at Brother Jerome in astonish-

80

ment, Brother Clemence patted his elbow—his sleeve had slid down over it again—and said, "I know you don't, Jerome. This is our environment. We need this the way fish need water. We'll do everything we can to save the monastery."

"Prayer," said Brother Jerome.

"We are praying," Brother Clemence said. "Every one of us."

"Everybody," said Brother Jerome.

Brother Clemence turned to look at Brother Oliver, who had been listening with a pensive frown and who now said, "I agree, Brother Jerome. We've tried to keep this to ourselves, to not disturb the others, and we just can't do it. We'll have to tell them, if only so they can add their prayers to ours."

"I agree," said Brother Clemence, and the rest of us nodded our approval.

"Tomorrow morning," Brother Oliver said. "After Mass." He gave us all a somber look, and his gaze stopped at me. "Brother Benedict," he said.

"Sir?"

"You'll be getting the Sunday paper tonight?"

"I suppose so, yes."

He closed his eyes, then opened them again. "Don't find anything else," he said. "If you can possibly help it."

SIX

UT I DID find something else. Or that is, she found
me.

But before that I went to confession, with Father
Banzolini. I was far more flustered than usual when
I entered the confessional, and got off at once on
the wrong foot—or the wrong knee—by saying, "Bless me,
Father, for I think I'm in love."

"*What?*" Never had I heard him so irritated, never, and
Father Banzolini was an absolute opera of irritation.

"Oh," I said. "I'm sorry." And I started again, doing it right
this time: "Bless me, Father, for I have sinned. It has been
three days since my last confession."

"And in three days you've managed to fall in love?"

"Ahhh."

"Sexually in love?"

"Ohhhh."

"With that girl on television?"

"What? Oh, *her*."

"Fickle in your affections, eh, Brother Benedict? Well, you might as well tell me about it."

So I told him about it. He already knew about the threatened destruction, so I started my story with the onset of my Traveling, the circumstances of my meeting with Eileen Flattery Bone, and the effect on my brain—waking and sleeping—ever since. His little breathing sounds of exasperation and impatience faded away as I went on, and at the end he was unusually soft-voiced and even-tempered. "Brother Benedict," he said, "I believe you are suffering from what has been called culture shock. I did an article on it once for a missionary magazine."

"I didn't know you were a writer, Father Banzolini."

"In a modest way," he said modestly.

"I'd like to read something of yours."

"I'll bring around some tearsheets," he said, in an offhand way. "But to get back to culture shock. It happens to some people when they are suddenly thrust out of the culture, the environment, that they know and in which they are comfortable. There were volunteers in the Peace Corps, for instance, who underwent culture shock when suddenly flown to some remote Central American village, where all at once everything was different. Right down to the basics, the attitudes about food and sex and dead bodies. Some people just cease to function, they become catatonic. Others lose touch with reality, they try to *force* reality to conform with their preconceptions about what society *should* be like. There are a thousand kinds of symptoms, but the cause is always the same. Culture shock."

I had the feeling I needn't read Father Banzolini's article on the subject, that I'd just heard his article on the subject. "That's very interesting," I said.

"It's a problem in the missionary field, as you can guess," he said. "And I believe it's what happened to you, Brother Benedict. You had become so settled in your way of life inside these walls in the last ten years that you couldn't take a sudden

83

transfer to a totally different environment. In the language of the street, it shook you up."

"Culture shock."

"Exactly," he said. "These feelings you have toward this girl are certainly real, but they're nowhere near as specific as you seem to think. It could have been any girl, any flesh and blood girl that you would meet and talk to in the middle of a brand new environment. We already know from your television watching, Brother Benedict, that celibacy has not entirely quieted your sexual nature."

"Mm."

"In the grip of culture shock," he went on, "you struggled for something familiar, toward which you could give a familiar reaction. The girl was it. You reacted to her as though she were something seen on a television set."

Hardly. But you don't argue with your priest in confession. "That's very interesting," I said. Which wasn't a lie. He might have been as wrong as Martin Luther, but he *was* interesting.

"You asked, a moment ago," he said, "whether your dreams could be considered sinful. Normally I would answer that the dream itself must be regarded as neutral, but that your *reaction* to the dream might constitute a sin. If, for instance, you dreamed of committing a murder, the dream would not be sinful, but if on awakening you relished the thought of having murdered that particular person, the reaction would be a definite sin."

"Well, it wasn't murder," I said, "but I guess it was a sin."

"You're rushing ahead," he cautioned me. "I said *normally* I would answer that way. But in truth, Brother Benedict, I believe in this case *everything* has been a dream to you, from the moment you started Traveling. A victim of culture shock is no more guilty of his thoughts and actions than is a victim of schizophrenia. In fact, I did an article once on moral culpability as it is affected by mental disorder. I could bring you the tear sheets, if you like."

"I'd like that very much," I said. I was utterly astounded: the depths one finds in the unlikeliest people!

"I'll bring it next time," he said. "As to your current problem,

I think you should ask Brother Oliver not to take you along on any more expeditions he might make."

I surprised myself with my reaction to that. I should have been delighted; I should have been relieved to have at last a legitimate excuse to stop all this Traveling. But I wasn't delighted, and I wasn't relieved. Quite the reverse—a sinking feeling filled me, a sudden great sense of loss, as though something important, vital, had been taken away from me.

So I really *was* suffering from culture shock. And it was being nipped just in the nick of time. "Yes, Father," I said. "I definitely will." One or two more excursions outside, and I might very well have lost my Call.

Father Banzolini said, "And until the effects of your recent Traveling wear off, I don't think you should worry too much about any stray thoughts that might meander through your head. At this point, you aren't entirely responsible."

"I'm glad to hear that, Father," I said.

✠

One Our Father and *one* Hail Mary! I felt almost guilty as I scampered through my penance, as though I had somehow sneakily put one over on Father Banzolini and were now wallowing in the rewards of that slyness.

But I guess I'm too shallow to be depressed for long. By the time I'd rapidly recited my prayers and was heading up the aisle and out of the chapel I was no longer bowed down by either of my guilts. (I did have two to dwell on, had I the character to do so. First, there was my shameless toadying of Father Banzolini, resulting in the lightest penance of my penitential career. And second, there was the sense of loss I'd experienced and kept secret to myself when he'd told me I should Travel no more.) Not only was I unbowed by this double evidence of my own worthlessness, I actually gloried in them both. The penny-ante penance, it seemed to me, made up for a lot of heavyweight penances I hadn't deserved. And there was a kind of exhilaration in the thought that Travel was not only philosophically wrong for me but was actually dangerous to my mental health. There was a titillation in the idea of Travel now that was probably very like the heroin addict's view of his drug. Dangerous, but exciting, and finally exciting *because* it is dangerous.

Ah, well; my fling with Travel was over. I was to be reduced again to a bearable level of addiction, being my weekly sojourn for the Sunday *Times*.

Meaning now. Off I went to the office for the necessary sixty cents and permission to leave the monastery. Brother Eli was on duty at the desk, surrounded by the shavings from his whittling. Brother Eli, a brooding slender long-necked young man in his late twenties, had after an apparently normal California childhood deserted from the United States Army in Vietnam. He had Traveled extensively incognito through Asia, and along the way had picked up a smattering of half a dozen exotic languages. He had also picked up a skill in woodcarving with which he claimed to have supported himself for three years in southeast Asia. Returning unofficially to this country he had presented himself at our gates two years ago, saying he had heard of us in a lamasery and that his own experience of Travel agreed with our philosophical stance. He had asked us if we had any objection to a wanted fugitive joining our number. Brother Oliver had assured him the laws of Man, being transitory, contradictory and invariably in error, meant much less to us than the laws of God, and so this young man had given up the name under which his government thought of him as a felon and had become Brother Eli, a woodcarver.

Oh, yes, a woodcarver. Lean Josephs striding next to plump mules bearing plumper Marys, androgynous angels rolling massive boulders from allusive cave entrances, wise men on camels, saints on their knees, martyrs on their last legs, all were discovered by his busy knife lurking in this or that stray piece of wood. And Christs, how many Christs: Christ blessing, Christ fasting, Christ preaching, Christ rising from the dead, Christ permitting the washing of His feet, Christ carrying His cross, Christ attached to His cross, Christ being taken down from His cross.

If Brother Eli were ever to become Abbot, none of us would be safe.

Our business now was quickly transacted. Brother Eli gave me a quick greeting, a quick sixty cents, and a quick farewell, before returning to the Madonna and Child emerging from this latest block of wood. (Shades of Brother Oliver!) And out I went.

Was it my imagination, or was the world different tonight from the normal Saturday evening? The usual glitter seemed harsher somehow, the gaiety more frantic. Danger and lunacy seemed to lurk behind every facade and every face on Lexington Avenue. I strode more rapidly than is my wont, I took less pleasure in this excursion, and even the newsy who sold me my paper seemed less familiar and less friendly tonight. "Evening, Father," he said, as usual, but somehow the tone was different.

On the way back, I paused at my regular trash basket to rid myself of the unwanted sections of the paper. Classified, Travel, Business, the advertising supplements. But then I paused at Real Estate. Might it be a good idea to keep that section? Perhaps a greater familiarity with the world of real estate would be useful to us in the weeks ahead. I returned it to the bundle of saved sections, and hurried homeward.

She must have been lying in wait for me. I was coming along 51st Street, barely half a block from home, when Eileen Bone stepped out of an automobile parked some distance ahead, walked around the hood of the car, and stopped on the sidewalk to wait for me.

She was perhaps twelve paces away, close enough for me to see her clearly in the streetlight glow, but far enough so that I could have taken evasive action. I could have turned about, for instance, walked back to Lexington, left to 52nd Street, left to Park Avenue, left past the Buttock Boutique, and thence half a block home. All in all, that's probably exactly what I should have done.

Well, I didn't. I continued the twelve paces forward, holding tightly to my newspaper and looking directly at her. She was wearing pants, and a dark-colored sweater, and some sort of hip-length jacket. She looked tall and slender and darkly beautiful. She was the refined essence of every electric peril I had sensed in the world tonight.

I stopped when I reached her. It didn't seem possible merely

87

to nod and say hello and walk on by, so I stopped. But I didn't speak.

She did. "Hello, Brother Benedict," she said, and both her smile and her tone of voice were far too complex for me to unravel. Several kinds of humor and several kinds of somberness were so entwined in her voice, her eyes, the set of her head, the lines of her lips, that I merely let it all wash over me like a Russian symphony and didn't even seek for meaning. "I'll drive you home," she said.

"It isn't far," I said.

"We'll make it far," she said. Then she looked slightly more somber, slightly less humorous. "I want to talk to you, Brother Benedict."

"I'm sorry," I said, "I have strict orders to return to—"

"About your monastery," she said. "About the sale. I might be able to help."

That stopped me. Frowning at her, trying to read her despite the complexity, I said, "Why?"

"You mean how," she said.

"No, I mean why. It's your father that's selling the place."

"That might be a good reason right there," she said. "And there might be others. I'm hoping you'll tell me."

"Brother Oliver is the one who—"

"You, Brother Benedict." Humor was returning, glinting in her eyes and creating soft pale shadings on her cheekbones. "I have a sense of trust in you," she said. "If anyone can tell me the monastery's side of all this, you're that one."

"Tomorrow," I said. "If you were to come tomorrow, possibly I—"

"I'm here now. I might change my mind by tomorrow."

"Come into the monastery, then, I'll show you ar—"

"No, Brother Benedict," she said. "My turf, not yours." And she gestured at her car. It was as long and sleek and graceful and competent and gleaming as she herself, and she was right about it. It matched her, as my monastery matched me.

I said, "I don't think I could get permission to—"

"Why get permission? We'll talk for ten minutes, and I'll drop you off at your door."

ı shook my head. "No. We have rules."

She was becoming impatient with me. "I'm beginning to be sorry I came here, Brother Benedict. Maybe my brother's right about you people, it doesn't matter what happens to you one way or the other."

"I'll ask," I said. I gestured with the newspaper, displaying it, saying, "I'll bring this in, and I'll ask Brother Oliver."

She studied me, frowning, as though trying to decide whether my insistence was weakness or strength. Then abruptly she nodded and said, "All right. I'll be waiting out front."

✛

I found Brother Oliver in the calefactory, watching Brothers Peregrine and Quillon in a boxing match. The purpose was salubrity rather than belligerence, this being an exercise campaign initiated by Brother Mallory, the former welterweight, who was quadrupling now as referee, trainer and both seconds. Brother Peregrine, our onetime summer theater operator, merely looked absurd in his long brown robe and huge sixteen-ounce boxing gloves, floundering around like a marionette with tangled strings, but Brother Quillon looked bizarre. They were circling one another like a binary star, with Brother Mallory bobbing and weaving intently around them as though an incredible display of fisticuffs were taking place somewhere or other. In truth, Brother Quillon backed in great eccentric circles, his eyes very round and his mouth very open and both boxing gloves held out in midair in front of himself, while Brother Peregrine stalked along in his wake, delivering confused flurries of punches at Brother Quillon's gloves.

I waited till a round had completed itself before attracting Brother Oliver's attention. While Brother Mallory bounded from corner to corner, giving his pugilists good advice and firm reassurance, I told Brother Oliver what I had found outside. "Hmm," he said, and frowned. "What did she want?"

I repeated the conversation, and her invitation, and the threat that she might change her mind by tomorrow. "The question is," I finished, "should I go?"

Brother Oliver thought it over. The next round had begun, and

89

he watched as he pondered. Out in the middle of the floor Brother Peregrine's face was becoming very red, while Brother Quillon's was dead white.

"I think," Brother Oliver said at last, "you should go."

"You do?"

"I see no harm in it," he said.

I did. I wasn't exactly sure what the harm was, but I saw it or felt it or tasted it; I sensed it with some sense or another, and I was torn about what to do. I'd been hoping Brother Oliver would refuse to let me out, thereby taking the decision out of my hands. But he was giving me permission, and now what was I going to do?

"All right, Brother Oliver," I said, not happily, and left the scene of battle.

So I would Travel. That was clearly where my duty lay, if by means of my Traveling I could at all help to save the monastery. And, I must admit, it was also what I really *wanted* to do, despite our Order's thoughts on the subject, despite Father Banzolini's warnings, and despite my own awareness that I was becoming very badly addicted. Very badly addicted. "God judged it better to bring good out of evil than to suffer no evil to exist," Saint Augustine wrote in *Enchiridion*. Or, putting it another way, "I can resist anything," said Oscar Wilde, "except temptation."

✛

It was awkward getting into the car. Through some miracle of design the seat managed to be several inches below street level, and the door opening was a weirdly shaped parallelogram through which it would have been difficult to pass anything larger than a doughnut. However, I did effect entry, though without much grace; at the last I had to release all my handholds and simply drop backwards the last few inches onto the white upholstery. Then I tucked my knees up under my chin, tucked my robe under my legs, and practically had to leave the car again in order to reach the handle so I could close the door.

Mrs. Bone—I thought it safest to think of her under that heading—watched my progress with amusement. "I guess you're

90

not used to this kind of car," she said, when I finally completed my labors.

"I'm not used to any kind of car," I told her. "This is my first automobile ride in over ten years."

She raised a surprised eyebrow. "Is that right? How do you like it so far?"

Shifting position, I said, "I didn't remember the seats as being so uncomfortable."

More surprise, plus amusement. "*Un*-comfortable? The people at General Motors will be sorry to hear that."

"I suppose one gets used to it," I said.

"That must be it," she agreed, and shifted the gear, and away from the curb we moved.

The sensation was pleasant, if more startling than Travel by train. The outer world was very close, almost as close as if one were on foot, but it was approaching and receding much more rapidly. Mrs. Bone's delicate hands made small adjustments of the steering wheel and we crashed into none of the obstacles that leaped into our path.

Neither of us spoke at first. Mrs. Bone was concentrating on her driving, and so was I. We Traveled north to 55th Street, where we turned left under a traffic light that I thought of as having already switched from amber to red, we made a green light at Madison Avenue, and we came to a stop rather reluctantly before a red light at Fifth. During this time I studied her profile in those instants when I could spare some attention from our driving, and I realized that in my dreams I had altered her somewhat. I had made her more ethereal somehow, more liquid, softer and slower and less totally present.

The process of comparison brought to mind again the content of that dream—as well as my waking thoughts the following morning—and I'm afraid I must have had a rather ambiguous expression on my face when she turned to look at me while waiting for the Fifth Avenue light to change. Her own expression became quizzical, and she said, "Yes?"

"Nothing," I said, and looked away. Out the windshield, somewhere, looking at the lights and darkness of Saturday night. "Where are we going?"

"For a drive." The light having changed, she glided us forward.

As we continued west on 55th Street I forced myself to concentrate my attention on the car. It was one of those small luxury vehicles I would occasionally see advertised on television —an impression of great massive form, yet in actual fact it was very low to the ground and could only comfortably accommodate two people. There was a back seat, but it wouldn't be much use to anybody with legs. Still, in the most wasteful and pretentious and transitory way possible, it did suggest that combination of wealth and self-indulgence that is called luxury.

And Mrs. Bone, of course, was exactly like the girls usually filmed with these cars on television.

A red light at Sixth Avenue. The car stopped, Mrs. Bone glanced at me again, and by God *I* was looking at *her,* no doubt with the same equivocal expression as before. And I had been *trying* to think about the *car.*

She frowned at me. "How long have you been a monk?"

"Ten years."

The light changed; she spun the wheel and we turned right onto Sixth Avenue. "Well," she said, her eyes on her driving, "that's either too long or not long enough."

There was nothing I could possibly say to that, so I turned away, looking out at the traffic, seeing in front of us now a yellow taxicab with a bumper sticker reading *Put Christ Back In Christmas.* An excellent sentiment, only slightly marred by the fact the lettering was colored red and white and blue, as though Christ were a good American running for re-election. But it's the thought that counts, however muddled.

Finishing with the bumper sticker, I looked out my side window at the activities of the world. It was not yet eleven o'clock on Saturday night, the thirteenth of December, and the streets were full of people, most of them couples, most of them holding hands. The pagan Christmas icons—pictures of that fat red-garbed god of plenty—were displayed in store windows everywhere, but most of the pedestrians seemed concerned with more personal pleasures: movies, the theater, a nightclub, a late dinner out.

Neither of our Western gods—Christ and Santa Claus, the ascetic and the voluptuary—seemed much in the thoughts of the citizenry tonight.

Put Christ back in Christmas. The next thing they'll say is, *Put Jehovah Back In Justice*. Think about *that* for a minute.

How the gods change. Or, to phrase it more exactly, how our image of God changes. Long ago, human beings became uneasy with that stern and unforgiving God the Father, the thunderbolt who lashed out so violently and unpredictably. Western man replaced Him with Christ, a more human God, a kind of supernatural Best Friend, a Buddy who would take the rap for us. (The Holy Ghost has always been too . . . ghostlike, to pick up many fans. What's His personality, where's the character hook, where's the worshipper identification?)

But even Christ carries with Him that sense of austerity, that implication of duty and risk and the possibility of truly horrible loss. So on comes jolly Santa Claus, a god so easygoing he doesn't even ask us to believe in him. With that belly and that nose, he surely eats too much and drinks too much, and more than likely pinches the waitress's bottom as well. But it doesn't matter, it's all harmless fun, the romping child in all of us. Bit by bit over the centuries we have humanized God until we have finally brought Him down to our own level and then some; today, with Santa Claus, we can not only worship ourselves but the silliest part of ourselves.

"Four cents for your thoughts."

Startled, I twisted my head around to gape at Mrs. Bone. "What?"

"Inflation," she explained. "You were brooding about something."

I rubbed my hand over my face. "I was thinking about Christ," I said.

"I see by your outfit that you are a cowboy."

"What?"

"Nothing," she said. "Just quoting the Smothers Brothers. We could talk now, if you're ready to come back to the Church Militant."

I looked around, and we were no longer in the city, which

93

made not the slightest sense. It is true that over the years my habit of meditation has improved to where I can almost automatically shut out the natural world completely, but I do retain an awareness of time, at least roughly. And I hadn't been thinking about the manifestations of God for more than three or four minutes, of that I was positive.

Yet here we were in the country. Or not quite the country. Trees and greenery surrounded us, but we were also amid fairly heavy traffic, all moving in the same direction, and the darkness out there was spotted with frequent streetlights. "Where are we?"

"On the Drive in Central Park," she said. "We can circle in here and have our chat without being distracted by traffic."

"You want to talk while Traveling?"

"Why not?"

"Well," I said, "I'm willing to try."

"Good." She adjusted her position, as though settling down for some serious activity, and kept her eyes on the cars ahead while she talked. "Your position is," she said, "that your lease with my father ran out, and my father sold the land, and you people will be evicted so the new owner can tear down the monastery."

"That's the position, all right."

"Why shouldn't it happen?"

"I beg pardon?"

She shrugged, still watching the road. "My father's a decent man," she said. "In his way. He owns property and he wants to sell it. Nothing wrong with that. These other people—what are they called?"

"Dwarfmann."

"No, the little word."

"Dimp."

"Yes. Dimp is a useful functional part of our social system, providing jobs for the working man, putting capital to work, increasing the value of the city and the state and the nation. Nothing wrong with them either. Now, you people, you neither sow nor reap, do you? You're decent, too, you don't harm anybody, but what do you have to offer that's stronger either than my father's property rights or Dimp's usefulness to society?"

"I don't know," I said. "I can't think of anything."

"So why not just pack up and move? Why make a fuss?"

I didn't know how to deal with such questions. "If you're asking me," I said, "to justify my existence on the basis of my usefulness, then I guess I don't have any justification at all."

"What other basis is there?"

"Oh, you can't mean that," I said. "Do you really mean that usefulness is the only thing that matters?"

She glanced at me, with a quick ironic smile, and faced the traffic again. "And do you really intend to talk about beauty and truth?"

"I don't know what I intend to talk about," I said. Then I said, "This is a nice car."

She frowned, but didn't look at me. "Meaning what?"

"A cheaper, less attractive car would perform the same function."

Now she did look at me, and her smile was almost savage. "So. You admit it. You *are* a luxury."

"Am I?"

"We all like luxuries," she said, "as you just pointed out. But wouldn't you have to agree yourself that where luxury and function clash, it must be luxury that gives way?"

"Mrs. Bone, I don't—"

"Call me Eileen," she said.

I took a breath. "I think I'd rather call you Mrs. Bone," I told her.

Again she turned her eyes from the traffic, this time giving me a searching look. In a softer voice she said, "Am I an occasion of sin for you, Brother Benedict?"

I didn't answer immediately. She watched the road again and I watched her profile. "Until I met you, Mrs. Bone," I said, "I never really knew what the phrase 'occasion of sin' meant."

She laughed, but in a friendly way, and said, "I'm not sure, but I think that may be the nicest thing anybody ever said to me." Then she suddenly leaned over the wheel, determination clenching her features, and the car surged forward. We rocked around a clopping hansom cab, threaded through a minefield of moving cars, and suddenly turned off, coming to a stop in an otherwise empty parking lot. Darkness surrounded us, but I could see her face when she turned to me, saying, "You've got to help me, Brother Benedict. I want to help you, I really do, but first you have to help me."

"How? In what way?" I responded to her intensity with a helpless intensity of my own. "I don't know what you want from me."

"Don't you realize," she said, "that those are my father's arguments? I want you to beat them down, Brother Benedict, I want you to win the battle for my allegiance. I am the sincerest of Flatterys, I want to help you but I can't do it unless I can believe it's *right* to go against my father."

"I'm sorry, I'm not very good at argument. Now I wish I were."

"I'm not asking to be conned," she said. "I don't want you to bring out some clever Jesuit to sell me a bill of goods. I want honesty. I *can* help your monastery, Brother Benedict, believe me I can, but you'll have to convince me I *ought* to."

"How can you help? What could you possibly do?"

"Never mind. Just take my word for it. And convince me, Brother Benedict." And she sat there, leaning sideways toward me, her burning eyes staring at me in the darkness.

Never had my mind been such a blank. Convince her? Beat down her father's arguments about the usefulness of usefulness, and the luxury of everything else? There were no words in my mind, no words at all, and certainly no words in my mouth. Staring at her, into those unblinking eyes, all I could do was pray for a distraction.

God answered my prayer almost at once. We were mugged.

☩

They yanked both doors open at the same instant, two tall skinny black boys with flashing knives in their hands. "Okay, Jack, get outa there," one of them said, and the other one said, "Come on out, honey, and meet the man."

Only *Eileen* was the one they called Jack, and I was the one they called honey.

It was an easy mistake. Eileen was driving, she was wearing pants, and my robe undoubtedly looked like a dress in the uncertain light.

But that realization came to me later, when I had more leisure to reflect on the situation. At that moment, all I could think was, *They're not going to hurt Eileen!*

The car was just as difficult to leave as it had been to enter. I squirmed out, clutching parts of it here and there to hoist myself up to ground level, and when I finally did get out and upright I stomped my attacker on the foot. The sneakered foot.

He wouldn't have been so careless if he hadn't thought I was a girl. He would have stayed farther away from me. But probably having some unseemly ideas about actions he would take toward me he had stood very close while I was getting out of the car, and that was why he was now hopping around on one foot, clutching the other with both hands and yipping like a dog that's been hit with a stone.

Now the other one, menacing Eileen. There was one advantage in a car as low as this; when in a hurry, you didn't have to go around it. Hiking up my skirts, I ran over the hood and fell on the other mugger like the Red Sea on the armies of Egypt.

Why, the nasty little creature, he tried to stick me with that knife of his. And me a man of the cloth. I whomped him two or three times, wishing I had Brother Mallory's expertise in punching people, and then he wriggled out from underneath me, got to his feet and took to his heels, disappearing almost at once into the surrounding darkness.

I struggled up, tripping over my own robe and running forward into the rear fender of the car. The second time, climbing up the automobile, I made it to my feet and looked across the auto roof to see the other one hobbling away as well. He gave one dirty look over his shoulder—aggrieved, that's what he was—and then he too was gone.

Panting, bewildered, I looked around and saw Eileen sagging against the side of the car. Her eyes seemed to be closed. I took two sudden strides to her, grabbed her by both shoulders, and cried out, "Eileen! Eileen!"

Her eyes opened. Beneath my hands her body was trembling. "My goodness," she said, in a much smaller and younger voice than I'd ever heard from her before.

"Are you all right?"

"—I—" She was more bewildered than I was, more thunderstruck. "I'm not . . . cut or anything, I'm . . . Oh!" And she squeezed her eyes shut again, the trembling becoming much worse.

"Eileen," I said, and pulled her in close, putting my arms tight around her to contain the trembling. My face was in her hair.

We both sensed the change. This slender body in my arms . . . the fragrance of this hair. . . . There *is* nothing else like it on earth, and I'd been celibate a long long time.

We drew back from one another. She wouldn't look at me, and I was just as glad not to have to meet her eye. She cleared her throat and said, "I'll, uh, drive you home. I mean, to the monastery."

"Yes," I said.

"To the monastery," she repeated, and fumbled herself back into the car.

SEVEN

UNDAY MASS. We had no regular celebrant, different priests from St. Patrick's taking turns at saying Mass in our little chapel. One of the newer young clerical clerics from the diocesan office officiated today, and after reading the gospel he asked us all, at Brother Oliver's request, to stay at the end of Mass for an announcement.

Even through the fevered swamp my brain had become since last night's occurrence with Eileen Flattery Bone, I could sense the unhappy atmosphere that filled the chapel while we all waited for the completion of Mass. Those of us who already knew what the announcement would be were of course saddened and disheartened at the necessity of making it, while those who did not yet know the details could certainly see, from the faces of Brother Oliver and we few others, that the announcement would be a gloomy one.

For me, it seemed doubly gloomy. I felt I was losing this home in two ways, both to the wrecker's ball and to my own frailty. Neither Eileen nor I had spoken a word on the drive back last night, except that as I was hoisting myself from the car at the end she did say, in a small and toneless voice, "Thank you." I had been unable to make any response at all, but had simply stumbled inside, where I'd pleaded fatigue and emotional upset with Brother Oliver, who of course had been waiting for me, anxious to know what Daniel Flattery's daughter had come after. I still hadn't told him, but would do so after Mass and his announcement. He would have to help me decide what to do.

It was strange all at once to have to think about my future. For ten years my future had merely been the present in finite repetition, and I had been happy and content. Now, without warning, I faced an unknown and unknowable future. Everything in my life was crumbling. Would this monastery be taken away, torn down to the ground? Would I be forced by the changes in my own mind to leave the monastery, no matter whether the building was saved or not? What was going to happen tomorrow? What did I *want* to happen tomorrow?

I had done little sleeping last night, and those questions had been ever-present in my mind, yet I still was nowhere near an answer. The habit of meditation, which had given me a brain (I like to think) as orderly as my room, had deserted me in my hour of need. My brain today was fudge. It was worse than fudge; it was last fall's macaroni salad accidentally left behind in the summer cottage and not found until this spring.

The Mass was nearing its end. When I finished telling the whole truth to Brother Oliver, as I would of course have to do, would he tell me to leave? He might, I wouldn't blame him. He might tell me to return to the outer world until I had become more secure again in my vocation. It was a possibility I'd already thought of for myself, without the slightest sense of pleasure or anticipation.

What did I want—what did I actually want for myself? I wanted the last week to cease to exist; I wanted it removed from history. I wanted to go directly from the Saturday night a week ago when I had in blissful ignorance brought that newspaper into these walls, directly from that Saturday to this Sunday, this morning, with nothing in between. No Travel, no Eileen, no threat to the monastery, none of it. That was what I wanted, and if I couldn't get it I just didn't have any alternate selection.

"Go, the Mass is finished." But we stayed. The priest departed, and Brother Oliver stood up from his place in the front row and turned to face us. He looked heavier and older and more care-worn than his usual self, and when he spoke his voice was so low I could barely hear him.

In fact, I didn't listen. I knew what he had to say, that stony center of fact that he would surround with cushioning layers of doubt and probability, and I spent the time instead looking about me at this place and the people in it.

Our chapel, like the rest of our building, was designed by Israel Zapatero and intended to be occupied by no more than twenty men. A long narrow shoebox of a room, its stone floor, stone walls, rough plank ceiling and narrow vertical windows were all part of the original plan, but other elements had been added in the two centuries since. The only one of Abbot Jacob's stained glass windows to remain out of the attic was here, centered above the plain table of an altar at the front of the room; a flowerlike abstract design in many colors, it had apparently been done shortly after some well-meaning relative had sent Abbot Jacob a compass and protractor.

More additions. The bas-relief Stations of the Cross lining both side walls were the work of some long-ago Abbot whose name I never knew, but who was also undoubtedly responsible for the bas-relief of St. Christopher carrying the Christ Child over the waters in our upstairs bathroom. Electrification had been delayed in this wing until the mid-twenties, when those brasslike helmet affairs had been attached to the corners of the ceiling, giving us a soft indirect lighting that almost perfectly duplicated the candlelight it had replaced. Due to the narrow-ness of the side windows, and the nonfunctional nature of Abbot Jacob's stained glass window—it had been affixed to a blank stone wall—the lights were needed as much in the day-time as at night.

The pews were a fairly recent addition; until about 1890 there had been no seating in here at all, and those attending Mass either stood or knelt on the stone floor. At that time, according to a story Brother Hilarius once told me, a church in Brooklyn underwent a severe fire, and the singed remnants of several pews had been given to our monastery. The Brother Jerome of that period had salvaged pew lengths each long enough for two people and had set ten of them in here, five on each side of a central aisle. Since there were only sixteen of us now, the last row was not in present use.

I was seated in the fourth row, against the right wall, from where I could see all my fellow brothers. In the front row, Brother Dexter was farthest to the left, his banker's features less confident than usual as he watched and listened to Brother Oliver, who had been sitting next to him. Across the aisle on my side were Brothers Clemence and Hilarius, Clemence with his face toward Brother Oliver, Hilarius with his head bent and face hidden.

In the second row began those who were hearing the story for the first time. Brothers Valerian and Peregrine on the left, Mallory and Jerome on the right. Valerian, whose fleshy face I had often thought self-indulgent and whose orange Flair pen I had stolen out of pique, looked so stunned that I couldn't help forgiving his having done that crossword puzzle. Peregrine, whose face was a bit too finely chiseled, too self-consciously actorish, but who had in fact been a set designer and summer theater operator rather than actor, seemed incapable of believing what he was hearing; as though he were being told the show would not after all go on. On this side of the aisle I could only see the broad backs and shoulders of Brothers Mallory and Jerome, the ex-boxer and the current handyman, like a pair of football players sitting on the bench.

In the third row, the faces were more expressive. Brothers Quillon and Leo were on the left, and Quillon looked crushed; I'm sorry, but he looked crushed in a very girlish way. Leo, on the other hand, looked enraged, as though he might lift that heavy fat forearm of his very soon and start pounding somebody into the ground. On the right, directly in front of me, were Brothers Silas and Flavian. Silas, onetime burglar and pickpocket, onetime author of his criminal autobiography, hunched lower and lower into himself as Brother Oliver talked, as though he'd just been picked up on a bum rap and was girding himself to tough it out without a word. Brother Flavian, the firebrand, started almost at once hopping up and down, coming very nearly to his feet, burning with the need to speak; the way he'd acted when he'd denounced my "censorship" and Brother Clemence had lawyered him to distraction.

Farthest to my left, across the aisle, were our two ancient Brothers, Thaddeus and Zebulon. Thaddeus, a large stocky man who had been a merchant seaman for years and years, had become sort of loose and shambling and disorganized in his old age, like an old car that hasn't been cared for very well. Brother Zebulon had shrunk with age instead, becoming tinier and more brittle almost every day. Both of them watched and listened with frowning concentration, as though unable to really come to grips with what was being said.

On my side of the aisle, seated next to me, was Brother Eli, whose face had the impassivity of a spectator at an automobile accident, but beneath whose impassivity I thought I could detect the fatalism, the nihilism, he so much struggled against, that turn-off drop-out conviction of his generation that stupidity and destruction are inevitable, that there's no point in struggle. Brother Eli's faith, I saw, was just as necessary and yet tenuous as my own.

Brother Oliver finished by saying, as he had to, "And please give us your prayers." And before he could sit down, or take another breath, Brother Flavian was on his feet, bursting up so precipitously he almost shot over the back of the pew and landed on Brother Jerome. "Prayers!" he shouted. "Of *course* we'll pray! But we have to do *more* than that!"

"We are doing more than that, Brother," Brother Oliver said. "I've just told you what we've done so far."

"We need public opinion on our side!" Brother Flavian cried, waving his arms about.

"Shaking one's fist in church is not quite the thing, Brother Flavian," Brother Oliver told him mildly.

"We have to do something," Brother Flavian insisted.

Brother Clemence got wearily to his feet, like Clarence Darrow in Tennessee. "If you'll excuse me, Brother Oliver," he said. "Brother Flavian, we *are* doing something, as Brother Oliver already outlined. Would you like me to repeat it, with another point-by-point summary?"

Brother Flavian waved that away with agitated—but unclenched—hands. "We have to do more. Why don't we picket them? Contact the media, get out there on the sidewalk with signs, bring our message to the public. They wouldn't *dare* make a move against us! Monks in a monastery?"

"I'm afraid they would," Brother Oliver said. "Mr. Snopes told me he didn't care about public opinion because he wasn't running for office, and I'm afraid I believe him."

Brother Peregrine jumped up. "Couldn't we raise the money somehow, buy the place ourselves? Couldn't we, oh, I don't know, maybe put on a show?"

"There's too much money involved," Brother Oliver said, and turned to Brother Dexter for confirmation.

Brother Dexter didn't stand, but he did half turn in his pew to nod back at all of us and say, "Land value in this neighborhood is in the range of twenty thousand dollars a frontage foot. Just our own parcel would cost over two million dollars."

That was a sobering number, and there was a brief unhappy silence, ended by Brother Leo, who demanded, "How did this happen anyway? If the lease ran out, why didn't we know about it ahead of time?"

"I must take the blame," Brother Oliver said, and spread his hands helplessly.

"No," said Brother Hilarius. Rising, he spoke directly across the way to Brother Leo, saying, "A ninety-nine-year lease doesn't call attention to itself like a three-minute egg."

Brother Leo was not appeased. "Somebody should have known about it," he said. "Where is this lease anyway? Who has it?"

"I should have it," Brother Oliver admitted, "but it's disappeared. I've searched high and low."

"If any of you knows where it is," Brother Clemence added,

"I wish you'd tell us. I've been wanting to take a look at the wording."

Brother Silas, betraying his background, said, "Maybe it was stolen."

Brother Clemence frowned at him. "What for?"

"So you can't take a look at the wording."

Brother Valerian said, impatiently, "Now, Brothers, there's no reason to get paranoid. From the sound of things, we have trouble enough as it is."

Brother Thaddeus, whose years of Traveling with the Merchant Marine had perhaps inured him to the thought of abrupt transitions more than the rest of us, said, "Brother Oliver, what happens if we don't save the place? Where do we go from here?"

Brother Quillon turned about to shake his head at Brother Thaddeus and say, disapprovingly, "That's very defeatist, Brother. We should be positive in our thinking."

"We have to consider the weather ahead," Brother Thaddeus told him gruffly, "no matter what it is."

Brother Oliver said, "That's true. And Dimp has committed itself to finding a suitable replacement structure for us, and to assisting us in making the move. They first suggested a college campus upstate, and this morning a messenger brought photographs and a proposal for a building in Pennsylvania which actually was at one time a monastery."

Brother Flavian, angry and suspicious, said, "Where in Pennsylvania?"

"A small town called Higpen."

Brother Silas said, "Higpen? You mean Lancaster Abbey?"

Brother Oliver said, "You know the place?"

"I was there for a while. It's no good, believe me. After this place, it's trash."

Brother Quillon called, "Tell us about it, Brother."

"Sure." Brother Silas got to his feet and half-turned so we could all see him. He was somewhat shorter than average, a fact which had apparently been useful in his burglary-cum-pickpocket career, and his face was composed of small sharp features bunched together. He had the appearance I had always visualized for race-track touts.

"This Lancaster Abbey," Brother Silas told us, "was a part of the Dismal Order. You know, dedicated to St. Dismas, the Good Thief, the one hanging on the right of Christ."

We all bowed our heads at the Name.

"I joined up with them," Brother Silas went on, "when I first went straight. They sounded like my kind of people, they mostly used to be in the rackets themselves. But it turned out all they did, these guys, was sit around and tell each other what master-minds they used to be, tell each other the capers they pulled and how they got out of this thing and how they knocked off the other thing and all that. I began to think, these guys, they didn't so much reform as retire, you know? So I split and I came here."

Brother Oliver cleared his throat, "I believe our primary interest right now, Brother Silas," he suggested, "is in the building."

"Right, Brother." He shook his head, telling us, "You don't want it. See, these guys, they'd spent most of their adult lives doing time, you know what I mean? When they thought of home, they thought of something with cell doors and an exercise yard. So what they built themselves out there in Pennsy was like a baby Sing Sing. Gray walls, metal doors, brown dirt courtyard. You wouldn't like it at all."

"Thank you very much, Brother," said Brother Oliver. The information seemed to have daunted him, but he turned bravely to the rest of us and said, "Of course, Dimp has promised to keep looking until they find something we can approve."

Brother Quillon, his voice rather shrill, cried out, "But how can we approve *anything*, Brother? After *this*. Our *home*."

"We all feel that way," Brother Oliver assured him.

Brother Clemence said, "Excuse me. Let me just raise this question of the lease one more time. Has no one seen it, or have any idea where it might be?"

There was silence as we all looked at one another, everybody waiting for somebody else to speak.

Brother Clemence spread his hands. "Well, that's it, then," he said.

Then little Brother Zebulon piped up, saying, "Whyn't you look at the copy?"

That got him more attention than he'd received in forty-five years. Brother Clemence actually stepped out into the aisle and took a pace in Brother Zebulon's direction, saying, "Copy? What copy?"

"Brother Urban's copy, of course," said Brother Zebulon. "What other copy is there?"

"Brother Urban's copy?" Brother Clemence looked around at us, his helpless expression saying as clearly as words that there was no Brother Urban among us.

Then Brother Hilarius spoke up. "A former Abbot," he said. "The one before Wesley, I think."

"That's right!" cried Brother Valerian. "Now I remember! He did illuminated manuscripts. There's a framed one of his hanging in the kitchen, near the sink, an illuminated version of I Corinthians V, 7: *Every man hath his proper gift of God, one after this manner, and another after that.*"

Brother Clemence looked groggy. "Illuminated manuscripts?"

"He did illuminated manuscripts on *everything*," Brother Zebulon crowed, suddenly breaking into laughter. "You should have seen his illuminated version of the front page of the *Daily News* the day Lucky Lindy landed in Paris!"

Brother Clemence shook his head. "Do you mean," he asked, "this Brother Urban did an illuminated manuscript version of our *lease*?"

"Of course!" cried Brother Zebulon. He was slapping his knees and cackling as though he were on some front porch somewhere and not in our chapel at all. I suppose in the excitement he must have completely forgotten where he was. "That Brother Urban," he cried, "was the looniest of them all, and they've *all* been loony! If he saw a piece of paper with writing on it, he'd do a copy, do it all up with pictures and big fancy capital letters and gold color all around the border and I don't know what all."

I noticed that none of us was looking at Brother Oliver. I too did not look at Brother Oliver, so I don't exactly know how he took what he was hearing. But I know how Brother Clemence took it; with the stunned joy of a miser who's been hit on the head by a gold bar. "Where *is* this copy?" he demanded. "The copy of the lease, where is it?"

Brother Zebulon spread his bony hands, shrugged his bony shoulders. "How should I know? With all his others, I suppose."

"All right, where are *they*?"

"Don't know that, either."

But Brother Hilarius did. "Brother Clemence," he said, and when Clemence turned to him he said, "Brother Clemence, *you* know where they are."

Clemence frowned. We all frowned. Then Clemence's frown cleared away. "Ah," he said. "The attic."

"Where else," said Brother Hilarius.

✝

The attic. Because the roof slanted down on both sides, the only place where one could stand up straight was in the very middle, directly beneath the ridgepole. And even then one could stand up straight only if one were less than five feet six inches tall. And barefoot.

That taller central area had been left clear as a passageway, but the triangular spaces on both sides were filled with the most incredible array of artifacts. Abbott Ardward's matchstick mangers —and his three partly damaged matchstick cathedrals—made a sort of sprawling Lilliputian city all about, intermixed with ancient cracking leather suitcases, copses and groves of tarnished candelabra, tilting light-absorbing examples of Abbot Jacob's art of the stained glass window, curling blow-up sheafs of Abbot Delfast's photographic studies of the changing of the seasons in our courtyard, piles of clothing, cartons of shoes, small hills of broken coffeepots and cracked dinnerware, and who knows what else. Over there leaned Abbot Wesley's fourteen-volume novel based on the life of St. Jude the Obscure, now an apartment house for mice. Old chairs, small tables, a log-slab bench and what I took to be a hitching post. Kerosene lanterns hanging from nails in the old beams, bas-reliefs on religious subjects jammed in every which way, and a rolled-up carpet with no Cleopatra inside. The wanderings of the Jews were recorded in mosaics of tiny tile glued to broad planks; some of the glue had dried out and the tiles had fallen off, to be crunched distressingly underfoot. Old newspapers, old woodcuts of sailing vessels, old fedoras, old stereopticon sets and old school ties.

You can really fill an attic in a hundred and ninety-eight years.

We came boiling up to that attic now, all sixteen of us, like escaping prisoners of war. Up we came and out we spread and down we bent and on we searched. Tiles and mothballs and mousedroppings crunched distressingly underfoot. Heads *thonked* into beams, followed by cries of pain or indistinct mutterings. The forty-watt bulb at the head of the stairs, our only illumination, gave little enough light to begin with, and we made matters worse by constantly casting shadows either in our own way or somebody else's. Brother Leo inadvertently knelt on a matchstick cathedral, Brother Thaddeus gashed his temple on a nail, Brother Jerome knocked over Abbot Wesley's novel, and Brother Quillon burst into tears. Brother Valerian found a stub of candle, stuck it into a candelabra, lit it, and the candle fell out and rolled burning into a little suburb of newspapers and shirts. Pandemonium ensued, but the fire was put out before it caused much damage.

And the dust. One man up here, just having a casual look around, could raise enough dust in five minutes to drive himself back downstairs again. Sixteen of us, all more or less frantic, all rooting and scrounging through the deepest and furthest recesses of accumulated junk, created the closest thing to the atmosphere of the planet Mercury ever seen on the planet Earth. We coughed and sneezed, our perspiration turned to mud, our wool robes itched, our eyes burned, and half the things we picked up fell apart in our hands. Creating more dust.

When in tribulation, when in discomfort, the good Catholic can offer his sufferings to be credited to the account of the souls in Purgatory, to shorten their punishments and gain them earlier release to Heaven. If we sixteen didn't empty Purgatory that day, I just don't know.

"Here!"

The voice was Brother Mallory's, and looking through the swirling gloom I saw his fighter's body in a fighter's crouch beneath the threatening beams. He was holding out and waving a large piece of stiff paper.

We all made our way in his direction, crushing anonymous crushables beneath our feet. Brother Clemence coughed and sputtered and called, "The lease? Is it the lease?"

"Not yet!" Brother Mallory shouted. "But it's the right stuff. And there's a lot of it here!" And he held that piece of paper out for our inspection.

Never had I seen *No Smoking* so beautifully rendered. The sinuousness of that S, suggesting smoke itself, was played off beautifully against the tendrils of green ivy encircling it, and the massive tree-trunk effect of that determined N was softened by the bank of daylilies in which it was embedded. The smaller letters were of a clear but soft black calligraphy, the whole surrounded by vines and leaves and floral arrangements. Small rectangular drawings of artisans in their rooms plying their crafts—writing, weaving, boot-making—were gracefully placed around the margins, and one noticed at once that not one of those artisans had a cigarette.

"There's a whole stack of these," Brother Mallory told us. "All different." Turning to show us some more of them, he gave his head a whack on a beam and dropped the *No Smoking* sign. "Damn that beam," he said, and looked toward Brother Oliver to say, "In a theological sense only."

"The lease," Brother Clemence said, leaning forward in impatience. "Never mind anything else, get that lease." Like half a dozen of the others, he had put his cowl up to protect his head slightly from beam-thumps, and I suddenly realized that by now, in this smoky dusty yellow light, in these cramped wooden quarters surrounded by strange bric-a-brac, we sixteen robed figures, half of us with hidden hooded faces, must look like one of the more disturbed paintings by Pieter Brueghel the Elder. Monks in Hell, at the very least. I half expected some little imp-figure, half toad and half man, to come scampering out of that nearby matchstick cathedral.

But he didn't; he stayed within. Brother Mallory, on the other hand, came up with a whole double armload of papers. "I don't know what your lease looks like," he complained. "Can't see anyway, not in this light, with all this dust in my eyes."

"We'll bring them all downstairs," Brother Clemence decided, "sort them out down there."

"This isn't all of them," Brother Mallory said. "There's hundreds back here." Thrusting the present handful at Brother Leo, he said, "Here, take this, I'll get the rest."

Brother Leo grasped the bundle of papers and hit his head on a beam. He grunted, and I waited for him to say something far worse than Brother Mallory's theological comment. But he didn't. For a few seconds he stood there biting his lips, and then he turned to say, "Brother Hilarius, was the Blessed Zapatero a tall man?"

"Short, I believe," Brother Hilarius said. "Under five feet."

"Pity," said Brother Leo.

Brother Mallory had come up with another armload, which he passed to Brother Peregrine. Sheets fluttered this way and that. I spotted a beautifully rendered version of a poster for the Louis-Schmeling fight, the letters cleverly entwined with knotted ring ropes. An outsize copy of what appeared to be a doctor's prescription featured stethoscopes, caducei, brass bedposts and cork-stoppered bottles in free-form style around the carefully reproduced illegible handwriting. Other sheets were too heavily encrusted with drawings, ivy-festooned capital letters, calligraphic curlicues and general grume to be comprehendible without a closer clearer look. But it was all very interesting.

And there was tons of it. When at last we all blundered back downstairs again armloads of the stuff were being toted by Brothers Mallory, Leo, Jerome, Silas, Eli and Clemence, while I stayed behind to gather up the half dozen sheets that had slipped and slithered out of the Brothers' embrace. None of them proved to be the wanted lease, but I carried them along anyway, and followed everyone else all the way down to the first floor and Brother Oliver's office, picking up other stray sheets along the way.

It's truly wonderful how intense group activity can take one out of oneself. From the moment this great lease-hunt had gotten underway I had completely forgotten all about my own personal troubles, the doubts and perplexities about my future. It wasn't until I was alone again, following the trail of paper left by the others, that reflection on my own situation returned to me. I felt the gloom descending, the unease and uncertainty, and I hurried to rejoin the safe anonymity of the crowd.

Brother Oliver's office looked like Bureaucrat Heaven: papers everywhere, teetering and tottering on chairs and tables, collapsing on the floor, heaped atop the filing cabinet. Brothers Clemence, Oliver, Flavian, Mallory and Leo were all simultaneously trying to create order, which meant that together they created chaos. Brothers Valerian, Eli, Quillon and Thaddeus were all waving sheets of paper in Brother Clemence's general direction and crying out, not at all in unison, "Is this it?" Brother Dexter looked across the mob scene at me, shook his head, and rolled his eyes. I could only agree with him.

It was Brother Peregrine who finally got everything channeled. Leaping up onto the refectory table as though about to break into a fast buck-and-wing—Brother Oliver gave him a startled and not pleased stare—Brother Peregrine clapped his hands together and shouted, exactly like the choreographer in every movie musical, "People! People!"

I think it was being called "People" rather than "Brothers" that did the trick. Silence fell, two or three syllables later, and everybody looked up at Brother Peregrine, who filled the silence at once by saying, very loudly, "Now, we need some organization here!" Two or three people would have restored chaos by simultaneously agreeing with him, but he out-shouted them and bore inexorably onward: "Now, Brother Clemence is the only one of us who knows *exactly* what we're looking for." Pointing at Brother Clemence, he said, "Brother, if you'll come around on the other side of this table. . . . Come along, come along."

You don't argue with the choreographer. I could see Brother Clemence begin dimly to understand that as, after a very brief pause, he pushed through the crush and went obediently around to the far side of the refectory table.

"That's fine." Brother Peregrine was suddenly so totally in command that he didn't have to *ask* anybody for anything. Pointing as he called out the names, he said, "Now, Brother Oliver, Brother Hilarius, Brother Benedict and myself, we'll go through those papers. It won't take more than four of us. I know the rest of you are interested, but if we all try to help we just won't get anything done. Now, if you want to watch, please just stand back there by the door. Brother Flavian? Over by the door, please."

Magnificent. In no time at all Brother Peregrine had chosen his cast *and* created his audience. (I noticed he'd cast himself in a leading role, but since he'd done the same for me I wasn't about to complain.)

Obedience was prompt and complete. Even Brother Flavian, though he hesitated, finally chose to keep his mouth shut and join the spectators. As those also-rans clustered themselves into the corner by the door, Brother Peregrine finished his staging. "Now," he said, "we four will each take a stack of manuscripts and go through them one at a time. If you find something that looks as though it might be right, take it to Brother Clemence for inspection. All clear?"

I noticed that he didn't ask us if we agreed; he asked us if we understood. You can't answer a question you haven't been asked, so we all nodded and mumbled our yesses, Brother Peregrine hopped gracefully down again from the refectory table, and the search got under way.

Brother Hilarius and I worked at stacks side by side, and very soon Brother Hilarius totally lost sight of the objective. The historian in him took over, and *he* thought we were here to admire the manuscripts. "Very nice," he would say, holding out a representation of the front of a Kellogg's Pep box. "Unusual commingling of Carolingian and Byzantine elements." Or, *in re* a supermarket flyer offering steak at forty-nine cents a pound, "A perfect example of the Ottonian Renaissance."

It made it difficult to concentrate on my own stack, but I did my best. And what a busy pen Abbot Urban had possessed! Anything in print, *anything* in print, that had passed before that man's

113

eyes had been copied in one or another style of illumination. Sheet after sheet after sheet I went through, finding nothing, pausing at a menu in which the capitals were constructed around the animals whose parts were being offered: fish, cattle, sheep.

"Look," said Brother Hilarius. "Look at these drolleries."

They didn't look very droll to me. Hangings, crucifixions, electrocutions and other forms of violent institutional death were represented with small stylized figures in the margins of a wanted poster. I said, "Droll?"

"Drolleries," he corrected me. "That's the term for these, it's a characteristic of the Gothic style, early sixteenth century."

"Oh," I said, and went back to my own array of drolleries.

"This Brother Urban," Brother Hilarius said, "was quite a scholar as well as being quite an artist. He knew the different styles and stages of illumination, and he had the wit to combine them for his own statements."

"That's wonderful," I said, and rejected a laundry list, all in gold and red.

"Is this it?" Brother Peregrine popped up, spraying sheets of paper off his lap, and rushed to Brother Clemence with his find. We all waited, tense, watching Brother Clemence's face. He studied the wording which, like many of these things, was hard indeed to read, and abruptly shook his head. "Seven cents off on Crisco," he announced.

Crushed, his star role reduced to a comic turn, Brother Peregrine turned away without a word and went back to his place. And my own humiliation followed almost immediately after.

I was positive I'd found it, positive, but Brother Clemence hardly gave it a look before dismissing it. "Birth certificate," he announced. "Somebody named Joseph something-or-other."

So we continued, more cautiously now, nobody wanting to be third in the chump sweepstakes, and then I got to something I couldn't read at all. There was lettering there—I could see that much—but I couldn't make out a word of it. Was that an L? Vines entwined themselves around the latticework of lettering, leaves fluttered, long-necked birds craned Heavenward, suns and

114

moons were scattered with a liberal hand, and all in all I just got a headache trying to look at it.

Finally I had to ask for help. But not from Brother Clemence, not just yet. "Brother Hilarius," I said. "What do you suppose this is?"

He looked at it, and burst out laughing. "Oh, that's priceless!" he said.

"It is?"

"That's very funny," he informed me. "What a wonderful joke. Don't you see what he's done?"

"Not in the slightest particular."

"He's combined the Irish style," Brother Hilarius told me, "right out of the Book of Durrow—look at that S right there—"

"Is that an S?"

"Of course it's an S." Brother Hilarius leaned over, chuckling, to study the joke in close-up. "He's mixed the Irish style," he said, "with Art Nouveau!"

"Oh really?"

"Art Nouveau! Don't you see? Art Nouveau is less than a hundred years old, it comes *much* later than the age of illumination. *Look* at the curve of that tendril there."

"Anachronism," I suggested, trying to get a handle on this alleged joke.

"*Wonderful* juxtaposition."

"Probably so," I agreed. "The question is, is it the lease?"

Brother Hilarius frowned at me, distracted from his admiration of Abbot Urban's humor. "What?"

"Is it the lease?"

"The lease?" He sounded astonished, as though he didn't know there was supposed to be any lease around here at all. "Of course not."

"Oh."

"Look! Look! Read it for yourself." His finger rippled across the leafy maze. "Lindy Lands," he said.

"Lindy Lands?"

"Lindbergh. That's the front page of the *Daily News*!"

Brother Zebulon, with that carelessness about rules characteristic of senior citizens, had wandered out of the audience and onto the stage. Now he was standing on Brother Hilarius' other side, leaning over to look at the manuscript in my lap and to say, "Yep, that's it. Lindy was all the way back here before Brother Urban ever got *that* one finished."

"I don't doubt it," I said.

Then Brother Zebulon looked around the room, squinting, obviously looking for something. "Where's the rolls?" he said.

Brother Hilarius and I, in close harmony, both said, "Rolls?" Visions of hard rolls danced in my head.

Brother Zebulon placed all his fingertips together, then pulled his hands far apart, like someone pulling taffy. "Rolls," he said. "Brother Urban did all the long things on rolls."

Brother Hilarius said, "*Papyrus* rolls?"

"Paper rolls, that's right," said Brother Zebulon. "He taped pieces of paper together, and then rolled them up."

Brother Clemence, who had been sitting at the refectory table twiddling his thumbs—literally physically twiddling his thumbs—now frowned in our direction, saying, "What's that?"

"There should be rolls," Brother Hilarius explained.

Brother Clemence spread out his arms to encompass the entire messy paper-strewn room. "You mean, there's *more*?"

✠

It was on one of the rolls. A select search party composed of Brothers Hilarius, Mallory, Jerome and Zebulon had found the rolls amid a lot of window shades and curtain rods, in behind the fourteen-volume novel based on the life of St. Jude the Obscure, and it didn't take long to find the one headed by a magnificent Romanesque capital L in the form of an ivy-covered tower or turret, leading to delicately etched E, A, S and E, superimposed on small detailed two-dimensional representations of outbuildings.

"All right," Brother Clemence said. "Let's unroll it, and see what it has to say."

More easily said than done. The roll wished to remain a roll, and not to become a tongue. When the end was released, it would immediately snap back to the main body. If just the end were held, the main body wished to barrel forward and enclose itself again. If both ends were held, the sides became determined to curl toward one another across the text.

Finally, four of us had to hold it down, like a sailor having his leg amputated in a pirate movie. I held part of the end and part of one side, with Brother Peregrine across from me and Brothers Mallory and Jerome down at the main body.

With the document thus spreadeagled, Brother Clemence could begin his inspection. Slowly he read, word by painful word, picking his way through two-hundred-year-old spelling, two-hundred-year-old legal phrasing, and nine-hundred-year-old calligraphy.

I grew tired, but I refused to let go, and in fact I saved the day when Brother Peregrine slipped and for just a second lost his grip on the other side. I held on, and Brother Peregrine quickly grabbed the curling corner again, but not before Brother Clemence gave him an annoyed look, saying, "Hold it steady, man."

"Sorry."

Brother Clemence read on. The audience crowded around, watching Brother Clemence's face. There wasn't a sound in the room.

Then Brother Clemence said, "Hm." We all looked at him more closely. The audience stood up on tiptoe. Brother Clemence, one finger marking his route, read slowly again through the same passage, and by the end of it he was nodding. "Yes," he said, and lifted his head to look around at all of us in grim satisfaction. "I got it," he said.

It was Brother Oliver's role to ask the questions now, and instinctively the rest of us deferred to him. And he asked: *"What do you have, Brother?"*

"Let me read this to you," Brother Clemence said. Returning to the lease, having a little difficulty finding the place and then at last finding it again, he read aloud, "The option of renewal lies exclufively with the leffee."

Brother Oliver turned his head a bit to one side, as though favoring a good ear. "It does what?"

"I'll read it again," Brother Clemence offered. And he did so: "The option of renewal lies exclufively with the leffee." And now Brother Clemence smiled. Turning that smile on Brother Oliver, he said, "You see what that does?"

"No," said Brother Oliver.

Brother Dexter said, "It says we can renew."

"It says," Brother Clemence said, "the option is *ours* to renew. Exclusively."

Shaking his head, Brother Oliver said, "There's that word option again."

"Choice," Brother Clemence told him. "In this case, Brother Oliver, it means choice. This lease says that *we* have the choice as to whether or not we want to renew."

Hope lit Brother Oliver's eyes. "It does?"

"I *thought* there might be something like this," Brother Clemence said. "When there was no paper filed at the time of the first renewal, back in 1876, I thought there just might be an automatic renewal option, and I wanted to see exactly what that option might say." Patting the lease, which we four were still holding spread out like a patient etherized upon a table, he said, "And this is wording far beyond what I'd hoped for. At the best, I'd hoped it might say renewal was automatic unless one side or the other gave written notice of an intention not to renew at some specified interval before the due date. And that would have been enough, since we never were given any kind of notice. But this is even better. This lease says the lessor, the owner of the land, *cannot* refuse to renew the lease if we wish to stay on."

"Then we're saved!" Brother Oliver cried, and in the general hosannah that went up after that the lease got loose and snapped shut like a bear trap on Brother Clemence's hand. Extricating himself, Brother Clemence shouted for our attention, and then said, "No, it doesn't. I'm sorry, but it doesn't."

Brother Hilarius said, "It doesn't what, Brother?"

"It doesn't save us." Holding up the lease, which was now a tight double roll, he said, "This is not the actual lease. It doesn't contain the signatures of the participants. Nor is it, in any legal sense, a true copy. It isn't notarized and there's no original to compare it to for inaccuracies. It just wouldn't carry sufficient weight in a court of law to decide the case conclusively for our side."

Brother Flavian, ever the firebrand, cried out, "But it shows we're in the *right*! Would we *lie*?"

"Men have been known to," Brother Clemence told him drily. "Even clerics have on occasion dealt rashly with the truth."

Brother Quillon, obviously on the verge of tears again, said, "You mean, we went through all this for nothing? All we've done is find out we're the victims of a miscarriage of justice?"

"Not exactly," said Brother Clemence, and Brother Oliver sighed. Pushing ahead, Brother Clemence said, "We don't have the original lease, but we do have this version, and it may be able to help us. The courts have established a precedent that could be very useful to us here. When a primary document is unavailable, the contents of that document can be reconstructed by assumption from secondary documents and the matter treated as though the primary document had been produced."

"Oh, Brother Clemence," Brother Oliver said wearily, and he sat down at the refectory table, shaking his head.

"This is a secondary document," Brother Clemence said, waving the illuminated lease again. "In those messy filing cabinets over there, Brother Oliver, there must be other secondary documents that refer either directly or by inference to matters in the original lease. Letters, tax bills, account books, I don't know what all. What I will do, now that I have this copy to tell me what to look for, is go through every document we possess and construct the strongest possible profile of the original lease. I will then ask a friend of mine, an attorney who volunteered the other day to help us for no fee, to get in touch with the Flatterys' attorney, present our case, and suggest we settle out of court."

Brother Oliver said, "And you really think there's a chance?"

"It depends," Brother Clemence told him, "on what secondary documents I can find."

"And you'll start searching right away?"

"As soon as I've cleaned up," Brother Clemence said, "and broken my fast."

119

"Oh," said Brother Oliver. "Of course."

Of course. We'd all been so caught up in this quest that all the more mundane things of life had become mislaid and forgotten. Breakfast; yes, indeed. We never eat until after morning Mass, of course, and today we hadn't eaten at all. I was suddenly aware that I was starving, and I could see the same awareness in all the filthy faces around me.

Which was the other item Brother Clemence had mentioned; cleaning up. Scrounging around up there in that musty attic, smearing ourselves with dirt, cutting and bruising ourselves, getting ourselves severally muddied and bloodied, we looked now less like monks and more like the inhabitants of some medieval lunatic asylum.

As did our surroundings. This room, Brother Oliver's office, was a knee-deep swirl of incomprehensible papers. Dust that had come downstairs with us hung in the air or had already settled on the room's various surfaces. Brother Quillon now said, "Well, you won't be able to find a thing in here the way it is. I'll clean up."

"I'll help you," Brother Valerian offered.

"Wonderful."

The group was diffusing itself into separate conversations. Brother Leo, our cook, said, "I'd better get to the kitchen. Who's on duty with me this morning?"

It turned out to be Brothers Thaddeus and Peregrine. "Well, come along, then," Brother Leo said grumpily.

"Just a second," Brother Clemence said, and when we all turned to give him our attention he said, "I hope everybody realizes the implication of this discovery."

Brother Oliver said, "Implication? Besides the obvious?"

"This means," Brother Clemence said, gesturing with the rolled-up lease, "that Brother Silas may have been right after all. The original lease really might have been stolen, to keep us from proving we have the right to stay here. So I think none of us should say anything to anybody about this copy we found."

We all agreed, rather somberly, and then the kitchen trio went off to make breakfast while the rest of us headed upstairs to wash and change.

Brother Oliver stopped me briefly at the head of the stairs. "We'll talk after breakfast," he said.

"Yes, Brother," I said.

And as I washed the attic grime from myself I wondered if Brother Clemence—or any of the others—had thought about the other implication of our find. If Brother Silas was right, if the lease had been stolen by somebody working either for the Flatterys or Dimp, who could have stolen it? Who, but one of us?

EIGHT

E HAD our talk after breakfast, strolling in the cloister, past the refectory and the kitchen, with the courtyard on our other side. The high wall separating us from the street marked one boundary of our walk, and the chapel and cemetery marked the other, a symbolism that struck me as simultaneously pat and obscure.

We walked together one circuit in silence. I could feel Brother Oliver glancing sidelong at me from time to time, but he remained very patient, not speaking until we had passed our original starting point, and then saying, "Yes, Brother Benedict?"

"I don't know where to begin," I said.

"Why not at the traditional place?"

"Yes, of course." I frowned, scrinching my face up tight. I held my breath for several seconds, and at last I burst out with it: "Brother Oliver, I'm emotionally involved with that woman!"

"Woman?"

"Eileen Flattery."

"I know *which* woman, Brother Benedict," he informed me. "But what do you mean by the phrase 'emotionally involved'?"

What did I mean by it? Wasn't that the question I'd been asking myself? We walked as far as the front wall, then reversed. "I mean," I said at last, "that my mind is confused. She's in my thoughts waking and sleeping. I hardly know who I am any more."

Brother Oliver listened to this definition in silence, his somber gaze on the alternating toes of his sandaled feet licking out from under his robe as he walked. When I finished, he nodded slowly and said, "In other words, she has attracted your attention."

"Yes," I said.

He nodded again, continuing to watch his feet, and we walked the length of the cloister as far as the archway leading to the chapel and cemetery. Again we reversed, and he said, "Is this a sexual feeling?"

"I suppose it must be," I said. "I want to touch her the way an infant wants to touch a gold watch."

I must have spoken somewhat forcefully. Brother Oliver flashed me a quick startled look, but said nothing.

I went on. "Last night," I said, "I did touch her."

He stopped in his tracks, and looked at me.

"Not very much," I said.

"Perhaps you should tell me about it," he suggested. He didn't walk on, so neither did I.

"Last night," I said, "she took me for a ride in Central Park. She stopped the car and two young men tried to rob us. After I chased them off she was—"

"You chased them off?"

"It worked out that way. And afterwards she was trembling, and I put my arms around her."

"I see," he said.

"I hadn't done that with anybody for a long time," I said.

"No," he agreed. "And that was as far as it went?"

"Yes, Brother."

"I see." He turned and walked again, and I fell in beside him, and we walked in silence together as far as the front wall, and reversed.

I said, "I think she's emotionally involved with me, too." Then I frowned and moved my arms around and stared out at the courtyard on our left, and said, "At least I think so. I'm not sure of it, but that's what I think."

Brother Oliver shook his head, saying, "I wish you knew a shorter phrase than 'emotionally involved,' Brother Benedict. It's like talking with some giddy version of Brother Clemence."

"I do know a shorter phrase, Brother Oliver," I told him, "but I'm afraid to use it."

"Oh." He gave me a quick speculative look, then studied his feet once more. "All right, then," he said. "Whatever you think best." His voice sounded muffled all at once, as though he were talking into a turtleneck sweater.

"Thank you, Brother Oliver," I said.

We walked together. We reached the cemetery arch and reversed. Brother Oliver said, "So you think she is also emotionally involved."

"I'm not sure," I admitted. "Maybe she's just confused, the way I am."

"And is that what she wanted to talk with you about last night?"

"Oh, no, not at all. She wanted to talk about the monastery."

"And to say what about it, Brother Benedict?"

I said, "She told me the arguments her father used to justify the sale."

"His arguments?" Brother Oliver sounded more intrigued than surprised. He said, "I hadn't realized he'd done any arguing on the subject."

"Apparently so, Brother. At least with his family."

"Ah." That seemed to explain things.

I said, "His argument is mostly function, by the way."

"Eh?"

"Function," I repeated. "The claim that usefulness is the primary virtue, that all other considerations are secondary, and that this particular space would be most usefully employed as an office building."

"A barbaric set of values," he said.

"Yes, Brother."

He mused, then said, "Was Miss Flattery reporting this argument favorably?"

"No. She wanted me to counteract it."

He raised an eyebrow. "Really? Why was that?"

"She said she could help us," I explained, "but she wouldn't do it unless she was convinced it was right to go against her father."

"Help us? In what way?"

"I don't know, Brother. She wouldn't be more specific, she only said she could definitely help us if she chose. But first I had to defeat her father's argument."

He nodded. "And did you?"

"No, Brother."

We had reached the front wall again. We reversed, and Brother Oliver said, "Because of your emotional involvement, Brother Benedict?"

"Probably," I admitted. "And then we were mugged," I added, as though that felony had cut me down in brilliant mid-debate.

"Yes, of course," he said. "And did you suggest to her that she talk to one of the other residents instead?"

"Yes, Brother."

That answer surprised him. "You did?"

"I really didn't want any of this to happen, Brother Oliver," I said.

"I know you didn't," he said, his sympathy showing again. "This all came on you too suddenly and too forcefully. You weren't ready for it."

"Father Banzolini calls it culture shock," I told him.

"You've discussed this with Father Banzolini?"

"Only certain aspects of it," I said. "In confession."

"Oh."

"Father Banzolini thinks I'm temporarily insane."

Brother Oliver gave me a look of utter astonishment. "He what?"

"Well, he didn't phrase it that way," I said. "He just said I I wasn't responsible for my actions at the moment."

Brother Oliver shook his head. "I'm not entirely convinced a Freudian priest is a viable hybrid."

"I may not actually be insane," I conceded, "but I'm certainly confused. I don't have any idea what I should do."

"Do? About what?"

I spread my hands. "About my future."

He stopped. Frowning at me he said, "Are you seriously considering an involvement with this woman? And I don't mean an emotional involvement, I mean an *involvement*."

"I don't know," I said. "I want to stay here, I want things to be the way they used to be, but I just don't know what to do about it. I need you to tell me, Brother Oliver."

"Tell you? What to do with your life?"

"Yes, please."

We came to the arch. Brother Oliver stopped, but did not reverse. Instead, he stood there for half a minute or so, gazing at the stones over long-departed residents. There were about thirty graves in our small cemetery, all from the nineteenth century. These days, we bury our deceased residents in a Catholic cemetery in Queens, next to the Long Island Expressway. The linkages with Travel are distressing, but unavoidable.

Brother Oliver sighed. He turned to me and said, "I can't tell you what to do, Brother Benedict."

"You can't?"

"No one can. Your own mind has to tell you what to do."

"My mind can't tell me anything," I said. "Not the way I am now."

"But how could anyone else decide whether or not you've lost your vocation? This woman is testing the strength of your commitment to God and to this life. The answer has to come from within, it has to."

"There's nothing within me but mush," I said.

"Brother Benedict," he said, "you are not tied by vows the way a priest is. That gives you more freedom, but also more responsibility. You have to make your own decisions."

"I've given a vow of obedience," I pointed out.

"But that's the only one," he said. "You've made no vows of chastity or poverty. You have vowed only to remain obedient to the laws of God and of this Order and of the Abbot."

"That's you," I said.

"And my commandment to you," he said, "is to search your mind and your heart, and do what is best for yourself. If that involves either temporary or permanent separation from this Order, you should do so. The decision is yours."

The buck stops here. "Yes, Brother," I said.

✠

There's a flow, a cyclical movement to the life of the monastery, and the points of the cycle primarily involve religion and work. Our religious activities, Mass and prayer and times of meditation, are mostly recurrent on a daily basis, but our work assignments tend to cycle at a more stately pace. While some tasks are in the permanent care of residents peculiarly suited to them—Brother Leo being our cook, for example, Brother Jerome being our superintendent-handyman, Brother Dexter handling our paperwork—most job assignments rotate among us all. I had been free of work assignments for nearly two weeks when suddenly my turn came around for two in a row. At the evening meal on that Sunday, a few hours after my talk with Brother Oliver, I was on kitchen duty with Brother Leo and Eli, and on Tuesday I had a stint in the office.

The kitchen job was simple but unappealing; one obeyed all of Brother Leo's barked commands about batter beating and water boiling and so on, and at the end of the meal one washed all the dishes. Such tasks left plenty of time for meditation, and all at once I had more than enough to meditate about. Washing spinach for the salad should certainly be conducive, if anything is, to dispassionate thought.

The outside world eats three meals a day, of course, but we feel content with two. We never have breakfast till we've been up and about for at least three hours, and then that first meal is hearty enough to carry us till the evening, when we have a second meal just as hearty. It's a healthy regimen, and it assures we'll have a good appetite every time we enter the refectory.

Brother Leo cooks all the meals, not because the rest of us aren't willing to do our share of the work but because he isn't willing to eat anything that any of us might prepare. He made that point clear in several unforgettable conversations shortly after joining the Order (unforgettable to those present at the time, who have repeated the good Brother's remarks almost verbatim to later-comers like myself), but he's always been willing to take on assistants and bully them. Thaddeus and Peregrine today at breakfast, for instance, and Eli and myself at dinner.

I got myself in trouble with Brother Leo right away, for what he grumbled was "wool gathering." And by golly, he was right. I hadn't even been brooding on my troubles; far from it. In fact, I had been standing there oblivious, watching Brother Eli peel carrots. He did it as though he were whittling, the little curls of carrot spreading around him exactly like wood shavings, and I began to be convinced the twelve Apostles would soon be emerging from that bunch of carrots; twelve little orange Apostles, edible and crunchy.

"Brother Benedict! You're wool gathering!"

"Ak!" And back to the spinach I went, salad gathering.

The Apostles did not after all appear, nor did the solution to my problem. The meal got itself made, and it got itself eaten, and the dishes got themselves washed, but my head remained a mess. Every time I tried to think about Eileen Flattery Bone my brain began to jiggle and fuzz like the television set when a plane goes over. And every time I tried to think about myself in a future outside these monastery walls my brain simply turned to snow, and then the snow melted. So much for meditation, and so much for Sunday.

✛

Monday was a free day for me, meaning a day in which I could walk in circles in the courtyard and fail to think. I could also enter the chapel to ask God for assistance, and then realize I didn't know what assistance I wanted. The strength to stay? Or the strength to go?

For the others in our community, Monday was the day we learned we could hope for nothing from the Landmarks Commission. Brother Hilarius apparently spent much of the day on the telephone, and he reported the result to us all at dinner. Brother Leo and today's slaveys—Clemence and Quillon—came soapy-armed from the kitchen to listen, and Brother Hilarius began by telling us we couldn't hope for the Landmarks Commission to designate us a landmark because they'd already rejected us seven years ago.

A lot of people said, "That's impossible." Brother Oliver said, "We would have known about it. Why wouldn't we have known about it?"

"We're not the owners," Brother Hilarius pointed out. "The Flatterys were informed, and they attended the hearing to oppose the designation. I suppose they should have informed us themselves, but we won't get very far with that argument seven years later."

Brother Clemence, wiping his soapy hands and arms on everybody's napkins, said, "What was the reason for the refusal?"

Brother Flavian thought he already knew. "So the Flatterys have friends in high places, eh?"

"That wasn't the reason," Brother Hilarius told him.

"Then what was it?"

"We have a dull facade."

Everybody looked at him. Brother Peregrine said, "We're a *monastery,* not a burlesque house."

"But that was the reason," Brother Hilarius said. "And if you think about it, it's true. We *do* have a dull facade."

What a thing to be accused of; a dull facade. Brother Quillon, who in fact did not have a dull facade, said, "What does that *mean?* Facade? I just don't understand it."

"The Landmarks law at that time," Brother Hilarius explained, "limited the commission to consideration of a building's facade, the outer walls facing the street. Inside, you could turn a place into

129

a roller skating rink, but if you kept that nice Federal facade then everything was fine."

Brother Oliver said, "Wait, let me understand this. Does the Landmarks Commission preserve buildings or front walls?"

"Front walls." Brother Hilarius spread his hands. "The Commission itself wants to do more, but the real estate people get in and lobby against the laws, so they come up with compromises. And that one said the Landmarks Commission could *not* designate a building on any basis other than its street facade. Not an architecturally interesting interior, not a useful function, not anything at all except facade. And our facade is dull."

Now that he'd explained it, nobody wanted to argue the point. In truth, our facade *was* dull. Since the Blessed Zapatero had been constructing a retreat from the world, he and his fellow builders had devoted their attentions mainly to the interior of our building. Facing Park Avenue was a blank gray stone wall one hundred feet long and twenty-five feet high. It contained two doors on the first floor and three smallish windows on the second floor, and that was it. From the street one couldn't see, one couldn't even guess at the existence of, our courtyard, our cloisters, our chapel, our cemetery or anything else.

Brother Clemence, having made a sopping pest of himself with everybody's napkins, now broke our grim silence by saying, "Wait a minute. Hilarius, didn't you say that was the law *at that time?*"

"Yes."

"Meaning it's been changed?"

"Not in any way that can help us."

"What's the change?"

Brother Hilarius said, "In 1973, the law was changed to permit the consideration of *some* interiors."

Brother Clemence brightened, saying, "Oh, really? I'd love to hear a law that could open up consideration to *some* interiors and not include *this* interior." His spreading (dry) arms suggested a magnificence in our surroundings that was perhaps slightly overdone.

Many of us felt the same way, and I could see hope entering the faces around me. But Brother Hilarius was already shaking his head. "The interiors to be considered," he said, "in the direct language of the law, are those 'customarily open or accessible to the public.' If there's one thing we're not, Brother Clemence, it's open or accessible to the public."

"Then it looks as though," Brother Clemence said, "I'll just have to save us myself, with my secondary documents."

Several of us turned to ask him how he was doing, and he gave us strong assurances. "Coming right along," he told us. "It's merely a matter of constructing the strongest possible profile." But somehow his air of self-confidence wasn't totally convincing.

✠

Tuesday I was on assignment in the office, another task which left the mind free to meditate. Though in my case the word wasn't meditate. In my case the word was *stew*.

There are actually two offices in the monastery, being the Abbot's Office and the Abbey Office. The Abbot's Office was where we'd been having our meetings and where Brother Clemence was now going through the chaos of our filing system. The Abbey Office, also called the scriptorium (inaccurately, I might say; a scriptorium in the old days was a room where monks hand-copied manuscripts), was at the front of the building, containing a desk and a telephone and a visitor's bench. Our rare incoming phone calls and in-person visitors were dealt with in this room. Our petty cash (all of our cash was petty) was also kept here, to be tapped by me on Saturday evenings for the price of a Sunday *Times*. One of us was usually on duty here afternoons and evenings, and Tuesday was my turn.

I spent the first hour or so sitting at the desk, leafing through the airplane magazines Brother Leo keeps in the bottom drawer there, and from time to time mooning into the middle distance, my brain turning in fretful circles like a dog trying to figure out how to lie down.

All of this cogitation was entirely self-centered, concerned only with my own future. I had virtually abandoned all thought about Dimp and the demolition deadline fast approaching. We had only sixteen days left to save ourselves, but I spared that fact hardly a thought.

Nor had I done anything about my suspicion that one of the

residents must have stolen the original lease. I'd mentioned the idea to nobody, and in fact I didn't even think about it myself. It was too grim to contemplate.

Whom would I suspect, out of my fifteen fellow monks? Brother Oliver? Brothers Clemence or Dexter or Hilarius? Brother Zebulon? Brothers Mallory or Jerome? Brothers Valerian or Quillon or Peregrine? Brothers Leo or Flavian? Brothers Silas or Eli or Thaddeus? There wasn't one of them I could suspect. How could I think about such a thing?

And my own problems did seem so much more acute. Brooding about them, it occurred to me at one point that I hadn't been considering Eileen Flattery's mental state in all this. Shouldn't I care what *she* was thinking? Didn't it matter that I might leave this monastery and then discover she didn't want me after all?

Well, no. In some strange way, she wasn't what really mattered. Brother Oliver had been right about that; her existence was the *form* of the test I was undergoing, but my vocation was the subject. Whether Eileen Flattery wanted me or not had finally nothing to do with my staying or going. The question was, would I remain Brother Benedict, or would I go back to being Charles Rowbottom? Everything else was confusion and irrelevancy.

It was nice to have the question defined, of course, but it would have been even nicer if it had come equipped with its own answer. I was continuing to ponder that little black spot in my thinking when all at once the street door opened and in came a lot of loud traffic noise and a tiny forceful man who slammed the door on the noise and then said, "All right, I'm here. I'm a busy man, let's get this over with."

I've been snapped back from meditation by the exterior world before, but never quite like *this*. In the first place, that street door was almost never opened, most of us preferring to use the courtyard door instead in our rare expeditions outside. In the second place, I'd assumed the street door was locked, since it usually was. And in the third place, who *was* this forceful little man?

I must have been gaping. The little man frowned at me and snapped, "You an unfortunate?" He darted quick impatient glances around the room, apparently looking for somebody swifter to talk to. "Where's the head man? Oliver."

"Brother Oliver? Who are *you*?"

His look grew even more impatient. "Dwarfmann," he said. "This Abbot wants a face-to-face, I'm here." He tapped a watch which was nervously displaying skinny red numbers on a black background: 2:27, it trembled, and the tiny brisk fingers tapped it, and it changed its mind. 2:28.

"Time flies," Dwarfmann commented.

Dwarfmann?

Dwarfmann! I jumped to my feet, displacing airplane magazines. "*Roger* Dwarfmann?"

He couldn't believe how I was wasting his flying time. "How many Dwarfmanns you expecting today?"

"None," I said. Then, "Wait. Yes, yes of course. Mr. Dwarfmann. Why don't you, uh, sit down." I looked around, my brain ascramble, trying to work out what piece of furniture people used when sitting down. "On that," I said, pointing, spying the bench. Then I remembered its name. "That bench," I said. "I'll go tell uh, I'll find Brother— I'll be right back."

He frowned after me as I fled the room. I couldn't help it if he thought I was an unfortunate; I'd been startled, that's all. I'm not very good at being startled. In the last ten years, before all this current craziness began to happen, I lost all of my training at being startled. There isn't all that much of a sudden nature that takes place in a monastery. Once, about six years ago, Brother Quillon tripped on the door jamb coming into the refectory and dumped a tray containing twelve dishes of ice cream on me, and of course the other week Brother Jerome had dropped that wet washcloth on my head, but other than that my life had been fairly placid for a long long time. It wasn't as though I were a cabdriver or something.

Brother Oliver was not in his office, though Brothers Clemence and Dexter were, both of them elbow deep in paper and looking mildly hysterical. I asked them if they knew where Brother Oliver was, and Brother Clemence said, "Try the library."

"Fine."

"Or the calefactory," said Brother Dexter.

Brother Clemence looked at him. "The calefactory? What would he be doing in *there*?"

"I saw him in there just the other day," Brother Dexter said.

Brother Clemence said, "But what would he be doing in there *now*?"

"Thank you," I told them both.

They ignored me. Brother Dexter said to Brother Clemence. "I just said he *could* be in there."

I hurried on, hearing their voices rising somewhat behind me.

Brother Oliver was not in the library. Brother Silas was sitting there, reading his book—when joining this Order, he had donated to our library fifteen remaindered copies of *I'm No Saint,* the memoir of his life as a professional criminal, and he frequently came here to glance through one or another copy—and when I asked him about Brother Oliver he said, "He *was* here. I think he went upstairs."

"Upstairs. Right." I turned back down the hall, and then I realized I'd have to go back through the office—the one contain- Roger Dwarfmann—to get to the stairs. Well, there was nothing for it.

The sounds of Brothers Clemence and Dexter in contention rippled from their doorway as I retraced my steps. I trotted back to the front office and found Roger Dwarfmann not sitting. He was standing, and he was pacing, and he was looking at his watch with the trembly red numbers. He paused to lower his eyebrows at me, but I didn't pause at all. "Upstairs," I said, *en passant.* "I'll just be—" And up the stairs I went.

Brother Oliver's room was second on the left. I could see it was empty through the open doorway, but I knocked anyway, and Brother Quillon came out of his own room diagonally across the hall to say, "Did you want somebody?"

"Brother Oliver."

"I think he's in the calefactory."

Two votes for that suggestion. "Ah," I said.

Brother Quillon went back into his room, leaving the door open. Starting for the stairs, I paused to look in at him and say, "What's he doing in there?"

Brother Quillon was puzzled. "I beg your pardon?"

"Brother Oliver. In the calefactory."

"Oh. Calisthenics," he said.

"Calisthenics? In the calefactory?"

"Brother Mallory thought it was getting too cold in the courtyard."

"Ah. Thank you." And I hurried back down the stairs, wondering fretfully what little red numbers were showing by now on Roger Dwarfmann's watch. But I really didn't want to know.

He was pacing again. He stopped to glare at me, frowning like a rock fault, and I said, "Calefactory. I'll go, um—" And down the hall I went again.

Brothers Clemence and Dexter were very angry at one another. I paused on the way by to close that door, not wanting Roger Dwarfmann to hear monks shouting at one another that way, and then hurried on down the hall to the calefactory.

The original idea of a calefactory was that it was a room that was kept warm in winter. Until this century, most rooms of most buildings were left unheated, and the calefactory in a monastery was where one could find heat if it was needed. The great fireplace in one wall demonstrates that this room was originally employed as its name suggests, but in more recent years it has become a general sitting room, our communal parlor. We most particularly like it in summer, perhaps, when it is one of the coolest spots in the building.

And Brother Mallory seemed to be taking it over for himself, gradually turning it into a gymnasium. Last Saturday he'd held his boxing matches here, and now his calisthenics class was spread out on the floor, raising one leg after the other with a great whiffling of robes. Brothers Valerian, Peregrine and Hilarius, looking like tipped-over wind up dolls, with Brother Mallory marching around them and counting out the cadence.

But no Brother Oliver. I shouted out my question, breaking into Brother Mallory's count, and while the three on the floor permitted their legs to flop and did a lot of gasping for breath, Brother Mallory mused a moment and said, "I think I saw him going into the chapel."

Would this never end? "Thank you, Brother," I said, and

135

trotted out the calefactory's side door, through the cloakroom past the sacristy, and into the chapel by the door behind the altar, where the reports of exploding knees told me Brother Zebulon was present long before I actually saw him.

Yes, there he was, sweeping the floor, and genuflecting every time he passed the center aisle. Crack! Bang! Kapow! He sounded like a Civil War battle.

Brother Oliver wasn't here, of course. I hurried over to Brother Zebulon—adding my own rattle of gunfire when genuflecting along the way—and whispered, "Where's Brother Oliver?"

He ignored me. I don't think he even knew I was there.

Well. One should whisper in church, but whispering to a deaf old man is self-defeating, so I raised my voice: "Brother Zebulon!"

He dropped his broom and jumped a foot. Turning, he said, "What? What?"

"Brother Oliver," I said. "Do you know where he is?"

He was annoyed with me, and so didn't answer till he'd picked up his broom. Then he said, "Try the kitchen," and turned his back on me.

I went out the far door of the chapel, intending to go through the cemetery to the cloister and thus into the kitchen, but turning out the cemetery arch I stopped and frowned and decided no. The way things were going Brother Oliver would *not* be in the kitchen but Brother Leo would, and he'd tell me to try the refectory, where some other Brother would tell me to try the second floor on this side—there are two separate second floors, which don't connect—where yet another Brother would tell me to try the tower, where a passing pigeon would suggest I try the undercroft, which is the basement, back over on the other side. Directly beneath, in fact, the pacing feet of Roger Dwarfmann.

No. Enough. Leaving the cemetery, I went instead directly out to the courtyard, a big grassy area crisscrossed by stone walks and dotted with plane trees, a few struggling evergreens, a couple of birdbaths, a flower garden which was not at its best this time of year, and along the chapel wall our grape arbor. I strode now out to the middle of this space, lifted my head, and said, *"BROTHER OLIVER!"*

"Yes, Brother Benedict?"

He was right next to me. He came mildly around the nearest evergreen, his paintbrush and palette in his hands, and blinked gently at me, wondering what it was I wanted.

"At last," I said. "It must be 2:43 by now, maybe even 2:44."

"Brother Benedict? Are you all right?"

"I'm fine," I lied. "Roger Dwarfmann is in there."

Brother Oliver looked pleasantly surprised, but no more. "He called?"

"He came! He's here, right now, he's walking up and down in the office!"

"He's here *now*?" Brother Oliver fussed with his paintbrush and palette, not knowing where to put them. "In my office?"

"No, the other one. The scriptorium. Brother Clemence is in your office, I didn't think I should—"

I stopped talking, because Brother Oliver had disappeared around the tree again. Following him, I saw him place his brush and palette at the feet of his latest murky Madonna, who oddly enough seemed to have been influenced by Picasso—I assume that treatment of the eyes was deliberate—and then he gathered up his skirts and trotted toward the side door, which led via a short hall to the scriptorium. I jogged after.

Dwarfmann had continued to pace. He stopped at our arrival and I tried to read those transient red numbers on his wrist, but his hands and arms were constantly involved in expansive gestures. "Well?" he said, glaring past Brother Oliver's shoulder at me. "Well?"

Apparently I was to make introductions. "Brother Oliver," I said. "This is Roger Dwarfmann."

"So here you are," Dwarfmann said. He bobbed on the balls of his feet, as though to make himself taller, and frowned severely upward at Brother Oliver's bulk.

"Have I kept you waiting? I'm so sorry," Brother Oliver said. "I was painting, in the courtyard. This winter light is so perfect for—"

Dwarfmann gestured that away with an impatient flick of his numerical wrist; I couldn't see the numbers. "My days," he said, "are swifter than a weaver's shuttle. Let's get down to business."

I'm sure Brother Oliver was as taken aback as I was. The imagery, in Dwarfmann's rattly style of speech, seemed wildly inappropriate. Then Brother Oliver said, in distinct astonishment, "Was that from Job?"

"Chapter seven, verse six," Dwarfmann snapped. "Come, come, if you have something to say to me, say it. Our time is a very shadow that passeth away."

"I don't know the Apocrypha," Brother Oliver said.

Dwarfmann gave him a thin smile. "You know it well enough to recognize it. Wisdom of Solomon, chapter two, verse five."

"Then I can only cite One Thessalonians," Brother Oliver said. "Chapter five, verse fourteen. Be patient toward all men."

"Let us *run* with patience," Dwarfmann or somebody said, "the race that is set before us."

"I don't believe," Brother Oliver told him, "that was quite the implication of that verse in its original context."

"Hebrews, twelve, one." Dwarfmann shrugged. "Then how about Paul to Timothy, with its meaning intact? Be instant in season, out of season." Again he tapped those little red numbers, and now I saw them: 2:51. I don't know why I felt so relieved to know the exact time—something about Dwarfmann's presence, I suppose. And he was saying, "I'm a busy man." *That* couldn't be Biblical. "My man Snopes told you all you needed to know, we'll give you every assistance in relocation, given the circumstances we'll go farther than the law requires. *Much* farther. But that wasn't enough for you, you have to hear it from me direct. All right, you're hearing it from me direct. We're building on this site."

"There *is* a building on this site," Brother Oliver said.

"Not for long."

"Why not look at it?" Brother Oliver made hospitable gestures, urging our guest to come look the place over. "Now that you're here, why not see the place you intend to destroy?"

"Beauty is vain," Dwarfmann said. "Proverbs, thirty-one, thirty."

Brother Oliver began to look somewhat put out. He said, "Wot ye not what the Scripture saith? Romans, eleven."

With that sudden thin smile again, Dwarfmann answered, "What saith the Scripture? Galatians, four."

"Pride goeth before destruction," Brother Oliver told him, "and an haughty spirit before a fall. Proverbs, sixteen."

Dwarfmann shrugged, saying, "Let us do evil, that good may come. Romans, three."

"Woe unto them that call evil good, and good evil. Isaiah, five."

"Sin is not imputed when there is no law," Dwarfmann insisted. "Romans, five."

Brother Oliver shook his head. "He that maketh haste to be rich shall not be innocent."

"Money answereth all things," Dwarfmann said, with a great deal of assurance.

"He heapeth up riches," Brother Oliver said scornfully, "and knoweth not who shall gather them."

"Unto every one that hath shall be given, and he shall have abundance." Dwarfmann permitted his own scornful expression to roam around our room, then finished, "But from him that hath not shall be taken away even that which he hath." Another quick look at his watch. "I think we've played enough," he said, and turned toward the door.

Brother Oliver had two pink circles on his cheeks, and his pudgy hands were more or less closed into ineffective fists. "The devil is come down unto you," he announced, "having great wrath, because he knoweth that he hath but a short time."

Dwarfmann's hand was on our doorknob. He looked back at Brother Oliver, flashed that thin smile again as though to say he was glad we all understood one another now, and with another quick glance around the room said, "He shall return no more to his house, neither shall his place know him any more. Job, chapter seven, verse ten." And he left.

Brother Oliver expelled held-in breath with a sudden long whoosh. Shaking my head, I said, "The devil can cite Scripture for his purpose."

Brother Oliver gave me a puzzled look. "Is that New Testament? I don't recognize that."

"Uhh, no," I said. "It's Shakespeare. *Merchant of Venice.*" I cleared my throat. "Sorry," I said.

NINE

ATHER Banzolini's tear sheets were perhaps the most difficult penance he'd yet given me. What an earnest writer he was! His articles were clearly the work of a slow but serious man who very sincerely wanted to explain every last detail of whatever subject he had chosen to gnaw. Unfortunately, he knew only one kind of sentence—the kind that has a subject and a verb and a comma and another subject and another verb and a period—and he used that sentence to tell us *everything*. A straightforward compound sentence is perfectly all right, of course, but seven thousand of them in a row can get wearing. After a while, the only question left was whether the word after the comma would be "and" or "but" or "or."

But I did have to read them. Father Banzolini had given me these tear sheets at confession with a kind of shy pride, and I knew I was not only going to have to read them, I was going to have to *like* them. Or at least find something in each of them that I could think of as likable for the next time I met with their author.

Because I was on the horns of a dilemma, a true dilemma. If I lied to Father Banzolini, I would then have to admit to him in confession that I had told the lie. In the abstract that might make for what mathematicians call a pretty problem, but in real life it made for a very ugly problem indeed.

And so I read. I learned more than I cared to know about missionary obstacles in newly independent African states, the attitude of the Church toward the "Protestant Ethic," Women's Lib for Catholics, feudalism versus mass transit, translation difficulties with the Bible, and several other topics both sacred and profane. By the time I finished I was feeling both sacred and profane myself.

Well, at least I was distracted for a while from my own more personal dilemma, which could very neatly be defined in the Father Banzolini Format: "I will stay in the monastery, or I will leave the monastery." Meditation was getting me nowhere on that topic, so perhaps distraction would help. As Father Banzolini himself had pointed out in *The Subconscious and the Holy Ghost*, "We think we are thinking about something else, but we are still thinking about Topic A."

So I read all the articles, starting them Tuesday night and finishing early Wednesday afternoon. Then I took a walk in the cloisters, trying to think of something both truthful and flattering to say about them. I could call them "interesting," which was true of at least a few—*The Great Catholic Boxers*, for instance, and *Why Animals Don't Have Souls*. I could say of all of them that they were "fact-filled," and I could hear myself saying enthusiastically to Father Banzolini, "I hadn't known about
————." (I'd fill in the blank as seemed appropriate at the time.)

But it was going to take more; I could feel it in my bones. I doubted that Father Banzolini, in the ordinary course of his days, had been so inundated with praise for his writing efforts as to become jaded or blasé on the subject. It was my very strong suspicion, in fact, that he was hungry for shoptalk and "positive feedback," as he'd phrased it in *The Confessional: A Two-Way*

Street. It was going to take more than a couple of carefully phrased ambivalent sentences to satisfy that hunger.

The more I thought about it, the more I realized I was going to need professional—or at least semiprofessional—help. Brother Silas did a lot of reading in the Sunday *Times* Book Review, and I suspected there was still something criminous buried deep within him. Could he be of assistance? Not so much with specific phrases as with a general wishy-washy attitude. I firmly intended to waffle, but I wasn't exactly sure how to go about doing it.

Come to think of it, though, Brother Silas just didn't strike me as the waffling type. Criminal and literary though he might be, there was still something very direct about his approach to life. I would certainly talk to him, but I doubted he was the expert I needed.

Who else, then? Pacing back and forth in the cloister, trying to think of someone who could help, I looked out over the courtyard where several of my fellow residents happened at the moment to be in view. Brother Oliver, for instance, seated on a three-legged stool, was hard at work on his latest Madonna and Child; but no, he didn't have the devious cast of mind I was seeking. Brothers Mallory and Jerome were packing mulch around some shrubbery near the front wall, but they were even more remote from the necessary subtlety of approach. And who else was there?

Someone came out of Brother Oliver's office across the way, turning to walk along the cloister on that side. His cowl was up, making identification difficult, but in his build and movements he reminded me of Brother Peregrine.

Of course! Brother Peregrine had operated summer theaters! Would anyone be more experienced at the ambivalent compliment, the tender treatment of tremulous talents? "Brother Peregrine!" I cried, waving one hand over my head, and dashed out across the courtyard in his direction.

He didn't seem to hear me. He was striding quite purposefully toward the front wall, more or less in the direction of Brothers Mallory and Jerome, angling out now away from the cloister and across the courtyard toward the front doors.

"Brother Peregrine! Brother Peregrine!" I altered my own

course to intersect his, trotting around birdbaths and plane trees, and he just kept moving. Such concentration I would normally respect, but this time I could think of nothing but my own problems, so when I reached him I put out my hand to grab his forearm, his head turned in my direction, and inside the cowl he was not Brother Peregrine.

A familiar face, but not—

"Frank Flattery!" I shouted his name out loud, more from astonishment than anything else. Dan Flattery's unmarried son, Eileen's brother.

Eileen's brother, but not ours.

"What—" I said, bewildered, and then everything happened at once. Flattery pulled away from me, with an imprecation that didn't blend well with his costume. Brother Clemence came dashing out of Brother Oliver's office, crying, "Fire!" And Flattery made a run for the doors.

"Brother Mallory!" I shouted. Flattery's cowl had fallen back, revealing him as a stranger and thereby greatly simplifying the message I had to transmit. When Brother Mallory looked up from his mulching, I pointed at the running impostor and shouted, "Smite him, Brother Mallory!"

Well, he tried, but years in a monastery do take their toll of the belligerent instincts. Brother Mallory dashed over between Flattery and the doors, feinted with his left and threw an overhand right. Flattery stepped inside the punch, gave Brother Mallory a short left chop to the breadbasket and a quick right uppercut on the button, and as Brother Mallory went pinwheeling backward Flattery flung himself at the doors, yanked them open, and dashed out.

I went running in his wake. Cabs, trucks, pedestrians, that great churning agitated other world boiled away outside there, and Flattery ran into it like a man in an asbestos suit running through a fire. A florist's delivery truck was parked at the curb, and Flattery ran around it and disappeared. I gave chase, but by the time I rounded the truck he was gone. Into a passing cab, perhaps, or zig-zag across this busy street. Gone, in any event. Gone.

✠

And so was the lease. Abbot Urban's illuminated lease, its old dry paper burned to ashes, along with a dozen other documents. "Our whole case," Brother Clemence said bitterly.

The physical events were simply stated. Frank Flattery had disguised himself in a robe like ours and had come on the grounds through either of our front doors—we were very very sloppy about keeping them locked. He had hung around Brother Oliver's office until Brother Clemence, working alone in there today, had been called away by nature. Then Flattery had entered, made a pile of all the valuable documents on the refectory table, put a match to them, and walked out again. If I hadn't mistaken him for Brother Peregrine he would have gotten away scot-free.

Well, apparently he'd gotten away scot-free anyway. When we had our hysterical meeting in Brother Oliver's smoke-reeking office five minutes after the event, with all sixteen of us present, it turned out I was the only one who could identify the arsonist, and Brother Clemence assured me my unsupported testimony would not be sufficient in a criminal action. "Particularly," he pointed out, "when you're already a party in a civil dispute against his family."

Brother Flavian, who was practically eating the woodwork in his frustration and rage, cried at Brother Mallory, "Surely *you* know what he looks like! The man knocked you down!"

Brother Mallory, who had a swollen jaw and a sheepish expression, flushed a dull red and muttered, "It all happened too fast. We were both bobbing and weaving, I wouldn't recognize him if he came walking through that door over there. All I know is he was white."

"Well, *that* narrows it," Brother Flavian said.

Brother Mallory looked as though he'd like to rehearse awhile on Brother Flavian in preparation for a return bout with Frank Flattery, but he said nothing.

The main subject, in any event, was the loss, which turned out to be considerable. Brother Oliver asked Brother Clemence, "Had you been getting close to what you wanted?"

"Close?" Brother Clemence's manner combined outrage and weariness in a very delicate balance. "We had it," he said. "We had it in the palm of our hand."

Brother Dexter said, "We were just talking about it this morning, Brother Oliver. Clemence and I, right in this room, with the papers around us."

"It took nearly a dozen separate secondary documents," Brother Clemence said, "and some *very* fancy inductive reasoning may I say, but we had put together a profile of the lease that I am *certain* would have stood up in any court in the land."

"All we needed," Brother Dexter added, "was to assemble the documents in the proper order and write our brief."

"That's what I was doing when it happened," Brother Clemence said. "I was writing it all out, laying every document in place, demonstrating what each one meant, how they reinforced one another, how the implications of *this* paper supported the implications of *that* paper, making sure it was absolutely airtight."

"It was becoming a beautiful piece of work," Brother Dexter told us.

Brother Clemence shook his head. "The rest of today to finish the draft," he said. "Tomorrow I'd intended to go over it with you, Brother Oliver, and anyone else who was interested. By Friday my friend could have been meeting with the Flatterys' attorneys."

We all looked silently at the ash-and-water mess on the refectory table. Brother Oliver said, "Isn't there any way to start all over?"

"None," Brother Clemence said. "The secondary documents are gone. All of our substantiation is up in smoke."

"Couldn't they be reconstructed?"

Brother Clemence smudged his forehead with his smudgy hand. "Use tertiary documents to reconstruct the secondary documents, and then by implication reconstruct the primary document? Brother Oliver, I doubt there's a human brain on this planet that could do a thing like that, and certainly not in two weeks."

Brother Peregrine joined the conversation, saying, "But they won't start tearing the building down in two weeks, will they? That's only when the sale is completed."

"Once the sale is made," Brother Clemence told him, "it will be too late. Nothing can save us unless we stop the sale from going through, that's our only hope."

Brother Eli, who rarely had anything to say, now said, "They'll come with the bulldozers. Bright and early on the first of January."

We all looked at him. Brother Peregrine said, "What makes you think so?"

"We're troublemakers," Brother Eli said. "The longer we're around, the more trouble we can make, but once this building is knocked down the trouble is gone."

The Vietnam generation has a slightly different view of life from the rest of us; colder, and I suspect more accurate. Brother Oliver said, "You mean, whether they intend to start construction right away or not, they'll get rid of us for the advantage of getting rid of us."

Brother Eli nodded.

Brother Oliver shook his head. "It isn't the world that Christ had in mind," he said. Turning to Brother Clemence he said, "And was this our last chance? Do we have to give up now?"

The heaviness in Brother Clemence's stance and voice seemed to indicate that the answer to that question was yes, but he said, "Not necessarily. There may be things we can do, delaying tactics at least, and maybe some—"

"Excuse me," I said.

Brother Clemence paused, and looked at me. "Brother?"

"I don't think," I said carefully, hating to have to talk this way, "you should be specific about your plans, Brother Clemence."

He didn't understand me. "You mean it's bad luck? Superstition, Brother Benedict?"

"No, that isn't what I mean," I said. "I mean, how did Frank Flattery know what to burn? How did he know there *was* something to burn?"

I had everyone's attention now. Brother Oliver said, "What on earth are you saying to us, Brother Benedict?"

"I'm saying what Brother Silas said the other day," I said. "And Brother Clemence said it, too. That *our* copy of the original lease was stolen. And who stole it?"

"Frank Flattery," Brother Clemence said. "He obviously came in here the same way he did today."

"How did he know where to look? And how did he know today *where* to look and *what* to look for?"

Brother Hilarius said to me, "Speak it plain, Brother Benedict. Say it right out."

"He had to have help from one of us," I said.

✝

What a miserable evening we spent. There was silence in the refectory throughout the evening meal. And silence from the kitchen as well; Brother Leo could not be heard tonight, chewing out his current slaveys in his usual style.

No calisthenics tonight, no boxing matches. No discussions, no chess. No one even had the heart to turn on the TV. We brooded separately, most of us alone in our rooms, and how strange it seemed to see all those doors closed; almost always, we left them open.

At first, most of the others had argued against what I had to say, or at least they'd tried. But what counter-argument was there? The original lease *had* been stolen, that no longer seemed in doubt. Frank Flattery had without question burned the copy and its supporting documents, and so *must* have known in advance of their existence. Would he have risked exposure to come inside these walls on a fishing expedition? No, he would have come in here only because he already knew there was a serious threat to the Flatterys' interests.

How could we suspect one another? And yet, how could we not? And suspicion of one meant automatically suspicion of all, since if it was impossible to believe in the guilt of any of us than it must be equally impossible to believe in the innocence of any one of us.

Say Brother Jerome. Impossible? More or less impossible than Brother Quillon? And was Brother Quillon more or less impossible than Brother Zebulon?

Oh, it was *all* impossible.

Defeated by it, our community destroyed by an idea more thoroughly than it could ever be destroyed by Dimp's bulldozers, we separated into silent, unhappy, mistrustful lumps of matter. No one could meet anyone else's eye; no one wanted to look at a suspicious face, or be caught with one. And everyone slunk around as though we *all* were guilty.

While I was the guiltiest of all. Which was ridiculous, I know, but there it was. Although I hadn't been the one to betray us to the Flatterys, I had been the one to bring the bad tidings and I felt guilty for the effect they'd had. Sitting in my room after dinner, listening to the miserable silence all around me, I dearly wished I'd kept my deductions to myself.

I didn't do much sleeping that night. If I hadn't already had the Father Banzolini dilemma to think about, and if I hadn't already had the Eileen Flattery dilemma to think about, and if I hadn't already had my own future here to think about, and if I hadn't already had the onrushing destruction of the monastery to think about, I had this damned traitor in our midst to think about.

In the theological sense, that "damned." Oh, very much in the theological sense.

✢

"Brother Oliver," I said, the next morning.

He looked as sleepless and bleary-eyed as I felt. He was sitting on his three-legged stool before his latest Madonna and Child, but his hands were empty and he had half-turned away from his painting to brood at nothing in particular. Now he squinted up at me in the cold clear winter light that he was wasting, and sighed, and said, "Yes, Brother Benedict?" In his tone, he seemed to be asking me what dreadful news I had to bring him this time.

I said, "May I have your permission, Brother, to Travel?"

That caught his interest, though only marginally. "Travel?"

"I was thinking last night," I said, and he sighed again in agreement. I went on, "I feel responsible for the way everybody feels, I was the one who told you all that it had to be one—"

"Oh, no, Brother," he said. Rising from the stool, trying to rouse himself to express concern, he rested a hand on my arm and said, "You shouldn't blame yourself, Brother. You merely pointed out to us something that was there for all to see. I should have seen it myself, but it was just so, so—" He made a helpless gesture, by way of finishing the sentence.

"Yes, I know," I said. "But I want to do something, I want to make amends somehow."

"There's nothing to make amends for, Brother."

"I want to do what I can," I said.

Again he sighed. "Very well. And what is it you want to do?"

"See Eileen Flattery."

He reared back in astonishment. "*See* her? What on earth for?"

"I believe she was telling me the truth the last time I saw her," I said. "I don't believe she was being two-faced, like her brother and her father. I believe she really would try to help us, if she believed her father was in the wrong."

"Help us how? What could she do?"

"I don't know," I said. "But if I went to her, if I told her what her brother has done, that might put her on our side. At least I could try."

He thought about that. "And what about . . . your own quandaries, Brother?"

"Under the circumstances," I said, "I believe I could sublimate them."

Again he patted my arm. "Bless you, Brother Benedict," he said. "You have my permission, and my thanks."

✣

I was an old hand at Travel by now, practically a commuter. Although this was my first experience outside the walls completely on my own, I strode off across 51st Street with barely a qualm. I made it to Penn Station without incident, re-excavated the Long Island Railroad without difficulty, and boarded a train for Sayville almost at once.

In the first part of the trip, in the two-level train with the tiny compartments, I shared the ride with a Santa Claus who drank something sweet-smelling from a pint bottle he kept in the pocket of his red Santa Claus coat. The white beard and red nose and huge paunch all seemed real enough, but instead of a deep ho-ho-

ho sort of voice he had a raspy cracked-pottery sounding thing, as though he'd been left outside in the damp for too many nights. Drinking, wiping his mouth on his red sleeve, offering the bottle to me—I shook my head, thanking him with a small smile—he said, "Tough racket."

"I'm sure," I said.

He glugged again, offered the bottle again. "Change your mind?"

"Thanks just the same," I said.

He shrugged, screwed the cap on the bottle, and stuffed it away in his pocket. "Fuckin little kids," he said.

"I suppose so," I said.

He nodded, brooding at his reflection in the window. We were still in the tunnel, with only blackness outside the train. Then he looked at me again and said, "What do you do off season?"

"I beg your pardon?"

He gestured, with a thick-knuckled hand. "You know. After Christmas."

Understanding the misunderstanding then, I smiled and said, "I go on being a monk."

He looked interested. "Oh, yeah?"

"A real monk," I said.

Then he got it, too, and he grinned widely, showing stumpy brown teeth inside the snow-white beard. "No shit," he said. "You're a real monk?"

"That's right," I said.

He laughed at that, with his hands on his knees. It wasn't a Santa Claus laugh, but it was a laugh. "A real monk," he repeated.

I nodded, smiling back at him.

He leaned forward, tapping my knee. "Whadaya think," he said. "Maybe I'm the real Santy Claus.

"Maybe you are," I said.

He tugged at his beard. "This ain't fake, you know."

"I can see that."

"Damn right." He sat back, studying me, pleased with himself, and abruptly said, "So whadaya want for Christmas?"

"What?"

151

"Sure," he said. "Whadaya want for Christmas?" His grin was huge.

I grinned right back at him. "I want my monastery back," I said.

He nodded, chuckling to himself. Laying a finger beside his nose, he said, "You got it." And he winked at me.

✝

They told me she wasn't there. I spoke to her mother first, and she said, "Oh, Eileen went away for the holidays. Aren't you the monk that came here last week with that other one, the stout one?"

"That was Brother Oliver," I said.

"Oh, he made Dan *very* upset," she said. She hadn't invited me into the house, and I could see she wasn't going to. "I think Dan would be *very* angry if he saw you here," she said.

"I'm sorry we upset him," I said. "Could you tell me when Eileen will be back?"

"Oh, not till after the first of the year," she said. "But I'll be certain to tell her you called. Brother—what was it?"

"Benedict," I said. But I was thinking that our deadline was the first of the year. Fifteen days from now. After that it would be too late.

"Brother Benedict," the mother was saying. "I'll be sure to tell her." And she was starting to close the door.

"Uh, Mrs. Flattery. Wait."

"Yes?" She didn't want to be impolite—I could see that—but on the other hand she didn't want this conversation to continue any longer either.

I said, "Where is she? She's gone away where?" Thinking that it might be somewhere close by, that I could still get in touch with her.

But Mrs. Flattery said, "Oh, the Caribbean. She loves to get down there two or three times every winter. I'll be sure to tell her you called." And she firmly closed the door.

The Caribbean. She might as well have gone to the Moon. More

152

wasted Travel. I'd come out here for nothing. Gloomily I turned away from the door.

To see a small dark green automobile turning in at the driveway, with a female at the wheel. Had Mrs. Flattery lied to me? I waited, hope fluttering in my throat, and when the automobile stopped it was Eileen's sister-in-law who clambered out. Peggy, her name was, married to Eileen's brother Hugh. Not the brother who had burned our papers, that was the unmarried one, Frank.

Peggy was a pleasant enough girl, and she recognized me at once. "Well, Brother Benedict," she said, with a big open smile, "what brings you way out here?"

"I wanted to see Eileen," I said. "But I understand she's gone away."

"Down to Puerto Rico for the holidays," Peggy agreed. She was so open and friendly with me that I couldn't believe she was a part of the plot against us, or knew anything about it.

"Puerto Rico, eh?" The vague concept of writing her some sort of letter entered my head, and I said, "Would you know her address? I'd like to, uh, send her a Christmas card."

"How very sweet," she said. "Yes, I'll give it to you; wait, um—" She rummaged in her shoulder bag, produced a stub of pencil and an envelope with LILCO in big letters for the return address, and carefully printed on the back of the envelope Eileen's address in the Caribbean, using the top of her little green automobile as a writing surface. "There you are," she said.

"Thank you very much."

"Nice to see you again," she told me.

"And you," I said, giving her a smile and a bow. I was becoming quite the lady's man.

TEN

Y USELESS JOURNEY didn't help improve the atmosphere in the monastery, but I doubt at that point anything could have. I returned without incident, reported to Brother Oliver, and sank back at once into the silent morass that still enveloped everybody else. There seemed nothing to do, no action that anyone could take that would get us out of this pit we were in.

Brothers Flavian and Silas had talked at first about conducting an investigation, and for a little while they'd even had Brother Clemence involved with their idea, but when all was said and done what was there to investigate? There were no secrets in our lives; we knew one another as well as we knew ourselves. Could we interrogate one another? "Where were you on the night of December first?" Or any other date you chose, the answer would always be the same: "Right here, and you know it, because you saw me. Because you would have noticed my absence." We couldn't do timetables of people's movements, because we *had* no movements. We couldn't check the suspects' associates, because we associated with no one but ourselves. Failing a confession by the guilty party, what was there to do?

Nothing.

And without that confession, without knowing certainly and finally who the guilty party was, how could we go on with one another? We couldn't, that's all. We could only sit and mope and wait for some outside force to change things.

Until my brainstorm.

What is there to call a brainstorm but a brainstorm? There are two kinds of reasoning, and a brainstorm is the other one. The first kind, deductive reasoning, the process of arriving at D on the basis of A and B and C, is easily explained and easily seen, but inductive reasoning, the process of arriving at D when all you've had to go on is 7 and B and K, is utterly impossible to describe. When people say to writers or inventors, "Where do you get your ideas?" they are really asking them to explain inductive reasoning.

Sir Arthur Conan Doyle, creator of Sherlock Holmes, more or less had to try a definition of inductive reasoning, and so he wrote, in *The Sign of the Four*, "When you have eliminated the impossible, whatever remains, however improbable, must be the truth." Although he didn't go on to tell us how to draw that thin and snakelike line between the impossible and the improbable, the definition has a certain comfortable solidity to it, and I suppose it could be used to explain my brainstorm. For instance, I suppose some corner of my brain could have been saying to itself like so:

1) It is impossible that any of the Brothers in this monastery betrayed us to the Flatterys.
2) It is impossible that Frank Flattery could have known to come in here and burn those papers without having been told of their existence, their importance and their location.
3) It is impossible that Frank Flattery could have been told

these things by anybody *except* a member of this community.

4) However improbable it may sound, Frank Flattery must have been told those things by someone who didn't know he was telling.

All of which is hindsight. None of that was in my conscious mind prior to the brainstorm. It simply struck me, that's all, and I rose up from my bed and went downstairs, where I found Brother Oliver coming long-faced out of his office. "May I go in there?" I asked him.

He seemed slightly surprised. "Did you want to talk to me, Brother Benedict?"

"No, I just wanted to be alone in your office for a few minutes," I said. Alone, because although I was certain in some non-rational way, at the rational level I thought I was probably crazy.

Suspicion crossed his face—what a strange thing to see there—and then cleared away again. Was it because he realized he could trust me, or because he'd remembered the damage had already been done?

"Of course, Brother," he said, trying to smile as though he hadn't hesitated, and he stepped aside, gesturing me the hospitality of his office. "Are you going to meditate?"

"Fumigate," I told him, and went on in.

✛

I found the bug, taped to the back of a Madonna and Child. It looked like a large button, and yet it didn't. What it was most like was those enlarged photographs of the eyeball of a fly, and it had for me the same eerie inhuman effect. The human race lost something when people stopped bashing one another with sticks and started using technology in their disputes, and what they lost was their humanness. We'll all wake up some morning and find that *we're* the Martians.

But didn't this thing need wires? Apparently not. It was all alone here, a little Flattery outpost in our midst. And where would the receiver be, the nest of ears, listening to every word spoken in this room?

Well, maybe that florist's truck had also been parked in my subconscious at the time of the brainstorm. Consciously, though, it was only now that I realized it was far too often parked outside our door. Every time I went out it had been there, sometimes noticed and sometimes not. Frank Flattery had run around it and disappeared; inside it, of course.

Outrage is not an emotion I'm that used to, and in this instance it made me do something foolish. Pausing for nothing, I stormed out of Brother Oliver's office through the outer door to the cloister, strode across the courtyard, threw open the great doors to the outside world, ignored the midafternoon crush of pedestrians and traffic, bore directly to the rear of the florist's truck, yanked open its back doors, and Alfred Broyle punched me very hard on the nose.

I sat down on the pavement. Eileen's "young man" pulled his doors closed again, and the florist's truck drove immediately away.

✝

"You made a very serious error there," Brother Clemence told me.

"I know," I said. I felt miserable. Not only had I made a very serious error, I'd been punched in the nose for my pains and it still hurt. I was puffy around the eyes, I couldn't breathe through my nose, and I talked like a long-distance telephone operator.

Brother Oliver said, "Oh, Brother Clemence, don't be hard on him. He did *wonderful* work this afternoon! That cloud of suspicion, that sense of gloom—"

"I know that," Brother Clemence said. "You're absolutely right. We all owe Brother Benedict our deepest thanks for what he did. I only wish he'd taken along a witness when he went out to that florist's truck."

This conversation was taking place an hour later, in Brother Oliver's office, sans microphone. (The bug itself was in the sacristy, under a stack of altar cloths.) Brothers Clemence, Oliver, Dexter and I had been joined by an old friend of Brother Clemence, a distinguished-looking attorney named Remington Gates

157

who sported both a hat *and* a cane, and who pursed his lips a lot to display a sense of dubiousness.

The sequence of events had now been pretty clearly worked out. The Flatterys had undoubtedly been planning this sale for several years, at least since that Landmarks Commission hearing, and had been waiting only for the lease to be up. Their difficulty had been with that clause giving us the option to renew. Learning that the lease had not been recorded with the County Clerk, that they and we had the only copies, they had broken in here at some point, rifled our files—what an undertaking *that* must have been—and stolen our copy of the lease. Either then or later they'd planted that bug, so they would know if we planned any moves to save ourselves. They'd hoped we wouldn't learn about the sale until after next January first, when it would be over and done with, when Dimp might have some small trouble with us but the Flatterys would be in the clear. But we did find out, so at once they'd put us under constant surveillance, just to be on the safe side. Naturally they'd heard us discover the copy of the lease, and they'd heard Brother Clemence discuss his plan involving secondary documents, and they'd waited till Brother Clemence had told Brother Dexter—in their hearing—that we now did have all the documentary evidence we needed. Then they broke in and burned the papers.

And we couldn't prove it. I was the only one who could identify Alfred Broyle as the man in the florist's truck, and in fact I was the only one who could identify the florist's truck. I was also the only one who could identify Frank Flattery as the arsonist. If only I had brought someone else with me today, a second witness to the presence of that truck and the presence in it of Alfred Broyle, we would now have a presentable case. Instead of which, we had Mr. Remington Gates pursing his lips and saying, "I really don't see that we have enough."

Brother Oliver said, "But we have so *much*. We have that, that microphone thing, and several of us saw the man running away after he set fire to our papers."

Mr. Gates said, "But none of you can identify him, except Brother Benedict here. And Brother Benedict found the microphone. It's all Brother Benedict. Do you know what I would say if I were the attorney on the other side?"

Brother Clemence rather gloomily said, "I know what you'd say, Rem."

"Yes, you do, Howard," Mr. Gates said to him. (So Brother Clemence's civilian name had been Howard; how strange. I squinted at him, trying to see him as a Howard, but failed.) "But let me," Mr. Gates went on, "try to make it clear to your friends here." Turning a stern eye on me, pursing his lips mammothly, he said, "I am now the attorney for the other side, Brother Benedict."

"Yes, sir," I said.

"And I put it to you, Brother Benedict, that you are happy in this monastery."

"Of course."

"You do not want to leave this monastery."

Did I? Oh, but that wasn't what he was talking about; he was talking about all this other business. After only the slightest hesitation, I said, "Of course not."

"You would do almost anything to save the monastery, wouldn't you, Brother Benedict?"

"Anything I could," I said.

"Then let me suggest to you, Brother Benedict," he said, his stern eye getting sterner by the second, "that what you *have* done to help save the monastery is plant evidence, present a fraudulent and trumped-up case, and malign and libel my clients, the Flattery family, who are decent well-thought-of members of society."

I said, "*What?*" Around me Brother Clemence was nodding moodily, as though he'd always known I was capable of such things, while Brothers Oliver and Dexter were both looking just as shocked as I felt.

"I put it to you, Brother Benedict," this horrible man went on, "that *you* planted that microphone in the office, *in order to find it again.* I further put it to you that there was no florist's truck parked outside, and that you did not see and were not punched in the nose by Alfred Broyle."

"I wasn't? Look at my nose!"

159

"Three weeks from now in court? Besides, Brother Benedict, the self-inflicted injury is a cliché of the legal profession."

"But—"

"I further put it to you, Brother Benedict," he rolled on, "that the man who burned those papers was a confederate of yours, that he did so at your request and because you believed an insufficiently strong case for your side would be built by those papers, and that you willfully and knowingly misidentified this man as my client, Frank Flattery. And I finally put it to you, Brother Benedict, that you have not one shred of proof for any of your assertions and that you lack the slightest capability of confounding my version of the facts."

"But," I said, and then, although no one interrupted me, I stopped. I had nothing to say.

Mr. Gates' stern eye became kindly and sympathetic. "I'm sorry, Brother Benedict," he said. "But you do see the situation."

"Yes," I said.

Mr. Gates turned to Brother Oliver. "I've offered to assist in any way I can," he said, "and now that I see the dastardly level these people will descend to I am more than ever available. And I will go and present our case to the Flatterys' attorney if you insist, but I must say I dislike being laughed at in another man's office."

✠

I made my decision on Friday, December 19th, at ten-thirty in the morning. It wasn't 10:30 by Roger Dwarfmann's red-and-black watch; it was ten-thirty by the grandfather clock in the scriptorium, which is always a little off one way or the other, so it probably wasn't exactly ten-thirty at all. But it was a decision, and I stood by it.

The atmosphere in the monastery had altered again. From that stagnant depression of mutual mistrust we had leaped to a sudden joy of reunity, which had lasted only until we'd all had time to think out our current position. Trust and brotherhood might have returned to our lives, but the monastery was still under a death sentence, and our present state was more perilous than it had ever seemed before. An answer had come to us from Ada Louise Huxtable of the *Times*, responding to my letter by assuring us of her support, urging us to both hire a good attorney and get in touch with the Landmarks Commission, and pointing out quite rightly that there was nothing she personally either could or should do. But we knew now that the Landmarks Commission couldn't help us, the law couldn't help us, the lease couldn't help us, and neither the Flatterys nor Dimp were prepared to help us. Brother Clemence was doggedly at work on tertiary documents, Brother Flavian was writing inflamed letters to his congressman and the United Nations and most of the other politicians of the world, Brother Mallory was shadow-boxing all over the calefactory in hopes of a return bout with Frank Flattery, Brother Oliver was studying the Bible in the event of a return bout with Roger Dwarf-mann, Brother Dexter was phoning relatives and friends of relatives to see if anybody had any influence on the two banks involved, and Brother Hilarius was reading Abbot Wesley's fourteen-volume novel based on the life of St. Jude the Obscure just in case it might include something useful to us; but none of these activities was being done out of a positive spirit. A sense of defeat was pervasive among us now, and those who struggled against it were doing just that, and no more; not really trying to save the monastery but merely fighting against their own sense of defeat.

Others had given up the struggle. Brother Leo was preparing breakfasts and dinners of such opulence and variety that each of them was obviously intended as a last meal. Brother Silas had retired to the library, surrounding himself with his book. Brother Eli was whittling figures from the Tarot deck; hanged men, doomed towers. And Brother Quillon had taken to his bed with a head cold, possibly terminal.

We had twelve days. But help was not going to come to us from Brother Dexter's relatives or Abbot Wesley's novel or Brother Clemence's old fuel bills. Help could only come from one place.

Me.

✠

"Brother Oliver," I said, "I would like two hundred dollars and permission to Travel."

I had found him seated at the refectory table in his office. He looked up at me, appropriately startled, having been deep in Deuteronomy: ("Then shall his brother's wife come unto him in the presence of the elders, and loose his shoe from off his foot, and spit in his face, and shall answer and say, So shall it be done unto that man that will not build up his brother's house. And his name shall be called in Israel, The house of him that hath his shoe loosed.") Brother Oliver gaped at me across the centuries, apparently hearing my question from back to front. He said, "Yes? Travel? *What*? Two hundred *dollars!*"

"Transportation and miscellaneous," I explained.

He closed the book on his hand. Then he opened it, withdrew his hand, and closed it again. "You're leaving us, Brother Benedict?" He sounded saddened, but not surprised.

Was I? That wasn't the question I had asked myself, nor was I prepared with an answer. "I don't know," I said. "But I think I can help save the monastery."

"Eileen Flattery again," he said.

"Yes, Brother."

"Next you'll be telling me you want to Travel to Puerto Rico."

"Yes, Brother."

He reared back, studying me as though I might have something contagious. "*Yes*, Brother? What do you mean, *yes*, Brother?"

"I want to Travel to Puerto Rico, Brother Oliver, and talk to Eileen Flattery face to face, and try to persuade her to help us."

He thought about it. He gazed past me, in the general direction of the windows and the courtyard, and when he looked back at me again his expression was deeply troubled. He said, "Are you sure you want to do this, Brother Benedict?"

"Yes, Brother."

"And you feel . . . emotionally secure enough? You're sure you can deal with it all?"

"No, Brother."

He cocked his head to one side, studying my face. "No?"

"Brother Oliver," I said, "I don't really want to do this. I don't want to go anywhere, I don't want to involve myself further with Eileen Flattery, I don't want to confuse myself to distraction, I don't want to break up a comfortable way of living, but I just

162

don't have any choice. If we can possibly save the monastery that's what we have to do, and no one can help us, no one at all can help us, except Eileen Flattery."

"Who may not choose to, Brother Benedict."

"I know that. But she's still our last hope." I sat in the chair opposite him, and put my elbows on the refectory table. "I thought of writing her a letter," I said, "but I know it wouldn't do any good. Because I know why she went away. She went away because the thing that happened the other night shocked her just as much as it shocked me. She doesn't want this any more than I do, and if I send her a letter she'll probably throw it away unopened. She certainly won't answer, won't decide to involve herself again."

He was nodding. "Yes, I agree. If she's run away, it means she doesn't want reminders."

"But if I *go* there," I said, "if I meet her face to face, then we can work on *through* that emotional involvement, we can get past it and *then* she might be willing to help."

"What if she isn't even willing to see you?" he asked me. "What if she refuses to talk to you or have anything to do with you?"

"Then it will have been a waste," I said.

We looked at one another, and I suppose my expression was as troubled as his. I had nothing else to say, and he hadn't decided yet what he would say, so we sat there for two or three minutes in silence, each of us mulling his own thoughts. Brother Oliver's thoughts were on my request, of course, while mine were on what I would do if he came to the conclusion that for one reason or another I shouldn't go. I knew the answer to that; I'd known it before I walked in here. I would leave.

I'd have to. The monastery and my own peace of mind were both too important to me. I had no idea how I'd get to Puerto Rico without money—aside from its being too far to walk, Puerto Rico is an island surrounded by water—but somehow I would do it.

"All right," Brother Oliver said.

"What?"

163

He didn't look cheerful. "I'm very reluctant," he said, "but I'm going to agree."

A weight on my shoulders and back that I hadn't realized I'd been carrying was suddenly lifted off. Unable to repress my smile, I said, "Thank you, Brother Oliver."

"I'll tell you my reason," he said.

"Yes?"

"If I had said no," he told me, "you would have gone anyway." I probably looked sheepish. "Yes, Brother," I said.

"Rather than have you break your vow of obedience, Brother Benedict, I will give you my permission."

We smiled together. "Thank you, Brother Oliver," I said.

✛

Most of the others weren't entirely sure why I was making this Journey, but everybody wanted to help. The concept of Travel is obviously a profound one; even among a group such as ours which had forsworn Travel except in the most extreme circumstances, the prospect of a Journey created ripples of excitement, a glitter in every eye, and the unexpressed but obvious specter of general jealousy. Father Banzolini would be hearing about all this several times tomorrow night.

Envy, however, converted itself into participation in one form or another, so that Brother Leo went out to find a travel agency where he could purchase my ticket, Brother Valerian climbed to the attic to seek out a presentable piece of luggage, and Brother Quillon rose from his head-cold bed to offer to do my packing. Brother Mallory, who had performed as a boxer in San Juan in the old days, and Brother Silas, who had lain low in Mayaguez for six months at one point in his criminal career, both had an infinite quantity of tips and general information for me. Spanish is the major language of Puerto Rico, and it turned out that Brothers Thaddeus and Hilarius both spoke it, or at least claimed to. They both presented me with word lists, and then fell to disputing between themselves over nuances of meaning and pronunciation.

Brother Leo returned from his own somewhat shorter Journey rather red-faced and disheveled but triumphant. It appeared that the holiday season was popular with Travelers—I can't think why—and all the seats on all the planes going to Puerto Rico from New York over the next several weeks had already been reserved in advance. What a lot of Traveling! But Brother Leo had used a combination of his religious affiliation, his bulldog tenacity and his natural bad temper to obtain for me someone else's last-minute cancellation: I had a seat on an American Airlines plane leaving this very night, Friday night, at midnight. Or almost midnight; in the terms of Roger Dwarfmann's watch, the plane would depart at 11:55. "I had to leave the return open," he told me, handing me the ticket which had cost our community nearly two hundred dollars. "You'll have to deal with that yourself when you're down there."

"Thank you, Brother Leo," I said.

"It's a seven-oh-seven," he told me. "I tried to get you on a seven-forty-seven, but I couldn't do it."

"I'm sure I won't mind. And thank you again."

Brother Eli had worked out my other transportation question, which was how I would get from here to Kennedy International Airport, where I would board the plane. In his soft-spoken manner, like an urban guerrilla describing a raid, he told me what to do: "There's a subway entrance at Lexington Avenue and Fifty-third Street."

"That's right," I said. "I've seen it."

"You go there," he said. "You get on the platform marked 'Downtown.'"

I nodded. "Downtown."

"Take the E train," he said. "*Not* the F."

"The E train," I said.

"Take it to West Fourth Street."

"West Fourth Street."

"You'll change there to the A train, on the same platform."

"Same platform."

"*A* train, same platform."

I nodded. "*A* train, same platform."

"Make sure the train says it's going to Lefferts Avenue."

I frowned at him. "The train *says*?"

"There are signs," he told me. "Small signs on the side of each car."

"Oh. All right."

"You want the train that goes to Lefferts Avenue."

"Lefferts Avenue. Is that the same as the E train?"

"You just got *off* the E train. This is the A train."

"That's right," I said. "Off the E train, on the A train, same platform."

"Right."

"Lefferts Avenue," I said.

"Right," he said. "Now, you're going to take this train to the end of the line."

"Where's that?"

He looked at me oddly. "Lefferts Avenue," he said.

"Oh! I see, it's the train that goes to Lefferts *Avenue*."

"Yes," he said. "The A train."

"That was a Billy Strayhorn song," I said. *"Day-*yam, oh, take the A train, that's the only way to get to Harlem. Am I going to Harlem?"

"No, Brother Benedict," he said. "There are no airports in Harlem. You're going the other way."

"I see. To the end of the line. Whatsit Avenue."

"Lefferts Avenue."

"I knew it started with L," I said. "Lefferts Avenue, I've got it now."

"Fine," he said. "Now, when you get there, you'll be at the intersection of Lefferts and Liberty. You should turn right."

"Right."

"Right. Turn right, and walk along Lefferts southbound."

"Southbound."

He closed his eyes briefly, nodding. "Yes," he said. "You'll walk till you get to Rockaway Boulevard. It's five long blocks."

"Rockaway Boulevard."

"Turn left on Rockaway Boulevard."

I nodded. "Turn left on Rockaway Boulevard."

"Now you'll walk to One Hundred Thirtieth Street."

"One Hundred Thirtieth Street."

"It's eleven short blocks."

"Eleven short blocks."

He looked at me. "You don't have to say that," he said.

"Oh," I said. "I see. Does it bother you if I say everything back?"

"A little bit," he admitted.

"All right," I said. "It's a memory aid, that's all. I'll just use it for the high spots."

"The high spots," he said.

"Yes."

He nodded. "Okay. You're at One Hundred Thirtieth Street and Rockaway Boulevard."

"Yes, I am," I said, as a substitute for repeating.

"You turn right."

"Okay."

"You'll walk on a bridge over the Belt Parkway."

"Right," I said.

He gave me a quick suspicious frown, as though suspecting I'd snuck a repetition past him but made no comment. "Just past the bridge," he said, "is One Hundred Fiftieth Avenue. You turn left."

"Wait a minute," I said. "This is the intersection of One Hundred Thirtieth Street and One Hundred Fiftieth Avenue?"

"Yes."

"I think I love it," I said. "Where is it?"

"In Queens, in South Ozone Park."

"South Oz—sorry."

"It's okay," he said. "Now, you've made your turn onto One Hundred Fiftieth Avenue. You walk just a little way, and you're on the airport."

"There at last," I said.

"Not quite," he told me. "You'll have to take the airport road to the right down to the terminals."

"Is that very far?"

"About as far again as you already walked."

"It must be a big airport!"

He nodded, unimpressed. "It's a very big airport." Studying my face, he said, "Have you got it now?"

"No problem," I said.

He considered that for a few seconds, then said, "I'll go write it down."

"Good idea," I said.

✛

Brother Valerian had found a small canvas bag in the attic that had once belonged to Brother Mallory, and Brother Quillon had packed it. Giving it to me, he said, "I put in some aspirin, in case you get a headache."

"Thank you."

"And a cake of soap, wrapped in aluminum foil."

"That was thoughtful."

"You never know what conditions are going to be like," he told me. "Oh, and I put in your toilet things, toothbrush and toothpaste, razor, all of that."

"Fine. Thank you."

"And some extra Kleenex."

"Good. Nice."

"And I must say I didn't much care for your socks, so I put in two pair of mine."

"You didn't have to do that."

"Well, you're representing all of us down there, so you really should look your best. I'll darn those other socks while you're gone."

"I'll get to that, Brother Quillon, I was just putting it off, I meant to—"

"Yes, yes," he said, "I know all about that. I'll just darn them while you're gone, and then they'll be done."

"Well—thank you."

"It's nothing really." He handed me the packed bag, and sniffed; from the head cold, I suppose. "Don't have any—disasters or plane crashes or anything," he said.

"I'll try not to."

✛

I left after dinner, at around nine o'clock. The last thing I did before departure was get Father Banzolini's tear sheets and give them to Brother Peregrine, asking him to return them for me when Father Banzolini came tomorrow night. He promised he would. "Tell him I found them very interesting," I said. "And fact-filled."

"I'll do that," he said.

I patted his arm, encouraged by him. "You'll know what to say."

ELEVEN

HAT DID I feel as I walked up Park Avenue in the darkness, past the Boffin Club and the, uh, shop and around the corner onto 52nd Street, putting the monastery out of sight behind me? What did I feel? Nothing.

I did not feel frightened, apprehensive, uncertain, insecure, inadequate to the demands of Travel. I had Traveled so much in the last two weeks that I felt a seasoned campaigner by now. Why should there be terrors in the simple transitional movements of a Journey?

I did not feel excited, expectant, curious, agog at the anticipation of adventure. I had never craved adventure, so why should I embrace it when it was thrust upon me?

I did not feel tender, flushed, earnest, ardent, eager to be in the presence of Eileen Flattery Bone. Like adventure, I had not craved her existence, so why should I embrace her now that—

Well. The phrasing may be unfortunate, but the point is, I did not want Eileen, or at least I did not want to want her. What I desired from her, or what I desired to desire from her, was two salvations, and no more: I wanted her to save the monastery, and I wanted her to save me *for* the monastery. I had a round trip ticket in that nicely packed bag, and I very much wanted to use all of it.

I suppose, in truth, I really was feeling all those emotions I've just denied, and more as well: self-doubt, cosmic rage, a slight digestive disturbance. But the result of all this was an emotional overload, a mutual cancelling out, the same effect you get if you throw a little paint of every possible color together in a vat and mix; it all blends down together into a neutral and not very interesting gray.

Protected, I suppose, by that coat of gray, I set off on my Quest.

⁘

Is the subway always full of such people? When I boarded that E train at Lexington Avenue and 53rd Street—having previously boarded an F train and then hopped off it again as the doors were closing on the skirts of my robe—it was full of scruffily neat people who gave the impression they had dressed themselves up to attend a public execution. Since it was now nine-something of a Friday evening, they were undoubtedly provincials from Queens coming into Manhattan for a night on the town, but did they absolutely have to look as though their parents had been first cousins?

Over the next several stops most of these people left, to be replaced by a shabbier and yet more appealing group: older men and women, many of them stout, who were finishing work somewhere and were on their way home. (Three of them were Santa Clauses.) This transition was complete by 14th Street, and the very next stop was mine. West 4th Street, just as the long detailed printed directions in Brother Eli's crabbed whittler's hand had promised.

This was a much larger station, with two long concrete platforms, each flanked by a pair of tracks. Along both platforms, flights of concrete steps led down into the bowels of the earth where, signs informed me, D and F trains were to be found. F trains? Hadn't I rejected an F train back at Lexington Avenue and 53rd Street? Then what was it doing here?

Well, perhaps there were complications with the F train and Brother Eli hadn't wanted to confuse me. I was here, that was the important thing.

But where was the A train? Trains kept coming into the station, all with letter codes and destinations spelled out in little windows on their sides, roaring in by both platforms—and from the bowels of the earth came the occasional rumble and grumble of restless D and F trains as well—but where was my A train? Perhaps it had been stolen in Harlem.

No, here it came, covered with nicknames and numbers in brightly colored spray paint. It stopped, the doors slid apart—that kept startling me, doors opening with no one touching them—and I stepped aboard. I sat next to a young black man in wide-cuffed plum trousers, chartreuse platform shoes with red-and-white-striped laces, a mustard-colored shirt that zipped up the front with a pair of dice dangling from the zipper tab, a pinch-waisted long coat in panels of two shades of green, and a big floppy cap in a black-and-white check design. He was also wearing sunglasses, for which I did not blame him.

This train was more full, and the occupants more varied. I looked at their faces and their clothing, still not being used to masses of strangers, while the train lunged from station to station. After a few stops I began to notice the station names, beginning with Jay Street–Boro Hall, then Hoyt–Schermerhorn. The people were strange, the names were strange, everything was already alien and foreign and I'd barely left Manhattan. I held my bag tight on my lap and felt myself drawn irresistibly away.

✢

When I emerged from the train at the end of the line, signs informed me the Q10 bus would take me to Kennedy Airport, but I saw no point in wasting either the money or Brother Eli's directions. They had done very well by me so far.

172

My only trouble on the subway ride had been with the names of the stations. Kingston–Throop? Euclid? Ralph? Perhaps the City of New York had hired Robert Benchley to name its subway stops.

A more serious problem had been names that echoed Brother Eli's instructions. Soon I was to walk on Rockaway Boulevard, for instance, and it had been a momentary shock when a station emerged out of the night—the subway had become an elevated train by that time—*calling* itself Rockaway Boulevard. (Previously, while still underground, a station named Rockaway Avenue had given me a similar start.) Liberty Avenue also figured in my walking instructions, and had also blossomed along the way into a place where the train stopped and the doors slid invitingly open. In retrospect, it seemed as though I'd done nothing all the the way out but paw through my robe for the instructions, clutch at my bag, half-rise from my seat, and not quite dash out to the platform.

Von Clausewitz once said, "The map is not the terrain," and he was right. Brother Eli had been working from maps, of course, in preparing these directions, and when I now descended to the street I learned that Lefferts Avenue had become Lefferts Boulevard. Being by now a seasoned Traveler, however, I ignored the anomaly. Turning to the right, as per my marching orders, I marched.

This was a working-class residential pocket of the city's fringe, blocks of narrow two-story houses packed closely together, all of them with front porches that had been enclosed into rooms years and years ago. Some of them had separate garages in back, with one narrow driveway frequently serving two neighbors. Most of the tiny lawns were defended with metal fencing, and there were lots of "Beware the Dog" signs. There was also a lot of lawn statuary, about evenly divided between geese and Blessed Virgins. The time now was around ten P.M., but a number of the houses were already dark, and most of the rest showed wavering blue television light in their front windows. I was the only pedestrian on the narrow sidewalk, though in the street there was a steady pulse of automobile traffic.

Turn left on Rockaway Boulevard. A busier thoroughfare, with heavier traffic, this street was devoted almost totally to the auto-mobile, being flanked by gas stations, used car lots, body repair shops and the like. Again I was the only pedestrian, and the strangeness of it made me realize that *I* was the alien and *this* was normal life. Of course I was used to automobiles in Man-hattan, which is usually clenched into one huge traffic snarl, but Manhattan is full of pedestrians as well. People still walk on that narrow island, as they just don't do anywhere else. Here, in South Ozone Park in Queens, was the edge of the real world; people who either drove their automobiles or stayed home.

Now, here was a question about Travel to be considered. Our attention in the monastery had been devoted almost exclusively to the sacred uses of Travel, but might there not be distinctions as well between various forms of Mundane Travel? If a person limits himself to Travel by car or no Travel at all, can there be any virtue in his staying home? If enslavement to the automobile is a simple habit, a tick, isn't the choice of life-style—living where it is necessary to drive to work, or to school, or to the super-market—a part of that habit as well? A person who chooses a place to live which makes it *necessary* for him constantly to Travel by automobile might be said to be undergoing Travel even when inside his own house. His existence then is Transitory, consisting of Latent Travel (at home) and Kinetic Travel (on the road again). If Travel is too profound to be undertaken lightly—as we firmly believe it is—such a person could be said to be a Travel Junkie, as unquestioningly tied to his habit as any drug addict, and surely feeling many of the same debilitating effects.

The physical first: the man who alternates sitting at home with sitting at the wheel of his car is destroying himself as surely, and possibly as messily, as if he took heroin. Emotional: buffeted by the tensions of piloting his vehicle day after day, his emotions must become either rubbed raw or anesthetized, either of which must make him less than he might be. Cultural: the Transitory existence, alternating Latent and Kinetic Travel, is the existence of the nomad, and must eventually render its victim rootless and without a viable sense of community, without a tribal or cultural heritage to be called upon in the hour of need. And finally, the moral aspect: a physically disabled man with anesthetized emotions and no strong sense of community is an unlikely candidate for a strong moral awareness.

I was becoming excited; I could hardly wait to get back home and present this to the others, get their feelings on the subject. Did I have further indications leading to the conclusions I seemed to be drawing? Well, there was the growing trend among these people, when they reached retirement age, to buy a mobile home and spend their declining years rolling from one trailer court to the next; the ultimate Transitoriness, *combining* Latent and Kinetic Travel, forcing one's home to Travel with one!

And then there was Los Angeles.

And here there was 131st Street. Was that right? Under a streetlight I consulted Brother Eli's perfectly formed miniature lettering, and saw I'd overshot by a block. Turn right at 130th Street. Caught up in my meditations, I'd lost my bearings for a minute.

So I retraced my steps to 130th Street. Turn right. Well, coming from the other direction I should turn left. After facing in various directions, pointing this way and that, rechecking Brother Eli's directions, and attracting the (Transitory) attention of several passing drivers, I decided which way I was to go on 130th Street, and set off once more.

I was back in a residential section now, the houses being slightly newer, slightly smaller, and set just a bit farther apart. But I was also getting closer to the airport; a monster jet plane suddenly came coasting down an invisible wire in the sky, passing over my head no farther away than the top of an eight-story building, and I couldn't believe the painful intensity of its noise. It shrieked, it screamed, it sounded like a fingernail on a blackboard amplified a thousand times. And the thing moved so slowly! How could it move that slowly and not just fall to the ground like a television set dropped out a window? I cringed my head down into my neck, I pulled my cowl up around my ears, but the screaming went on and on until the plane finished sailing by, receding diagonally downward beyond the houses on the far side of the street.

And no one appeared. These houses should have emptied, shirt-sleeved people should have run screaming out of every door, clutching their ears, staring around in terror and astonishment, yelling at one another, "What is it? Is it the end of the world?"

But no one came out. Lights were on in various windows, television sets were running, surely human beings were inside all these imitation-brick structures, but nobody at all came out.

I continued walking, all thoughts of Transitory Travel and enslavement by the automobile vanishing from my head, and meditated instead on the adaptability of Man. Twice more jet airplanes followed that same invisible roadway down the sky, shrieking in the same blood-chilling manner, confirming the subject of my meditation, and then I walked over a smallish bridge over some major highway. Brother Eli had referred to it, in his directions; here it was: "Cross the Belt Parkway."

Belt Parkway. Three lanes of rushing automobiles coming this way, three lanes of rushing automobiles going that way. There was a momentary prettiness to it by night, the ribbon of white headlights next to the ribbon of red taillights, but the rush-rush-rush sound of the cars disappearing under the bridge distracted from the view and I didn't pause, but walked on.

Turn left at 150th Avenue. There proved to be a Department of Sanitation garage here, plus an open area filled with white-painted garbage trucks that looked like giant cockroaches dressed as ski troopers. There was no longer any traffic, there were still no pedestrians, there were few streetlights, and after the Department of Sanitation building there was no sidewalk. More highways were somewhere ahead of me, fitfully seen in the darkness. I passed a car rental agency, and the street I was on curved away to the right through an underpass beneath some other road. Buildings ahead, some sort of under-illuminated confusion. I approached, saw a sign reading "All Traffic" with an arrow pointing to my left, and looked that way to see a highway a little distance off, surmounted by great huge green signs. One of them said something about the airport, so I walked in that direction.

Yes, that was the main road into the airport, the one taken by all the cars and taxicabs. "JOHN F. KENNEDY INTERNATIONAL AIRPORT" the biggest sign said, and just beneath that, "MAIN PASSENGER TERMINALS 2 MILES."

Two miles? This was the entrance, and the terminals were two miles away? Shaking my head, telling myself it was a good thing I'd left myself plenty of time to get here, shifting my bag to the other hand, I went on walking.

There was a grassy patch between me and the highway. I crossed that, then turned in the direction of the terminals, and walked on the verge, with the traffic just to my left. It was going very very fast, creating its own wind, and I kept as far from the concrete as I could, though up ahead I saw an underpass that looked a little narrow for a pedestrian like me.

I never got that far, at least not on foot. A vehicle, just past me, bumped its tires up onto the grass and slowed to a stop quite some distance away. It was, I saw, a police car, and I wasn't surprised when a pair of white lights showed at the rear and the car backed up to me. I stood to one side, permitting the car to come between me and the roadway, and waited.

They both got out of the car, two hard-faced suspicious young uniformed cops with silly Groucho Marx moustaches. "Okay, Mac," one of them said, "what's *your* story?"

"I'm going to the airport," I said.

He looked scornful, as though he thought I thought he'd been born yesterday. "On *foot*?"

I looked down at the objects in question; sandal-covered, the toes getting rather dirty from all this walking in the outer world. "They're my own feet," I said. I couldn't think of any other response to suit the circumstances.

The other policeman gestured at the highway noisily beside us, as though it were an important piece of evidence against me. "You're walking on the Van Wyck Expressway?"

"Is that what it's called?"

The first policeman snapped his fingers at me. "Let's see some eye dee," he said.

"I beg your pardon?"

"Identification," he explained. Though it didn't sound like an explanation, it sounded like an additional order.

"Identification," I repeated, and frowned doubtfully at my bag. Would there be anything in my luggage with my name on it? My initial—B—was inscribed with laundry marker inside the neck of the robe I was wearing, but that hardly seemed sufficient for men as serious and self-important as this.

The policeman who had snapped his fingers was frowning at me more and more sternly. "No eye dee?"

"I have no idea," I said. "I could look, but I don't think—"

The other policeman said, "What's the bag for?"

"I'm going on a Journey," I told him. I'd thought that was obvious.

"You're taking a plane?"

I might have tried sarcasm, but it probably wouldn't have been lost on him. "Yes, I am."

"You have your ticket?" he asked me, and his design finally became clear.

"Of *course*!" I said, delighted with him. "It'll have my name on it!" And I dropped to one knee, unzipped the bag.

Movement made me look up. Both policemen had moved back a pace, closer to one another and closer to their car. Both were staring at me with rather frightening intensity, and both had their hands hovering near their holsters.

"Um," I said. I've watched enough television to be not *totally* unaware of the outside world, and so I understood at once that my intention to put my hand inside this bag had frightened and angered those policemen. It was incumbent upon me to reassure them; soon. "My ticket," I said, and pointed my finger at the bag. I was very careful not to point it at them. "It's in there."

Neither of them moved or spoke. They didn't seem quite to know what to do about this situation.

"I said, "Would you like to do it, get the ticket? Shall I give you the bag?"

"Just get out the ticket," one of them said, and I saw that he'd relaxed a bit, though his partner was still rigid with the suspicion that I was a bomber or a maniac or an escaped murderer.

The ticket, fortunately, had been the last item placed in the bag and was still near the top. I found it, left the bag unzipped, and handed it to the one who had originally asked to see it (and who had been the first to relax). He studied it, while his partner went on studying me, and behind them their car suddenly spoke in a squawking incomprehensible voice like a parrot. They ignored it. The policeman with my ticket said, "You're Brother Benedict?"

"That's right."

"What's this here? C–O–N–M."

"That's the Order I belong to, the Crispinite Order of the Novum Mundum."

The other policeman said, "What's that? That Catholic?"

"Roman Catholic, yes."

"I never heard of it." He seemed to think that fact significant.

The other one said, "You're going to Puerto Rico, huh? Missionary work?"

"No, uhh, not exactly. No."

"Vacation?"

"I have to see someone," I said, "on monastery business."

He gestured with my ticket toward my bag. "Mind if I take a look in that?" It was phrased like a question, but the toughness of their manner suggested I didn't have that much choice in my answer.

"Of course," I said. "I mean of course *not*. I mean yes, go ahead. Here." Picking up the bag, which was still unzipped, I handed it to him.

"Thanks." Another statement belied by its manner.

He unpacked my bag on the flat surface of the police car's trunk, while his partner continued to beetle his brows and give me long suspicious glares and the cars going by on the Van Wyck Expressway slowed to catch a no-doubt tantalizing glimpse of this roadside entertainment. Brother Quillon's socks, carefully rolled, rolled off the car and were retrieved by the policeman.

His partner, the starer, abruptly said, "What's the Assumption?"

Startled, I said, "What?"

He repeated his question.

"Oh," I said. "The Assumption. Well, in our present circumstances, it is the attitude you're supposed to have toward my innocence, but I think what you're referring to is Mary's Assumption into Heaven. Christ *ascended*, because being God He had the power to lift Himself, but Mary, being human and without Godly power, had to be *assumed*, drawn up through the power of God. Are you trying to find out if I'm really a Catholic?"

He didn't answer me. The other one, having repacked my bag, now returned it to me, saying, "We don't get walkers out here that much, Brother. Particularly dressed like you are."

"I don't suppose you do," I said.

He had retained my ticket. Looking at it again, he said, "American Airlines."

"That's right."

Now handing the ticket back, he said, "Get in, we'll take you there."

"Thank you very much," I said.

I rode in the back seat, holding my ticket in one hand and my bag in the other. The more mistrustful policeman drove, glaring at the other traffic and occasionally muttering to himself, while his partner spoke into a microphone. I suppose he was talking about me, but I couldn't make out what was said, and when the parrot-voice of the car's radio responded I couldn't understand a word of that either.

I leaned forward toward the front seat when I was sure the radio communicating was all finished. "You know," I said, addressing myself to the milder of the policemen, "there was a Ray Bradbury story exactly like this years and years ago. About a man walking, and being stopped by the police because walking had become a suspicious activity."

"Is that right," he said, not looking at me, and began flipping documents on a clipboard. And that was the last any of us said in the car—except for the radio, which squawked incoherently from time to time—until they stopped at the terminal and I said, "Thank you again."

"Have a good flight," the policeman said, but not as though he cared.

✠

180

Did I have a good flight? I don't really know, having no standard for comparison.

It was an experience, that's all. I was gathered together with a great crush of people, and we were all shuffled through a "checkpoint" where my bag was searched for the second time tonight and X-ray equipment was used to discover any weapons I might have concealed beneath my robe. After that we were shuffled down a long corridor with many left and right turns, and were suddenly on board the airplane.

How did that happen? I'd been expecting a walk across concrete from a building to a plane, but the corridor *ended* at the plane. In fact, it was difficult to tell exactly where the corridor stopped and the plane began. I was looking around at all that when a stewardess—pleasant-acting, but a bit plump—said, "Father, may I see your boarding pass?"

Boarding pass; the piece of pasteboard I'd been given at the desk where I'd first shown my ticket. "Brother," I murmured, and handed it to her.

"Yes," she said, with the same smile. She looked at my boarding pass, ripped it in half, gave half back, and said, "Three-quarters of the way down the aisle, on your right."

"Thank you," I said.

"My pleasure, Father." Her perky smile grazed my cheek and hit the passenger behind me. Why did she remind me so much of that policeman, the one who'd said, "Have a nice flight"?

Three-quarters of the way down the aisle another stewardess, somewhat older and more harried and human, placed me in my seat amid a *gigantic* Puerto Rican family on its way home for the holidays. (When I say gigantic, I do not mean to imply that any of them were tall.) (Nor do I mean to imply, by that disclaimer, that any of them were thin. I was a bit squeezed.)

They were a wonderful family. Their name was Razas, their original home was "near" the town of Guanica on the south shore, and they welcomed me into their midst (or their fringe; I'd been placed in a seat against the wall, next to a window) as though they'd just rescued me from a blizzard. Three or four of them helped me adjust my seatbelt, my footrest and my chairback, my bag was successively stowed in half a dozen different thoughtful locations, and it became utterly impossible for me not to accept a a pillow.

And then we were in the sky, and the airport lights outside my little oval window had been replaced by blackness, thinly populated by faraway stars. I had thought I might be nervous during takeoff, since that's the traditional time for first-flight jitters, but it had all happened so abruptly, while I'd been trying to comprehend Spanglish being cheerfully shouted at me by three Razas at once, that I didn't think to be frightened until the opportunity had passed.

It now developed that the Razas were under the impression they had come out for a picnic rather than a plane trip. Baskets of food, shopping bags of food, boxes of food, all blossomed into existence as though in some parody of the miracle of the loaves and fishes. Great thick sandwiches, chicken legs, fruit, beer, soft drinks, cheese, tomatoes—it just kept pouring out. Everybody's mouth was full, and everybody went on talking just the same.

There were other similar family groups around us, intermixed with nervously smiling Anglos. Songs were sung, stories were told, running children were spanked, visits were made up and down the aisle, and the stewardesses stayed pointedly away.

In some bewildering fashion, this rigid plastic environment with its three-seat pews and its narrow aisle had been turned into a front stoop, a series of front stoops, and December had been turned into spring. Enveloped in this atmosphere, full of chicken and beer and friendliness, soothed by the clamor all around me, I sat back at last in my little corner, my head resting on my pillow, and my thoughts turned again to Travel and its myriad manifestations.

It seemed to me the Razas were somehow the opposite of the automobile people, those who were in a state of Latent Travel even when at home and who finished their lives wandering from trailer court to trailer court, dragging a simulacrum of home behind them. The Razas, on the other hand, had such strong self-identification, such vital ties to one another and to their heritage, that without conscious effort they defeated Travel, they swept

182

away its qualities of isolation and disruption and disconnection. Where those others were Traveling even when at home, the Razas were at home even when Traveling. Their self-created environment overpowered the external environment. They had found an answer to the question of Travel that I didn't think had ever been dreamed of by anyone in our community. When I got back, I told myself drowsily, I would have a lot to tell the others about my adventures. So thinking, I dropped gently away into sleep.

✝

Our plane was to land, Dwarfmann-time, at 4:26; perhaps it did. The sun wasn't up yet, I know that much, and I felt bleary from too much food and too little sleep. And from the change in climate; New York had been chilly, becoming cold, but San Juan was warm and humid. The wool sweater I habitually wear beneath my robe in the wintertime had become an instrument of torture, hot and scratchy and confining.

The Razas were met by several platoons of relatives, and after much shouting and smiling and shaking of my hand they all straggled away together, a portable crowd scene. They offered me several lifts, but I knew they would be going now in the opposite direction from the town I wanted, and I refused to permit them to go twenty miles out of their way.

After I'd shaved and brushed my teeth in the airport men's room, and removed that heavy sweater, I began to feel more human again, but coffee in the coffee shop nearby caused a relapse. A pleasant girl at an information counter gave me a map of the island, on which she marked with a red Flair pen the route to Loiza Aldea. "Will you be driving a rental car, Father?"

"Brother," I said. "No, I'll be walking."

"But it's twenty miles!"

"There's no hurry about my getting there. Thank you for the map."

TWELVE

HE HOUSE could not be seen until you were almost upon it, coming around the curving dirt road through the heavy jungle underbrush. And when first seen, it was far from impressive, a squat, one-story-high, flat-roofed structure with gray stucco walls and small louvered windows. It was neat enough, and so was the bit of lawn and garden hacked out of the jungle all about it, but I suppose I'd been expecting a fairy castle. This was simply a small blunt house tucked into a fold in the coastline, with the Atlantic Ocean just in front, nibbling modestly at a small white sand beach.

I was very hot and very tired, and I'm sure my face was sweaty and dusty, but now that I was here I very much wanted to get this interview over and done with. No, the truth is, I didn't want to face Eileen at all. I shrank from it so completely that the only possible method was to leap forward, shove myself into the scene and hope for the best.

The dirt road, having approached the house from the side, now skirted around to the front. I followed it, glancing at the ocean with some longing—I would have enjoyed lolling in that cool-looking water for half an hour or so, clothing and all—and then I went up the cement steps to the tile-floored small front porch. Humming sounds from the air-conditioner rumps sticking out of two windows suggested that someone was at home. The front door consisted mainly of frosted glass louvers, tightly shut. There was no bell, so I knocked on the metal part of the door.

I had to knock twice more before I got any response, and then it was a sleepy male voice that called through the louvers, "Who is it?"

Raising my own voice to something just under a shout, I said, "I'm looking for Eileen Flattery."

"And who are *you?*" The door remained firmly shut.

"Brother Benedict."

"You're *what?*"

"Tell her it's Brother Benedict."

The louvers cranked open, and a puffy face squinted out at me. "Good Christ," it said. The louvers cranked shut again, and for quite some time nothing at all occurred. During that interval, I had much leisure to consider whether or not the puffy face was another "young man" of Eileen's, and to decide it couldn't possibly be. Couldn't possibly.

I was gazing seaward, trying not to think how hot and uncomfortable (and apprehensive) I was, when the louvers abruptly cranked open again. I spun back, but too late. There was a quick after-image of startled eyes peering out, but the louvers were already folding shut once more, like something in a Busby Berkeley musical number.

Had that been Eileen? Possibly, but I couldn't be sure, and when a minute later the entire door opened, revealing a dim wicker-bedecked interior and releasing a fall of tomblike air, the person who gestured gracelessly at me to enter, while saying, "Come on in," was puffy-face again.

"Thank you." Stepping from one tile pattern to another, I entered the house, with its cold dead air and its gauzy gray illumination, and my perspiration-soaked robe immediately froze solid.

185

Puffy-face closed the door and extended a puffy hand to me. Since he was wearing nothing but an open white terrycloth jacket, a skimpy red bathing suit and pink rubber shower clogs, I could see that he was puffy all over, a tall young man who had gone completely to seed twenty years ahead of schedule. "The name's McGadgett," he claimed. "Neal McGadgett."

"Brother Benedict," I repeated, and accepted the handshake. Within the puffiness, his hand was strong.

"Eileen'll be out in a minute," he said. He seemed neither hostile nor friendly, but merely cloaking impersonal curiosity. "Can I get you something? Coffee? Coke?"

I was beginning to shiver inside my cold robe. "Coffee would be fine," I said. "If it isn't too much trouble."

"No trouble," he said, with a shrug. "Sit down." And he went away through an arched doorway in the far end of the room, calling out, "Sheila! One more coffee!" Then he leaned back into the room: "How do you take it?"

I told him regular, he bellowed the information to Sheila, and I was left alone. Settling myself into the nearest wicker chair, trying to keep the colder and wetter parts of my robe from touching my body, I looked around at a large bare-looking room which seemed to have been furnished more for low-maintenance functionalism than for either personal style or general appearance. Airline posters were tacked to the walls, there were no personal knick-knacks on the small tables scattered among the wicker chairs, and the air-conditioner covering me with its icy breath had a blunt gray-metal facade. So this must be a rented house, rather than a place owned by Eileen or one of her friends. I don't know why that should have made any difference, but for some reason it increased my discomfort to know I would be meeting with her in a Travelers' way-station rather than a home; anyone's home.

A door in the side wall suddenly opened and Eileen walked out, barefoot and wearing a pale blue knee-length robe. She gave me a brooding troubled look, then turned away to close the door behind her, and when she faced me again she'd shifted to the old amused expression. But I didn't believe it.

Walking toward me, she said, "Well. Fancy meeting you here."

I got to my feet, unable to decide whether my face wanted to smile or be solemn. I left it to its own devices, so I suppose it looked seasick, which is the way I felt. "I'm as surprised as you are," I said.

"Sit down, sit down. Are they getting us coffee?"

"I think so, yes."

We sat in wicker chairs at right angles to one another, and she said, "I thought you people didn't believe in travel."

"Only when necessary," I said.

"Is this trip necessary?" She grinned, but it was still the mask.

"You told me you could help us save the monastery," I reminded her.

"Did I?" With half a grin still clinging to her lips she faced me for a few seconds, then looked away.

"That's why I'm here," I said.

Her eyes snapped back to mine, and she leaned forward, suddenly intense, and suddenly very angry. "Butter wouldn't melt in your goddam mouth, would it?"

I blinked. "What?"

"You've got the hots for me, you son of a bitch, and you know it."

"Yes," I said.

"What?"

"I said yes."

"Yes? That's all, just yes?"

"I haven't been able to think straight since I met you," I said. "But that isn't—"

"You mean you love me?" She thrust that out as fiercely as if it were a javelin.

"Love you? I think I *am* you," I said. "Some broken-off piece of you, trying to get home."

"You're crazy," she said. "Look at you, dressed in that robe, talking to me like that. You're a *monk*."

"I don't like it any more than you do," I told her.

"Then why don't you get out of my life?"

"Don't you think I want to?" We were arguing all at once, we

187

were glaring fiercely at one another, and yet I could feel an inane smile trembling about my lips, straining to reveal itself. Although I was hugely angry, enraged at this stupid girl for turning me into such a bewildered silly wreck, I knew somehow it wasn't really anger I felt at all. My brain was full of dammed-up emotions, contradictory and embarrassing and even frightening, and anger was simply the only way to let them all out.

And it was the same with Eileen. I could see that and sense it, the same relieved smile struggling to show itself on her lips, and (God help me) I rejoiced in the knowledge. Rejoiced angrily, of course.

She was saying, "You're lousing up my life, do you know that?"

"Well," I said, "you're doing the same thing to me. And I was *happy* in *my* life."

She ducked her head, the better to glare at me. "Meaning what?"

"Meaning you were unhappy," I told her. "Any fool could see that."

"Is that what you came down here for, to tell me I'm unhappy?" The joy of anger had drained out of her now, and she seemed on the brink of angry tears.

"No," I said, "I didn't want—"

"What are you here for anyway? Who asked for you?"

"The monas—"

"Oh, shut *up* about that stupid monastery!"

"All right," I said, and grabbed the lapel of her robe to yank her close, and when McGadgett came in to announce breakfast the girl in the blue bathrobe was being kissed by the runaway monk.

✠

The tall and irritable blonde wielding the spatula in the kitchen was introduced as Sheila Foney, "Neal's girl." Neal's girl; meaning that Neal was not Eileen's young man. And while there were four places set for breakfast, one of them had a certain indefinable air of afterthought to it, and I wasn't at all surprised when that one turned out to be my place. So there were no occupants of the house other than these three, Eileen and Neal and Neal's girl, and I was a fourth wheel, not a fifth.

188

That had suddenly become very important to me. Instinctively and self-protectively I recoiled from contemplation of what that kissing scene in the living room had actually meant, and remained for as long as I could at the level of bewildered delight: happy that I had kissed her, happy that she had no boy friend here. There was no possible way to think about my future, so I wallowed in the pleasures of the present.

Neal's girl, Sheila Foney, was in a mood as foul as mine was fair, though it seemed mostly a personality trait and not directed at anyone present. She stamped around like somebody who's just been insulted by a busdriver, and she was far too caught up in the grievances of her own life to take much notice of a robed and cowled monk abruptly at her table. McGadgett, on the other hand, ignored his girl friend's grouchiness and thought Eileen and me both very humorous. While he shoveled in great quantities of scrambled egg, fried sausage and toasted English muffin, he kept giving us sidelong smirks of confederacy, as though we were all conspirators together.

As for Eileen, she seemed mainly embarrassed. She avoided my gaze most of the time, acting calm and unruffled, as though determined to maintain her dignity in the face of some silly humiliation, but when perchance our eyes did meet she blushed and became suddenly flustered and awkward and at the same time soft, as though she were melting from within.

Myself, I was freezing from without. Breakfast was eaten in a large tile-and-plaster-and-formica combination kitchen-dining room equipped with its own chill-breathing air-conditioner, and my wet robe was just getting clammier and clammier no matter how much hot food I put in my stomach. Halfway through the meal I started to sneeze.

It apparently gave Eileen an excuse to look at me. "What's the matter? You're shivering!"

"My robe's a little wet," I admitted. "From the walk."

"Neal," she said, "find something for him to wear, until we can get to the store."

"Sure," he said, and turned his friendly look toward me. "Now?"

"Finish breakfast first," I told him. "It's not that bad." Though

189

it was. I was feeling queasy and light-headed, and I wasn't sure if that meant I was in love or had the flu. The symptoms seemed to be the same.

✛

All of McGadgett's clothing was too large and lumpish. I had become very self-conscious about my appearance all at once, so I spent a long time testing different items of clothing in front of the dresser mirror before finally settling on a pair of red boxer-style swimming trunks and a white pullover shirt that didn't look too bad in its billowy fashion. Then I dawdled in the bedroom another two or three minutes, hesitant to show myself.

But there was no point stalling any longer. Reluctant, awkward, self-conscious, I took my nearly naked body out of the bedroom and into the living room, where Sheila Foney, wearing an astonishing pink string bikini, was irritably on the telephone, saying, "You don't seem to realize you have certain responsibilities." Seeing me, she told the phone, "Hold on a minute," capped the mouthpiece with her palm, and said to me, "They're at the beach."

"Thank you," I said, and hurried outside, not wanting to hear any more of her conversation.

McGadgett was out at the pocket beach in front of the house, supine beneath the sun, wearing a multicolored cousin of the swimming trunks he'd loaned me. Great dark glasses covered his eyes and much of the rest of his face, and his pinkish flesh gleamed with either suntan lotion or perspiration. Out in the water, Eileen floated on her back in the easy swell, her body trisected by narrow lavender bands of bathing suit.

The heat and humidity seemed much worse now that I'd grown used to air-conditioning. Plowing barefoot across the sand, I felt myself growing soggy again, and was already anticipating the chill the next time I would go inside. Why did people treat themselves in such a way?

McGadgett lifted his head slightly at my arrival, grinning his overly familiar grin. "Welcome to civilian life," he said.

"Thank you. I guess I'll . . ." And I gestured vaguely toward the ocean and Eileen.

"Be my guest." And he lowered his smiling head to his beach towel again.

I removed the pullover shirt and ran into the water, which was cold but refreshing. I hadn't swum in years, but the movements came effortlessly back to me, and I stroked steadily out to where Eileen was now treading water and watching my progress with a dubious expression on her face. "You look like everybody else," she said, when I got there.

I couldn't help laughing. "You mean you only love me in my uniform?"

"Maybe so," she said, and swam away from me.

I didn't know how to take that—I didn't know how to take *anything*—so I didn't follow her. Instead, I floated awhile as she had been doing, my closed eyes toward the sun and my mind just starting to pick experimentally at the scab of my recent experiences. Who was I now, and what was I going to do with myself?

"Listen, you."

I opened my eyes, and she was back. Lowering my legs so I could tread water, I said, "Mm?"

She was squinting determinedly in the sunlight, as though she'd come to a firm decision to *take charge*. "Are you really going to hang around here with me?"

"If you want me," I said.

"Don't put it on me, you son of a bitch," she said.

I said, "I mean I want to stay with you, but if you tell me to go away I'll go away."

That disgusted her, for some reason. "Oh, go away," she said, and turned about as though to swim to some other part of the ocean.

"No," I said.

She swam in a circle and came back to me, frowning. "I thought you said you'd go away if I told you to go away."

"Only if you meant it," I explained. "Only if you really don't want me. Bad temper doesn't count."

She paddled about for a minute, thinking that one over, then came back and said, "I'm bad-tempered most of the time."

"Why?"

She glared at me. "If you're going to be my boyfriend," she said, "you'd better stop talking to me like some wise old priest."

"Sorry," I said. "I don't feel like any wise old anything."

"And that's something else," she said. "I'll be darned if I'm going to call you Brother Benedict."

"I agree."

"So, what then? Ben? Benny?"

"My real name," I said, the whole sentence being cumbersome in my mouth, "is Charles. Uh, Rowbottom."

"Charles. What did they used to call you? Chuck? Charley?"

"Charlie," I said.

"Which one? I E Charlie or EY Charley?"

I thought back, surprised at the question and trying to remember. Nicknames are mostly spoken, but from time to time there'd be notes . . . "I E," I decided.

"Good," she said.

"What's the difference?"

"E Y Charleys are irresponsible," she stated, then said, "I'm getting tired out here. Let's go in for a while."

McGadgett had disappeared, taking his beach towel with him, leaving behind the pullover shirt and one other beach towel. "I'll get you a towel," Eileen said.

"I'll get one," I said, and started for the house, but she held up a hand like a traffic cop and said, "Wait there, I know where they are. Besides, they might be screwing in there and we don't want to bring you along too fast."

So she went for the towel, and I stood on the beach and thought about screwing. I had not entered the monastery at age twenty-four completely inexperienced, but ten years is a long time, and now I stood before the concept of screwing the way a small child stands before the star-filled night sky, feeling its vast mystery and its close fascination in tiny tremors behind the knees.

By the time she came back I was a flustered wreck, unable to look her in the eye and certainly unable to look at any other part of her. But she didn't notice, or at least gave no sign that she'd noticed. "You better not stay out here too long," she said, handing me a folded-up towel. "It's your first day in the sun."

"That it is," I said. The towel, unfolded, showed a smiling

couple with their arms around one another in a sailboat. I sat on them, and Eileen sat near me on her own towel, and for a while we remained like that in companionable silence.

Then Eileen said, "I think you've had enough sun. We'll take the car and go get you some clothes."

"I don't see how," I said.

"What? I don't follow."

"Well," I said, "I spent the monastery's money to get here. I can't do that any more, and I don't have any money of my own."

"Don't worry about it," she said.

"But I have to worry about it. You need money to live in this world."

"Look, Buh—" She shook her head, in mock annoyance at herself, and said, "Don't worry, I'll get there. *Charlie*. Look, *Charlie*."

I smiled at her; she delighted me. "I'll answer to any name you want to use," I said.

She gave me an ironic look. "You've been saving up those zingers for years, huh? Just waiting to hit some poor girl with the whole bunch of them at once."

"I guess so," I said.

"But the subject," she said, "is money."

"And that I don't have any."

"You don't need any."

"Of course I do."

"Look, Charlie," she said, and nodded in satisfaction. "Got it right that time." Then she went on: "I live off my father, Neal lives off his mother, and Sheila lives off her ex-husband. You might as well live off us for a while, if only to even the score a bit."

I said, "I can't take money from a—"

She stopped me with a sternly pointing finger. "I'll have you know I'm a Ms," she said (pronounced Mizz), "and you'd better be very careful how you finish that sentence."

I closed my mouth.

"I thought so," she said, got to her feet and gathered up her towel. "Come on, pig," she said.

"Come on where?"

"First we get you out of the sun while I throw on my city clothes, then we drive to San Juan and get you decently dressed."

I felt as though there were arguments I should be presenting, but I couldn't think what they were. Besides, Eileen was already heading for the house, and the sun was in fact feeling very hot on my shoulders. So off I went.

✠

After the shopping expedition, we went to one of the beach-front hotels for a drink. I was dressed now in white slacks, a pale blue shirt and sandals which were much lighter and flimsier than the ones I'd always worn in the monastery. But those of course had been handmade by Brother Flavian, who made all our shoes.

As to Eileen, she was also in white slacks and sandals now, plus an orange halter. The attention she got from other men confirmed my own feeling that she was something special, out of the ordinary.

We sat in a shaded air-conditioned lounge, in a corner with windows on two sides. In one direction we could see the crowded swimming pool and in the other direction the big empty beach. We were both drinking some sort of rum concoction, pink and sweet and full of fruit juice. I was already light-headed, from the sun and the events of the day, and I doubted this drink would have much effect on me.

We seemed to have no small talk, Eileen and I, though that didn't mean our silences were comfortable. We were both twitchy and nervous, glancing quickly at one another and then away, and abruptly dropping into speech. For instance, after our second drink arrived I said, "What was Kenny Bone like?"

She looked at me. "Was? I'm not a widow, I'm divorced."

"I meant, what was he like during the marriage?"

"Like you," she said.

I stared. "What?"

"Don't take it as a compliment," she said. "He was an unexpected lunatic, a turn for the worse, a complicated crazy man."

"Oh," I said.

She made wet circles on the table with her drink, watching

them with great concentration. "I thought I could take care of him," she said. "Protect him from the world." Her lips curled in what might have been a smile, and she said, "Be his monastery."

"What was he?"

"A loony."

"I mean, what did he do?"

"I know what you meant," she said, and drank down half of her drink. "Sometimes," she said, "he claimed he was a poet, sometimes a playwright, sometimes a songwriter. And he could do it all just as well as the real thing, so long as the fit was on him."

"And in between?"

"Fifty percent mush and fifty percent paint remover."

"And you think I'm like that?"

"No." She shook her head, but not very enthusiastically. "I don't know what kind of hell you are," she said, "but I have my suspicions."

"Where is he now?"

She shrugged. "Probably London. But it doesn't matter, he wouldn't give me a reference."

"Did you divorce him or did he divorce you?"

"I divorced him," she said, "partly because I didn't want to talk about him any more."

"Oh. Sorry."

She reached over to place her nondrinking hand on my non-drinking hand. "I don't mean to be bad-tempered," she told me. "It just seems to come natural, under the circumstances."

I said, "What are the circumstances? Would you mind telling me what we're doing?"

"You ask too many questions, copper," she snarled, and finished her drink. "Come on, let's drive back to the house."

✠

It was strange to whiz back and forth in sunlight over the road I had walked in darkness. Strange, but not informative. The light showed me land and swamp and stunted trees and occasional sagging buildings, but it didn't show me anything I needed to know.

The car we were in, a rental shared by everyone in the house, was called a Pinto, even though it was only one color; yellow. At one point in the drive back I said, "Shouldn't a Pinto be two colors? This is more a Saffron, isn't it?" But Eileen didn't know what I was talking about, so I let it go. Also, I wasn't feeling very good.

Shortly after we turned off the main road onto the road to Loiza Aldea I said, "Eileen."

"Yes?" She half-turned her face toward me, but kept her eyes on the bumps ahead.

I said, "Can a grown-up be carsick?"

She gave me a startled look, then braked at once to a stop. "You look terrible!"

"Good. I wouldn't want to feel this way and look wonderful."

She touched my wet forehead and said, "You're all clammy. You're coming down with something."

"I'm also coming up with something," I said, and struggled out of the Saffron and did it.

‡

Maybe there's something to be said for this business of psychosomatics. If there is, Sheila Foney said it. She told me the whole story, in her brisk argumentative way, when I was once again healthy—that the body's illnesses reflect the mind's disturbances. "A runny nose is a way to deal with unexpressed weeping," she said, with her self-confident face that seemed never to have known either snot or tears.

But maybe so. I'd almost never been sick during my ten years in the monastery, and here I was barely into secular clothing when I got the flu, complete with vomiting and diarrhea and sweating and incredible weakness. Maybe I was, as Sheila bluntly explained, punishing myself with all that, and getting out my grief and confusion as well.

On the other hand, there'd been the night without sleep on the plane, the sudden transfer from the cold of December in New York to the heat and mugginess of Puerto Rico, the twenty-mile walk in the humid night air, the alternations between heat and air-conditioning, my damp robe freezing on me during breakfast, the unfamiliar dip in the ocean . . .

Well. Whatever the cause, I spent the rest of Saturday, all day Sunday and part of Monday in bed, mostly asleep except for occasional staggering runs to the toilet, and generally feeling like something that had been eaten by a dog. (It neatly, by the way, solved the problem of what I would have done about Sunday Mass, which is another one up for the psychosomatic theory.)

Toward the end I had a dream, in which I was twins, one of me hot and one cold, and when I awoke I was very hot because Eileen was asleep next to me with one arm and one leg thrown over me, weighing me down, and she was shivering with cold because the air-conditioning was (inevitably) on and she was on top of the covers. "Hey," I said, and she snarfled and moved somewhat, but didn't wake up, and for a while I didn't know what to do about it.

Then I took time out to realize I didn't feel as rotten as usual. I was generally so weak my ears were hanging down, but the clammy perspiration no longer sheathed me, my stomach no longer felt like a sailor knot, and there was no urgent need for me to run to the bathroom. The flu had gone, leaving the local population with the task of reconstruction.

And Eileen was shivering in her sleep. It would be really stupid if she caught the flu just as I finally got rid of it, so I dragged one arm out from under the covers and spent a while shaking her shoulder, trying to wake her up. She groaned, she thrashed about, and she exhaled a lot of sweetish rum aroma, but she absolutely refused to become conscious, so I paused and looked around the room, trying to decide what to do next.

This was Eileen's bedroom, and very dark. There was no sound from anywhere in the house, so McGadgett and Sheila were probably also asleep. They'd probably all been drinking together, and Eileen had forgotten about me being here until she'd come in to go to bed, and then she'd been either too sleepy or too drunk to make other arrangements. (I learned later that she'd spent Saturday night on a wicker sofa in the living room.) So she'd gone to sleep on top of the covers, wearing shorts and a halter, and now her skin was very cold.

Well, I couldn't just leave her there. I managed to shove her limbs off me, and then I climbed wearily out of bed and stood

197

leaning against the wall until the likelihood of fainting passed. Then I pushed the covers from my side over to the middle of the bed, exposing the bottom sheet, and yanked on Eileen until she rolled complaining over the bunched-up covers and onto the sheet, her head thumping onto my pillow. I stopped her before she could roll completely off the bed, and pulled the covers back again, bringing them over her and tucking them in along the side. Then I stumbled around the bed, got in on the other side, and fell almost immediately asleep again.

✝

Our arms and legs and noses were tangled. Early morning daylight squinted through the slats of the bamboo shades, and Eileen's open right eye was so huge and so close that I couldn't clearly focus on it.

We were both moving a bit fretfully, trying to become comfortable. Then we were just moving, and discomfort didn't seem to matter much any more. "I think we're going to do something," I said.

"You'd better," she said.

THIRTEEN

Y MONDAY AFTERNOON I was out of bed, though very weak what with one thing and another, and I spent the next few hours on the beach, soaking up sun through a thick smear of suntan lotion, applied by Eileen. That, plus a great quantity of food, made me feel almost my old self by evening, when the four of us got into the Pinto—Eileen and I crowding snugly together into the back, while Neal drove and Sheila gave expert criticism—and we traveled fifteen miles to another beach house currently occupied by well-off Long Island Irish: Dennis Paddock, Kathleen Cadaver, Xavier and Peg Latteral, plus some others who came later and whose names I didn't catch.

These people had all gone to the same parochial schools together along Long Island's south shore, the same Catholic high schools, even the same Catholic colleges: Fordham and Catholic University. Their parents had also grown up together in the same settings, and for some of them the linkages extended back to grandparents. The fathers were in construction or real estate or banking, and the sons were in advertising or law or the communications media. This was the generation which had severed the last of its ties with its heritage—they were only sentimentally Irish and only nominally religious—and I had been cautioned on the way over not to mention the fact that I was, or had been (the confusion on that score wasn't as yet settled), a monk. I had promised to say nothing about it.

In fact, I said very little at all. Like most groups of people whose relationships extend back nearly to the cradle, this bunch spent most of the evening talking about those of their friends who had been so incautious as not to be present. There must have been some ears burning in Patchogue and Islip that night. I sat quietly in the corner amid the talk, sipping rum-and-something-sweet while rebuilding my strength and meditating on the similarities and differences between a secular social grouping like this and the more cohesive and purposeful grouping at the monastery. We monks did our own backbiting, of course, but it seemed to me a less important part of our relationship there than it was of the social structure here. If this entire group was ever gathered together into one spot, for instance, with no absent friends to discuss, what on earth would they find to talk about?

(I asked Eileen that question eventually—not that night—and she answered, "Dead people.")

I was not the first monk to leave in the Crispinite Order's two-hundred-year history, but I was the only one in my experience and I had no idea how to think about it from the group's point of view. I tried to visualize one of the others leaving—Flavian, say, or Silas—and guess what my reaction would be, but it was impossible. Even if I surmounted the difficulty that I *couldn't* visualize either of those two, nor any of the others, leaving the monastery, I was still left with the problem that my reaction would be different depending which brother it was who had chosen to depart.

Well, I was the one who had departed, so what would the others think and say about me? Fifteen bewildered faces passed across my imagination, but no words issued from any of those open mouths, nor could I guess at any emotions deeper than or subsequent to the initial surprise.

Perhaps that was partly because my own reaction hadn't yet moved beyond bewilderment. In fact, it seemed to me as though no moment of decision had ever actually been reached, and yet somehow here I was on the other side of it. When had I decided I no longer had a religious vocation? When had I come to the conclusion that I could make my peace with God outside the monastery walls? When had I chosen to fling myself back into the river of the world?

I didn't know. But here I was, in over my head.

My only other reaction to myself, beyond bewilderment, was a great fluttery nervousness. Whenever I tried to see more than five minutes into the future—what I would do, where I would live, how I would earn my daily bread, what would eventually happen between me and Eileen—I began at once to twitch and itch, fidget and scratch, gulp a lot and feel very queasy in the stomach. My solution to that was to avoid thought of the future as much as possible, and I quickly learned that the ever-present rum drinks were a considerable help in that direction. And if a thought of the morrow did from time to time infiltrate through my rum defenses, the rum at least helped to lessen the resultant jitters.

It also helped me to think more calmly about Eileen. The ice had been broken between us, so to speak, and I had learned that swimming was not the only facility that remained undimmed in its details over a decade, but when I was utterly sober and in my right mind—or my usual mind—I still felt embarrassed at the lechery of my thoughts when I looked at her. A little rum helped me to relax and accept the fact that, for instance, in the back seat of the Pinto I really did want to stroke her leg. And other things of that sort.

✛

What a nervous time the morning was! But it wasn't considered acceptable to start drinking rum until lunchtime, so I distracted myself with as much activity as possible: swimming, talking, shopping, going for drives. And my tendency was to avoid Eileen until I'd had a little something to calm me down.

I was beginning to answer now when people said, "Charlie." Mostly I said, "Huh?" And there were always, it seemed, plenty of people around. The group I'd met Monday night continued to be a part of our landscape, a fluctuating informal grouping that tended to get together after lunch and more or less stay together until late at night. Joining them on Eileen's visa, I accompanied them swimming at Luquillo Beach, gambling in San Juan and drinking at one or another of their rented houses. The days were far more full—and yet emptier—than in my previous life in the monastery, and I was a neophyte, learning this vocation. I kept quiet, watched and listened, and allowed the group consensus to determine my course.

☩

Tuesday night I spent three hours at the crap table, betting against the shooter, and won two hundred seventy dollars. Eileen wouldn't take the money.

☩

Wednesday morning Sheila Foney spent an hour on the beach telling me why a Cancer like me was just perfect with a Scorpio like Eileen. Then she told me more about Kenny Bone than I could possibly have wanted to know, including sexual things that were certainly none of my business and even less any of hers. In her version, Kenny Bone emerged as something of a cross between Brendan Behan and Reinhard Heydrich, but with neither Behan's talent nor Heydrich's efficiency.

One interesting fact did emerge from that talk: Kenny Bone had not been a member of this social grouping. "You're certainly better than the first guy she came back with," was the remark by Sheila that gave me the hint. When I questioned her further, it developed that Eileen had always been slightly out of phase with the rest of the group, "even in grammar school." She had tended throughout childhood to find her friends elsewhere, in the local public schools, and she'd confirmed this habit later by not going

202

to any of the usual colleges but to Antioch, which Sheila for some reason apparently thought of as Jewish.

Kenny Bone had been one of the results of Antioch. As with her public high school sweethearts, it had been obvious to her in-group friends at once that the relationship could only end badly. "From the time she was twelve," Sheila said, with strict satisfaction in her voice, "she's been going away and going away, and she always comes back. Usually with her tail between her legs."

I doubted that last part; it seemed to me Eileen's pride would keep her from showing any emotional reaction to failure. But I had to consider Sheila's own emotional reactions in judging her choice of words. Her own well-guarded pain at these perpetual snubs from Eileen were combined with and shielded by her no doubt sincere belief that the in-group *was* the best place to be, with the best possible friends, the best possible values, enjoying the best possible times together. Eileen was both an affront and an enigma to Sheila, and no doubt to all the others as well.

Sheila didn't say so, but the impression I had of her opinion of me—and by extension the group's opinion, presumably—was that I was not to be taken seriously, since no one outside the group was ever taken seriously, but that I was certainly a step up from Kenny Bone and undoubtedly a therapeutic interval for Eileen until she was ready to settle down at long last with one of the currently available group males. (These people were far enough from their heritage for divorce to be as common among them as in the external society.)

I also learned from this talk that Eileen had not been exclusively alone during her stay down here. In fact, she'd been accompanied by a man until just the day before I'd arrived—not the infamous Alfred Broyle, but somebody named Malcolm Callaban, "a swell guy in television news in the city." Some sort of raging argument had taken place, lasting the final three days of Callaban's stay on the island, until he had at last departed in a fury, flying back to New York the afternoon before I showed up. Eileen's temper was apparently as famous with the group as her failed attempts to live away from them, though I had to say I hadn't as yet seen it. I would have asked for more detail—was she a screamer, a thrower, a silent seether, an insidious revenger—but Eileen herself joined us at that point, followed by lunch, and the subject was dropped.

✝

"Hey, Charlie, you want a drink?"
"Soon as I finish this one."

✝

We were alone in El Yunque, Eileen and I, looking at the greenery from the tower there, when next I brought up the subject of the monastery and the sale to Dimp. I hadn't really thought much about that since coming to this island, though it was certainly urgent enough, with barely a week to go before the sale would be final and all hope gone. But my own chaotic emotional life had driven the question from my mind, and when it had strayed across my consciousness from time to time I'd determinedly avoided it, feeling helpless. The El Yunque tower, though, brought it all back, in a manner too insistent to ignore.

El Yunque is a rain forest in the mountains of Puerto Rico, part of which has been semicivilized by the National Park Service into the Caribbean National Forest (Luquillo Division). One drives south from the main road, and after a mile of ordinary flat scenery the road begins to climb and curve and zig-zag and corkscrew up the steep mountain sides into the rain forest. Much of the road is kept in permanent damp twilight by huge overhanging ferns, and eerie trees crowd the blacktop from both sides, their roots coiled above the ground like gray snakes. Everywhere the trees and vines and shrubs are all snarled together like one of Brother Urban's illuminated manuscripts—twice on the drive up I thought I read "LINDY LANDS" in the vegetation—and from time to time we'd passed narrow, tiny, furious waterfalls rushing down over slick dark boulders.

And five miles in, rounding yet another climbing V-turn, one comes abruptly on the tower. Playful, silent, silly, unnamed, virtually useless, it stands on a rare flat spot in the forest, a round blue-gray tower about forty feet high, topped by a crenellated

Camelot fortress wall. There's nothing around it but the jungle and a smallish parking area, and nothing inside it but a circular staircase to the top, from which it is possible on a clear day to see as far as the Virgin Islands.

Though not today. A notice near the tower entrance had told us that when the tree leaves on the mountainside rising up across the road were all turned over, revealing their pale gray-green undersides, there would soon be rain, and when we reached the top of the tower the leaves were indeed all doing their mysterious flip-flop, looking as though that one mountain out of all the mountains here had been faded by the sun. Southward, thick black clouds like great pillows were humped around the mountaintops, and a damp mildew smell was in the air. To the north and east, the tangled valleys tumbled away, stopping at a narrow tan border of beach before the flat blue ocean.

But it was the tower that held my attention; reminiscent of so many other towers and turrets and castles and yet uniquely and ridiculously itself, in the wrong place and inexplicable and yet calm about its role in the scheme of things. Insistent and rather friendly and faintly comical, how could it not have reminded me of my monastery?

"This reminds me of the monastery," I said.

"Then let's leave," Eileen said. She took my hand and started for the steps.

"No, wait." I tugged back, keeping her from descending, and the look she gave me was worried and impatient and annoyed. I said, "I want to talk about it."

Annoyance became dominant. "That's the past, Charlie. Do I talk about Kenny Bone?"

"But they're still in trouble, and there isn't much—"

"All right," she interrupted. Withdrawing her hand from mine, she leaned her back against a merlon—a crenellated parapet consists of alternating crenels and merlons—and said, "You want to talk about that place, we'll talk."

Her face was closing against me; was this the beginning of the famous temper? Nevertheless, I had no choice but to push ahead, and so I did. "They're in trouble," I said.

"Uh huh." The very neutrality of it was hostile.

"If something doesn't happen by the first of the year," I said, "there won't be any hope left at all. The sale will go through, the building will be torn down, and we'll—*they'll* have to move."

"Where to?"

It seemed a strange question, under the circumstances, and even stranger in its delivery, flung out at me like a challenge. I said, "I don't know. The Dimp people are trying to find a place, but all they're thinking of is storage, not living. Some defunct college upstate, places like that."

"Did you go look at it it?"

"At what? The college? No, we just heard about it, that's all. That was enough."

"It doesn't matter, though, does it," she said. "Dimp could find the greatest place in the world, but that isn't the point."

"That's right," I said, eager to find her so unexpectedly on my side.

"They could offer you the Waldorf Astoria, you still wouldn't want it."

I didn't correct her use of pronouns. "They're happy where they are," I said. "And the building itself—"

"Fuck the building, Charlie," she said.

"Ah," I said. "People sure do talk different to you when you wear shirt and trousers, don't they?"

"The *point* is," she said, sounding like a hanging judge instructing the jury, "and the *only* point is, those precious monks of yours *don't want to move.*"

"Well, there's this philosophical viewpoint they have about Travel, the whole question of—"

"They don't want to move."

I hesitated. Explain at length? No, the moment seemed wrong for that. "Yes," I said.

"Big deal," she said.

"What?"

"Why *not* move?" she said. "A change of pace every once in a while is good for everybody. Get up and get out, blow the cobwebs out of your brain, get a new perspective on life. What's such a big deal about this bunch of monks, that they can't be moved? What are they, breakable?"

"They're a community," I said, "with their own view of life, and they ought to be permitted their own destiny. Surely the world can make a place for alternate points of view."

"Upstate," she said. "In that defunct college."

"Where they *are*," I insisted. "It's their setting, it's been their setting for two hundred years, they belong—"

"It's time they moved," she announced. "It's the wrong place for them, midtown Manhattan. It's a ridiculous idea to begin with."

"It's their right to be there."

"But it *isn't*. My father has property rights, they're perfectly legal and honorable—"

"They are not."

She lowered her brows at me. "Don't you play holier-than-thou with *me*, Brother Benedict."

"I'm not. I'm just telling you your father does not have legal and honorable property rights. There's nothing legal *or* honorable about it at all."

"Of course there is. The lease is up and—"

"The lease was stolen from us," I said. I hadn't intended to get into this—one doesn't like to accuse one's girl's relatives of being thieves and arsonists—but this callous point of view she was putting forth was becoming annoying. "And when we found a copy of it," I went on, "your brother Frank set fire to it."

She looked at me as though I'd just announced I could leap from this tower and fly. "Are you crazy? Do you have any idea what you're talking about?"

"I certainly do," I said. "There's a clause in the lease that gives the monastery the exclusive right to renew, and we've been cheated of that right because our copy of the lease disappeared under mysterious circumstances, and there's no copy of it on file with the County Clerk, and when we found an unofficial copy that one of the other Abbots had made your brother came in dressed up like a monk and burned it. I saw him."

"My *brother*?" She was still staring at me as though I'd just grown a second nose.

"Your brother Frank," I said.

"That's such a silly thing to say, I can't even think about it." She shook her head to show me how bewildered she was, and spread her hands out. "Why would you even say such a thing?"

"Because it's true."

"My brother Frank would never do— How would he even *know* you had a copy?"

"They bugged the monastery."

She gave me a flat look. "You *are* crazy," she said.

I said, "They put a microphone in Brother Oliver's office, and they had their equipment in a florist's truck parked out front. When I found the microphone I went out there and opened the back of the truck and your friend Alfred Broyle was in there. He punched me in the nose."

She had been shaking her head all the way through that recital, and now she said, "I don't see what you expect to gain. Do you think the story's so wild I won't believe you could make it up? My brother Frank, now Alfred, there's—" Then she stopped, and frowned, and looked away toward the upside-down leaves.

"Everything I've told you—"

"Shut up a minute." She was thinking hard. "Florist truck," she said, and looked at me again. "What was the name of the florist?"

"How would I know? It was just a florist truck, it was parked outside all the time, it finally occurred to me—"

"You must have looked at it," she said. "You saw the word *florist*. What else did it say?"

"What else?" I did some looking away myself, and some frowning, trying to picture that truck in my memory. Light blue, a badly done painting of flowers in a white vase, and a name followed by the word *florist*. "I think it started with a C," I said. "What difference does it make?"

"A C? You're sure?"

"No, I'm not, I— Wait a minute. Grynn! That was it, Grynn's Florists!"

208

She was giving me calculated looks. "If only I could be sure of you," she said.

"Sure of me about what?"

"About whether or not you knew that Alfred worked for Grynn's. Come on," she said, and turned away.

The first rain drops, huge and cool, splashed about us. "Come where," I said.

"Back to the house. I'm going to call my dear father."

✢

When I'd changed from my wet clothing into a dry bathing suit and returned to the living room Eileen was already on the phone. Back at the tower the promised rain had suddenly descended as though someone had slit open the black bellies of the clouds with a sword, so that by the time we'd hurried down the circular staircase to ground level the world was made entirely of water. It was like being in a play tower in a fish tank. Running from there to the car, whose windows we'd left open, drenched us to the skin and possibly to the bone, and how Eileen managed to see well enough to drive us away from there I still don't know. Though the rain stopped two miles later—or perhaps we'd merely traveled beyond its edge—the air remained humid and we remained sodden, and I changed at once upon reaching the house.

But not Eileen. Urgency had driven her to the telephone, and she was sitting there now with her wet hair lank around her head and her wet clothing plastered to her slender body as she repeated my story to somebody at the other end of the line, presumably her father.

Most of it had already been told, and she was down to the part about the florist's truck and the Alfred Broyle nose-punch. She seemed to be giving a mostly fair and neutral account, but I didn't like the way she kept inserting remarks such as, *"He* says," and, "According to *him.*" I wished I'd been here to listen to it all from the beginning.

At the end of her recital she said one word—"Well?"—and then sat back to listen, flashing me a sharp but enigmatic look and gesturing at me crossly to seat myself. I did, and watched her listening. With her wet hair molding her skull she looked younger, quicker, harder, more intelligent, less receptive. "No, it doesn't," she said, and went on listening. (Her father had most likely pointed out that the activities described didn't "sound like" normal doings of the Flattery family.)

I could faintly hear the crackle of the voice speaking into Eileen's ear. What was he saying? Would he deny everything? Would she believe him?

"That isn't the point," she said. I frowned, watching her, unable to guess what had been said to cause that response. Then she said, "I know I am. Nobody ever said I shouldn't be." The crackle went on, impassioned and impatient, and she interrupted it, saying, "You want me to come home right now? I'll get a job." Crackle, crackle *crackle*. She glanced at me, shook her head, looked away, and when next she spoke I felt she was as much describing the situation for my benefit as to continue the dialogue with her father. "Look, Daddy," she said. "Maybe we are broke, I don't know. This is the first I've heard of it." Crackle. "No, let me talk for a minute." Crackle. "I don't care, I want to say this. If we're broke somebody should have told me. And maybe it *is* a legitimate excuse, and I don't know what right those damn monks have to be smack in the middle of midtown either, and if we have to set fire to their papers and punch them in the nose then maybe we have to do it. What I want to know is, *did we do it?*"

There was silence now for quite a long time, and when the crackle started again it was lower and slower. And Eileen interrupted it: "You already said that, and I already agreed with you." More crackling. "That's a good point, I'll ask him." *Crackle?* "Of course he's here," she said calmly. "Hold on." And without covering the mouthpiece she said, "My father says, if there was arson and assault and illegal bugging and all that, why didn't anybody call the police?"

"Because we couldn't prove it," I said.

"Why not? You could identify Alfred, couldn't you?"

"Yes, but I'm the only one who could. Nobody else saw him."

"What about my brother? Didn't somebody else see *him?*"

"Not his face," I said.

210

She gave me a long calculating stare. "Next," she said, "you'll tell me you were the one who found the microphone."

Was I blushing guiltily? Why did I *feel* guilty, when I knew I was innocent? "Yes," I said, and had trouble meeting her eye.

Into the phone she said, "Just a minute, Daddy," and this time she did put her palm over the mouthpiece, to make our conversation private. She studied me, and she'd never looked more beautiful, but it was a very unhuman beauty. Her skin was thin and taut and almost blue over her cheekbones, and her eyes were so deep-set they seemed to be studying me separately from somewhere deep in the center of her head. I met her gaze—with difficulty—trying to look innocent and finally she said, "Is this whole thing a con job, Charlie?"

"No! Of course not, why would I—what would I *gain*, what's in it—what—?"

"I can't figure that out either," she said. "What do you hope to get out of it?"

"Look," I said. "I can't prove anything, I wasn't even going to talk about that part with you, I just wanted to know what you meant when you said you could help us and I got caught up in, in, in *everything*, and I don't know where I am any more."

"My father says we need the money," she told me. "When I said I could help, I meant I knew he was embarrassed about selling the monastery, he blustered with us and tried to justify himself, and I know how to handle him when he gets that way. But not if the family's broke. I wouldn't be able to talk him into changing his mind even if I wanted to, and why should I want to? If the family's broke *I'm* broke. I don't get any alimony from Kenny Bone, believe me."

"But what if it's dishonest?" I said. "What if the, the monks have the *right* to stay there, it's in the lease, and they're being cheated just so you can afford to go on hanging around with these, these, these *people* you're hanging around with?"

"What's the matter with these people?" She was really bridling at that.

"Nothing," I said forcefully. "I think they're all terrific."

The phone had been crackling petulantly for a while now, like a mosquito locked in a medicine cabinet, and Eileen spoke abruptly and severely at it, saying, "Will you *wait* just one *minute*?"

I said, "Does he deny about that clause? Did you ask him about the clause?"

She ignored that. Palming the phone again, she said to me, "Now, what's this about the people around here? They've treated *you* all right, haven't they?"

"They're fine people," I said. Me and my big mouth. "And they don't have anything to do with any of this. The point is—"

"The *point* is," she said, "this doesn't have anything to do with people punching one another and all this mystery movie nonsense about microphones and arson and all that silliness. You just think you're *better* than we are."

"No, I don't, I—"

"You think we're silly useless people who don't have any reason to be alive, and *you're* some sort of *saint*. A whole bunch of *saints* there on Park Avenue."

Knowing that she was accusing me of attitudes toward her friends that she herself held—or why else was she constantly trying to get away from them?—didn't help me a bit. "I never said I was a saint, or any of us was—"

She slammed the phone into its receiver, ending the call, and jumped to her feet. "You think you can shame me into helping you?"

"The clause!" I wailed, pointing at the phone. "You didn't ask him about the clause!"

"Just look at yourself!" she challenged me. "Just how holy are *you*? You come down here like any con man, you jump into the sack with me, you try to turn me against my own family, turn me against my friends, and you're the biggest fake of all!"

"I never tried to—"

But I was wasting my breath. Turning on her heel, she marched away into the bedroom and slammed the door behind her, shaking the house. And the click I heard an instant later was the lock.

✝

I was still standing there, trying to figure out what words exactly I wanted to try speaking through that locked door, when the phone rang. I looked at it, looked at the door, and it rang again.

No, she wasn't coming out. Not for me, not for a ringing phone, not for anything.

On the third ring I picked up the receiver. "Hello?"

"Is my daughter there? Eileen, let me speak to Eileen." It was a heavy and angry and yet hesitant voice.

I said, "I'm not sure, uh . . . Hold on, I'll just—"

"Wait a minute," he said. "Is that the monk?"

"Yes, sir."

"Just what the hell are you up to? You're pretty goddam cute, aren't you, attacking a man through his family."

"I *what*?" I was so flabbergasted I couldn't think of any answer at all.

"Do you call that Christian behavior?"

"Me!"

"Listen," he said, "I never said I was a saint. I'm just a fella trying to make it in one world at a time. This Dwarfmann deal here, this could pull me out of a real hole."

"The lease says—"

"Yeah, the lease," he said. "Does the lease tell you where I get my interest payments? I got loans outstanding, I got earthmoving equipment, I got heavy construction equipment, all of that stuff has to get paid for. You think I go to Mack Truck, I go to Caterpillar, I pull seventy-two grand out of my pocket and I say, 'Give me one of the big yellow things with the tires?' You think that's the way it works?"

"I have no idea how it—"

"No, you don't, I know damn well you don't. You hang around, you burn candles, you pray a lot, you got it made. Me, I'm financed up to my earlobes. I got major equipment, the interest *alone* costs me forty-one hundred dollars a month, I got no job to put them on. I default on the payments, they come take the stuff back, I lose the entire investment. And when another major job comes along, can I bid? Without equipment? Don't make me laugh."

"I'm not trying to make you—"

"Inflation's wiping me out," he said. "It isn't enough I backed the wrong candidates all over Nassau County, there's no mortgage money anywhere. Nobody's building. You want me to tell you about trade unions?"

"No, I don't think I—"

"No, that's right. You don't want to hear any of that shit. My red corpuscles are blowing up like firecrackers, I got a life expectancy of fifteen minutes, all you want is you should go sing Gregorian chants on Park Avenue. *Why on Park Avenue?*"

"We don't sing Gregor—"

"WHY ON PARK AVENUE? WHAT IN THE NAME OF CHRIST ARE YOU DOING ON PARK AVENUE?"

"We were there first," I said.

"Oh, my bleeding ass," he said.

"I'm sorry about your financial problems," I said. "I know you wouldn't go to these extreme measures if it wasn't—"

"Shut up," he said, but he said it quietly, almost calmly.

"What?"

"You talk about extreme measures," he said. "You're turning my daughter against me."

"No, I'm not. I—"

"Don't tell me what you're doing, you pasty-faced twit, you're turning my goddam daughter against me!"

"You mean by telling her the truth?"

"Self-righteous son of a bitch."

"I'll tell Eileen you're on the phone."

"No," he said, even more quietly and calmly than before. "Wait a minute. I want to make you a deal."

"A deal?"

"What's a construction business, right? It's only been in the family three generations, so it goes under, so what? I got a piece of a wholesale liquor business, I'm not gonna starve, right?"

I had no idea what he was talking about. "If you say so," I said.

"So here's the deal," he said. "You tell my daughter you were lying."

"I couldn't possibly—"

"Hear me out," he said. "My little girl is very important to me, and what I would most like to do is come break your arms and your legs. But that wouldn't do me any good."

"Me either."

"I don't care about you. Now, listen. You tell her you were lying, and you make damn sure she believes it. And then you go back to your goddam monastery, and you stay away from my daughter the rest of your life."

"Mr. Flattery, I can't—"

"You can listen. What you get in return is a copy of the lease."

I was silent. There wasn't a thing I could think of to say.

"*With* the option clause," he said. "Before the first of the year."

I went on being silent. There went on being nothing for me to say.

"Well? Is it a deal?"

The lady or the monastery. "Um," I said.

"What?"

"I—I don't know."

"Why *don't* you know? You think you're in *love* with her? You're a *monk*!"

"I know what I am," I said, although it wasn't the strict truth.

"How long you think you'd stay with her? Or her with you?"

I looked at the closed bedroom door. "I don't know," I said. Particularly if the price for keeping her was the loss of the monastery.

(And the monastery? If the price of keeping that was the loss of Eileen?)

"It's a good deal," Flattery was saying, "better than you deserve. You gonna take it?"

"I'll, uh, I'll call you back," I said, and hung up on his squawking voice. "Rum," I said, in distraction, and went away to the kitchen.

FOURTEEN

ND A very merry Christmas to *you*," said a female voice, and I opened rum-bleary eyes to see Sheila Foney sitting on the coffee table next to me, holding a glass of creamy foam out in my direction.

I gestured several of my pudgy right hands toward the glass. "What's that?"

"The cure," she said. "Can you sit up and take nourishment?"

"I don't know."

Yesterday, after the fight with Eileen and the phone conversation with her father, I had done a certain amount of rum drinking. After Eileen suddenly burst out of the bedroom and out of the house and into the Pinto and away from here I did some more rum drinking. Then Sheila and Neal had come back from wherever they'd been, received a blurry headline from me about the fight— I'd offered no details, though they'd both encouraged me—and they'd taken me more or less under their combined wing. A

216

Christmas Eve party was scheduled for the evening over at the Latterals' place, and they'd urged me to attend it with them, but I hadn't wanted to go anywhere without Eileen. Besides, what if I went out to a party and she came back here to make up? So I'd stayed home, with the rum bottle, and I'd done a lot of indiscriminate meditation, some of which had left tracks in my brain.

And on what had I dwelt? Christmas in the tropics, for one thing, beginning with the standard reaction of the northeasterner that a snowless Christmas amid warmth and palm trees was somehow "wrong," followed by the sudden realization that palm trees were an almost inevitable part of all manger scenes, that there had been no snow in Bethlehem, and that the first Christmas of all had taken place in at least a semitropical setting.

I had also brooded on the choice I'd been given between saving the monastery and keeping Eileen, and on the general question of secular love, and on the Church's ambiguous position *in re* fornication. (Married sex is sanctified and adulterous sex is condemned, but that leaves much of the world's sex in Limbo. Eileen, for instance, had never been married in the Church and was not at this point married either in or out of it, so what we'd been doing was morally neutral, though most priests would have lowered their eyebrows at the idea of it.)

Meditation under the influence of rum tends to be more wide-ranging but less substantive than meditation taken straight. Aside from the above matters, I had brooded on several lesser topics from time to time, until finally I had staggered into the living room and onto this couch, not wanting to use the bed before having peacefully concluded the argument with Eileen.

Who had not come home before I'd faded out, my last remembered thoughts having been on the comparative textures of glass and wicker. Was she home now? Sitting up, which activated a sudden violent headache, I said, "Ow! Is Eileen back?"

"Not yet."

What an incredible headache. "Ow!" I said again, and clutched my temples. "Do we have any aspirin?"

She held out the hand not holding the glass of foam, and two white pills were in the palm.

"Ah," I said, and made the mistake of nodding. Then I made the mistake of squinting. "You've seen these symptoms before," I suggested.

"It's a regular epidemic. Here. Drink them down with this."

I took the aspirin gladly, the glass of foam more dubiously. "What's in it?"

"Drink."

So I drank. Somewhere inside the foam was a sweet liquid with tastes that might have been milk, and egg, and sugar, and . . . rum? No. Impossible.

"Drink it all."

I gasped for breath, then drained the glass. "Gaaaa," I said. "Thank you."

"Don't mention it." Taking the glass from me and getting to her feet she said, "You still want the recipe?"

"Not even a little bit," I said.

⊹

"I'm sorry," Eileen said.

I was lying on the beach in front of the house, absorbing sun. Opening my eyes, shielding them with both hands, I saw Eileen seated beside me, looking troubled and contrite. "Hello," I said.

"I couldn't handle it," she said, "so I picked a fight."

"That's all right," I said.

She gave me a hesitant smile. "Can we start over?"

"Sure. You couldn't handle what?"

"The whole thing about you and my father." She turned away and looked out at sea, letting sand run through her fingers. "I just can't deal with that," she said.

I sat up. It was late afternoon now, I had done much eating and much resting and I was quite recovered from last night, thank you. What I wasn't recovered from was Eileen. Reaching out to touch her leg, I said, "What can't you deal with? Tell me about it."

She looked at me, upset and intense, then turned quickly away again. "You want me to choose between you and my father."

"No, I don't. I really don't."

"You really do." When she faced me again, I could see from the skin around her eyes that she'd been doing a lot of crying. "You say he's lying and he says you're lying, and I have to choose which one of you I believe."

Which was perfectly true, of course, so what could I say? Nothing. That's what I said.

"How can I make a choice like that?"

"Maybe you can't," I said.

She turned away again, releasing me from her staring eyes, and said, "I don't know who's right or wrong about that monastery, I don't know if they should be allowed to stay or forced to go or what should happen. All I know is—" And she looked at me again, and reached out to clutch my hand, "—it has to be without us. If we're going to make anything of *us*, Charlie and Eileen, you and me, we have to stay away from it."

"That's right," I said.

"It can't be part of our lives," she said.

"You're right," I said.

✝

But now the monastery was filling my thoughts. If I were there at this instant, at this instant, at this instant, what would I be doing, what would the others be doing, what would be happening? The sound of Brother Eli whittling roused me on the beach, and when I turned my head it was Sheila buffing her nails. An airplane flew over, a black dart high in the blue sky, and I could almost *see* the bulky shape of Brother Leo, leaning backward to point his nose and chin toward Heaven. "Boeing," he would say. "Seven forty-seven." One of ours.

Christmas Day. *This* was Christmas Day? Eating and drinking with a lot of pagan Irishmen on a tropic island that hadn't even *existed* when Christ was born. "There went out a decree from Caesar Augustus, that all the world should be taxed," Luke, chapter two, that's why Mary and Joseph went to Bethlehem, where there failed to be room in the inn; and Puerto Rico was no part of that world.

Neither was New York, of course, and neither was my monastery, but that didn't seem to matter. Christmas was Christmas in New York; here it was an appendix.

I'm not even sure I mean that in a religious sense, though certainly in the monastery we did keep the holiday holy. Traditionally, we have had moderately good seats reserved for us at the midnight Mass in St. Patrick's Cathedral, a tradition that goes back, I believe, to the Cathedral's beginning in 1879. Following Mass, it has been our custom to return to the monastery and to gather in the chapel for silent meditation until dawn, when we take a light snack of bread and tea and go to bed. At eleven we arise, have more bread and tea, and spend the daylight hours in our courtyard, regardless of the weather, in group prayers and hymns. (Occasionally in recent years *Rudolph the Red-Nosed Reindeer* leaps our wall from a passing transistor radio to tangle with our *Adeste Fideles,* but so far we have beaten back all such incursions.) And then we have dinner.

Ah, dinner. It is purgatory for Brother Leo, hell for his assistants, and heaven for the rest of us. It is our only grand meal of the year, and its memory easily sustains us for the next three hundred sixty-four days. Brother Leo provides the suckling pig, the roast beef with Yorkshire pudding, the yams, the brussel sprouts, the broccoli au gratin, the asparagus with hollandaise sauce, the baked potatoes in their rough thick jackets streaming butter. Brother Thaddeus produces one or another of his seafood specialties for our first course: oysters Rockefeller, perhaps, or a shrimp bisque, or trout in white wine. And to finish, Brother Quillon flutters out pie after pie like a compulsive stutterer: apple pie, mince pie, cherry pie, pecan pie, pumpkin pie, pear pie.

Then there's the wine. Our undercroft has been well stocked now for centuries, and it isn't often we really make use of it, but what is a more joyous time for celebration than the birth of our Lord and Savior? And so the wines come up for our table: German white with the first course, French red with the main course, Italian liqueurs with dessert, Spanish brandy and Portuguese port with Brother Valerian's coffee.

We don't exchange presents, of course. Individually we have nothing, and can give nothing, and can accept nothing. Besides,

220

the fat red god is not *our* God, and it's our God Whose birth we are celebrating.

It feels strange to talk about our community in a religious sense. We're a religious brotherhood, but we don't carry on about it. Similarly, we all of us dwell in a world ruled by the law of gravity, and every day of our lives we make one or more decisions based on the law of gravity, but how often do we talk about or think about gravity? It is simply a given, a basic postulate of our lives, and there'd be something foolish and self-conscious in an extended dissertation on the subject.

It isn't that I believe that God *requires* me to be a Crispinite monk, though I do believe He requires all of us to keep our promises. I merely believe that God exists, that this world is His, and that He has provided a place in His world for each of us if we will but seek it out. For the last ten years, it has seemed to me that God's place for me in His world was on Park Avenue between 51st and 52nd Streets. I have been happy there, and I have been delighted, once a year, to celebrate the birth of the One who made everything, to honor that birth with ritual and prayer and fasting, to welcome it with song, and to celebrate it with a communal feast.

But not this year. This year I was on a humid island in the dominion of North Pole Fats, in that great outer world where I don't know *what* Christmas is supposed to mean.

Dinner in the rented house on the beach consisted of chicken parts on a bed of stewed tomatoes and rice, fried plantains, and a rather nice California white wine in a big glass jug. Eileen and I ate all this alone, Neal and Sheila having tactfully vacated the place so we could kiss and make up. It *was* a pleasant meal, but when after the coffee Eileen handed me three gift-wrapped packages I couldn't think what they were for. "Your Christmas presents, dummy," she had to tell me, and then I had to admit I hadn't bought or made or invented anything at all for her. "You're my Christmas present," she said, unoriginally but passionately, and she kissed me again.

So I had to open the packages. I started with the smallest, and it unwrapped to display an alarm clock, a travel alarm clock that folded shut into a tan leatherette square clam. Open, it was a wind-up alarm clock with a neat squarish face and, when I tested it, a discreet but no doubt effective buzz. "That's very nice," I said. "Thank you."

"You really like it?"

"Yes, I do, honestly." I tried to put as much enthusiasm into my voice and face as possible.

"You were a real problem," she told me. "It's hard to know what to get someone who doesn't have anything."

I went on to open the second package, and this present was a razor, an electric razor with an infinity of settings. "Ah," I said, constructing fervour again. "I'll cut myself no more."

"And you can use it without plugging it in," she explained, her fingers intermixing with mine as she pointed out the razor's features. "You can either plug it in like any razor, or you can take it with you when you travel, and it will run for days and days without recharging."

"That's great," I said, and opened the largest package of all, and it was luggage, a tan vinyl overnight bag. "Ah hah," I said. "Something to put everything else in."

"Do you really like everything?" she asked me.

"I like everything," I told her, and then I told her a truth: "And I'm madly in love with you."

✝

Now I lived from moment to moment, like a blind man coming down a mountain. I awoke each morning full of tension and uncertainty and the wisps of bad dreams, I soothed myself with rum drinks each afternoon, and I devoted myself to the truth of my love for Eileen each evening and night. My problems were critical but not urgent, severe but insoluble. There seemed nothing I could do to help either myself or the monastery, so I settled into fretful inactivity instead, trying not to think.

On Sunday we went to Mass, all four of us from the house. There was a small ancient vine-covered church in the nearby town of Loiza Aldea, but this Mass attendance was as much a tourist expedition as a religious requirement, so we drove past that church

222

and on the twenty miles to San Juan and the Cathedral of San Juan Bautista, which features primarily the marble tomb of Ponce de Leon inside, and a statue of the same fellow out front, pointing rather languidly into the middle distance. (Aside from his famous search for the fountain of youth, instead of which he discovered Florida, Ponce de Leon was the first Spanish governor of Puerto Rico.)

The Mass we attended there seemed an older and richer rite than what I was used to in New York, somehow more properly Roman Catholic and yet much more remote. I had thought I might be embarrassed there, or alternatively that I might take the opportunity to seek guidance, but this version of God seemed unlikely to cast either an Eye or an Ear in the direction of some insignificant sex-struck erring monk; it would take fire and blood to attract the attention of this southern God.

Coming back from Mass, we stopped along the way for lunch and drinks, then continued on with Neal driving while Eileen and I were stowed together in the back seat. I touched her leg, which was my frequent habit, and she pushed my hand away. I said, "What's the matter?"

"Not right after Mass," she said. She wouldn't look at me, but frowned out her window instead. "Maybe tomorrow."

"Do you mean, never on Sunday?" The rum I'd taken on at lunch made me think things were funny.

"Not *this* Sunday," she said, and the way she frowned made her look like a stranger.

✝

We did, actually, late that evening, but there was a difference in it. My week of sex had awakened a hunger in me that had been dormant for a long long time, so that my hands seemed always now to be reaching out in Eileen's direction and I wasn't of a mind to be critical or analytical about individual encounters, but even I could tell this particular exercise lacked something. Eileen was more clinging and yet more removed, and I felt simultaneously sated and starved. We were like actors who had toured in a play together years ago and who now, on returning to the stage after a long absence, discovered that they remember all the lines and all the bits of stage business but have forgotten why they chose to do this play in the first place.

In the morning I called American Airlines. Eileen was not yet awake, and I spoke softly when I asked for a seat on the next plane leaving for New York. "I'm sorry, sir," said the Spanish-accented voice, "we're all booked for today."

"Tomorrow, then."

"Booked solid, sir," she said. She managed to sound both cheerful and regretful at the same time. "I could put you on standby, if you like, but I don't think there's much hope, to be honest with you."

This was absurd. Finally I *wanted* to Travel, and the gods of Travel wouldn't permit it. I said, "Well, when *can* you book me?"

"Let me see, sir. Mm-hm, mm-hum. We could give you a seat on Wednesday morning's flight."

"Wednesday." And this was barely into Monday: what would I do for the next two days?

"That's right, sir. Do you wish to make a reservation?"

"Yes," I said.

"That would be Wednesday, the three one of December," she said.

The three one of December. New Year's Eve, the last day of the deadline for the monastery. "That's right," I said.

✝

So I was going; but where? Back to the monastery?

They'd take me back, I knew that, no matter what I had done during my time on the outside, but could *I* accept my presence there ever again? If the monastery, if its existence and its destruction (and my failure to stop that destruction), was a perpetual barrier between Eileen and me—and it was—wouldn't it be just as much a barrier between the Order and me? When my brothers, some time this coming spring, were driven from their home to new quarters in some phased-out Job Corps campus or bankrupt soft-drink plant, how could I possibly include myself? How could

I live among them there? I had been their last hope, and I had failed.

At first I'd thought my choice was between Eileen and the monastery, but in truth my range of options wasn't even so broad as all that. I couldn't possibly stay with Eileen if the loss of the monastery was a permanent fact between us, but neither could I save the monastery by giving up Eileen. I *was* giving her up, I was doing it now, but that was only because the very silly idea of our being together had run its course. I had to leave, but my reasons were private ones and I couldn't use our separation to save the monastery. I couldn't bring myself to fulfill Dan Flattery's other demand. I just couldn't tell her I had lied.

Of course, I should have done so. As Roger Dwarfmann had said, citing Scripture for his purpose, "Let us do evil, that good may come." But I couldn't do it, and that was my failure. I couldn't go away leaving her to believe I was a liar and a con man, who had cheated her, who had not loved her.

✝

She got up late that day, while I sat on the beach in front of the house—I'd carry quite a startling tan with me back to the cold dark northeast—rehearsing different ways to tell her that I couldn't stay, that I was wrong for this world or any of her worlds. I was a monk again, whether I went back to the Crispinite Order or not. I would have to find some such place for myself; it was what I was fit for. Perhaps that Dismal Order of ex-thugs Brother Silas had told me about would take me in—I could join those felonious monks in whatever substitute San Quentin now housed them.

What on earth was I going to say to Eileen?

"I love you, but I can't stay."

"I was content and happy before all this started, and now I'm confused and miserable. Maybe I'm merely a coward, but I have to try to get back to where I was before."

"The monastery, that simple stupid building, stands between us and always will, particularly once it's been torn down."

"You won't want me forever. I'm merely a rest period between your struggles to find some way to live your own life."

225

"You knew yesterday, you knew last night, that we're finished, it's only a matter of time."

She came out at last from the house, wearing her lavender bathing suit under her blue terrycloth robe, and looking at her I knew the transition back to celibacy was going to be a difficult one. But it had been difficult the first time, ten years ago, until gradually the itch had faded, as it would do again; abstinence makes the heart grow cooler.

She was carrying a glass in her hand, obviously one of our rum drinks, which was unusual this early in the day. She was also very pinched-looking around the mouth and eyes, as though she'd lost the ability to withstand the sun and now it was beginning to shrivel her. And the look in her eyes was both tender and hard. When she reached me, she knelt beside me in the sand and said, "I want to talk to you."

"I have to tell you something," I said.

"Me first. You have to go back."

Suddenly it seemed too abrupt. My stomach fluttered, I needed things to slow down. "I do love you," I said, and reached out for her hand.

She wouldn't let me touch her. "I know that," she said, "but you can't stay. It isn't any good for either of us."

The she said, "All I've done is louse you up, make you confused and unhappy. You have to get back to where you were before I came along."

Then she said, "That monastery building, that hateful place, it won't let us get together."

Then she said, "I'm not a forever person, and you are. I'm always either running to something or away from something, I'll be that way all my life. If you stay with me, some day I'll walk out on you and that's a guilt I wouldn't be able to stand."

Then she said, "You know I'm right. You knew it yesterday, that we can't go on."

She had taken all my lines. I said, "I have a reservation on the morning plane Wednesday."

✠

226

Eileen drove me to the airport. I had slept the last two nights on that wicker sofa in the living room, I had avoided all rum since making my decision, and I was dressed again in my robe and sandals. I was also a physical wreck from lack of sleep, an emotional wreck on general principles, and a moral wreck in that I craved Eileen's body just as much as ever. More. We had had a week together, and turning off that faucet was easier said than done. Her nearness in the Pinto made me quiver.

But I was strong—or weak, depending on your point of view— and I didn't alter my decision. We arrived at the airport, Eileen walked me as far as the security checkpoint, and we said good-bye without touching. A handshake would have been ridiculous, and anything more would have been far too dangerous.

At the end, as I was about to leave her, she said, "I'm sorry, Char—I'm sorry, Brother Benedict. For everything the Flattery family has done to you."

"The Flattery family gave me love and adventure," I said. "What's that to be sorry for? I'll remember you the rest of my life, Eileen, and not just in my prayers."

Then she kissed me, on the mouth, and ran. It's a good thing she ran.

FIFTEEN

MY SEATMATE on the flight back was a skinny cranky-looking man of about fifty, who gave me one short curt glance when I took my aisle seat and then returned to his dour survey of the world outside his window.

The plane was less than half full, and most of the passengers—like the one next to me—were men Traveling alone. All holiday Travelers had presumably arrived at their destinations by now, leaving only these few solitary wanderers who were no doubt involved in Business Trips.

The plane took off, the stewardess provided my seatmate with Jack Daniel's on the rocks and me with a cup of very weak tea, and for some time we Traveled in silence. The Jack Daniel's was methodically dealt with and replaced by another just like it; I rather liked the little bottles, but could think of no way to ask if I might have the empties. I read the airline's house magazine,

228

I did the puzzles in it, and wondered how the Razas family was getting along. This was certainly a very different trip.

My seatmate pulled stolidly at his Jack Daniel's, emptying one little bottle after another, behaving not as though he were enjoying the drinks but as though they were a duty he was required to perform. Something midway between medicine and ritual. He drank and drank, in small and steady sips that were never ostentatious, never great thirsty gulps, but which in their inexorability suggested he could rid the world entirely of its store of Jack Daniel's if he put his mind to it.

I finished the magazine, returned it to its pocket in the seatback in front of me, and my neighbor said, in tones of the deepest disgust, "Travel. Gah."

I looked at him in some surprise, and found him giving a brooding glare at the seat in front of him, seeming to consider whether or not to bite it. He probably hadn't been speaking to me, but I was a bit curious about him and a bit bored (and trying very hard not to think about how much I wanted to leap from this plane and swim madly back to her and attach myself to her like a shirt full of static electricity), and so I said, "Don't you care for Travel?"

"I hate it," he said, in such a flat hoarse way that I instinctively drew a bit back from him. He went on glaring straight ahead, but now his near eye glittered as though his only pleasure in life was the contemplation of his hatred of Travel.

I said, "I suppose, though, people do get used to it."

Now he turned to stare at me, and I saw that his eyes were somewhat bloodshot. Also, his cheeks were drawn, his hair was thin atop his narrow skull, and the flesh around his temples seemed gray. He reminded me of the Marley knocker. He said, "Used to it? I'm used to it, oh, yes, I'm used to it."

"You are?"

"I do over a quarter million miles a year," he informed me.

"Good God! I mean, uh, good gracious. Why?"

"Have to," he said. He took one of his remorseless sips of Jack Daniel's.

"But if you hate Travel so much, why—"

"Have to!"

Violence seemed very possible from this gentleman, but my curiosity overcame my caution. "But why?" I persisted.

Sip. Brood. Sip. "I'm a Travel agent." He spoke more quietly, but also more desperately. "The airlines ship me, the hotels put me up, the restaurants feed me. And I have to do it, I have to know what's out there." He turned his head to glare out the window, hurling his hatred at everything "out there."

"I don't understand," I said. "I know very little about Travel, and—"

"You're a lucky man," he told me. "In my business, it's Travel or perish. The customer comes in, the customer says, 'What's the best hotel in Quito?' Well, say no one in my office has been to Quito in ten years, and we tell him the Asuncion. So he books it, because we don't know the family that ran the Asuncion sold it three years ago to a Brazilian hotel chain and they're running it into the ground. Is that a customer I'll ever see again?"

"I suppose not," I said.

"I suppose not," he echoed, but his sarcasm—if that's what it was—seemed more directed at life in general than at me. "I'm selling the world," he said. "You know what that means?" He held out one of his bony hands between us, cupped the fingers around an imaginary globe, hefting that imaginary globe in the palm of his hand. "The world is my stock-in-trade, and I have to know my inventory."

"I see," I said. I looked on him now with combined pity and awe. "And do *all* Travel agents have to go through this?"

"Pah!" he answered, and rattled the ice cubes in his empty glass at the passing stewardess.

"Yes, sir," she said, and glanced at me. "And you, sir?"

"Of course for him," growled my neighbor.

"Oh, no," I said. "I really don't—I don't have any money."

"You're my guest," he told me, and glowered at the stewardess. "He's my guest."

"Yes, Mr. Schumacher," she said, casting her smile uselessly against the rock cliff of his face, and moved briskly away, her thighs stroking one another within her tiny uniform skirt. I watched her stride along the aisle, realizing fatalistically that I would be fantasizing myself in bed with the next three hundred women I saw, and I was grateful when my seatmate, Mr. Schumacher, distracted me by saying, bitterly, "They all know me."

Could it be so terrible to be known by such an attractive girl? Wishing my thoughts elsewhere, I turned to him and said, "You were saying, about other Travel agents . . ."

"I was saying, 'Pah!' " he told me. "Glorified clerks, most of them. Writing an airline ticket to Disneyworld about strains the limits of their capacity. *I* am a *Travel agent*. My card."

He conjured the card from an inner pocket with a practiced stroke, extending it to me between the second and third fingers of his hand, and I took it to find a stylized globe centered in the rectangle, surrounded by the firm's name: *Schumacher & Sons*. Across the bottom were two small lines of print reading, "Offices in New York, London, Los Angeles, Chicago, Caracas, Tokyo, Munich, Johannesburg, Rio de Janeiro, Toronto, Mexico City and Sydney." On the upper right, in simple small block lettering, was the name, "Irwin Schumacher."

I was still studying this card, which managed to be so fact-filled and yet so uncluttered—unlike, for instance, Father Banzolini's tear sheets—when the stewardess returned with our drinks. She assisted me in lowering my little table from the seat back in front of me, which gave us a proximity I regretfully found delightful, and then gave me my glass of ice cubes and two little Jack Daniel's bottles. Well, it was one way to get my empties; souvenirs of my Travels, to put next to Brother Oliver's railroad timetable.

The stewardess returned at last to her other duties, and I returned to my examination of the card, saying, "Are you the father or one of the sons?"

"A grandson," he said gloomily. All facts seemed to embitter him. "My grandfather started the company with a small storefront in the Yorkville section of New York, booking Germans onto Lloyd Line steamships."

"I know Yorkville," I said. "I live not far from there."

"You live in one place," he said. He sounded envious, saddened, wistful.

"In a glorious place," I told him, forgetting for the moment that I might never live in that place again.

He looked at me as a starving man might look at someone freshly returned from a banquet. "Tell me about it," he said.

"Well, it's a monastery, It's two hundred years old."

"Do you leave it often?"

"Almost never. We don't believe in Travel."

He clutched my forearm just as I was about to sip my drink. "You don't believe in Travel! Can that be true?"

"We're a contemplative Order," I explained, "and one of the wishes of our founder was that we meditate on Earthly Travel. We have found most of it unnecessary and wrongheaded."

"By *God,* sir!" Animation lit his eyes for the first time. I wouldn't say he exactly smiled, but his intensity seemed all at once much more positive, much less despairing. "Tell me more about this place!" he cried. "Tell me everything!"

So I did. Between sips of Jack Daniel's—and a constant renewal of full little bottles from the full little stewardess—I told him everything. I told him of our founder, Israel Zapatero, and of his midocean visitation from Saints Crispin and Crispinian. I told him the history of those saints, and the history of Zapatero, and the history of our Order. I described our thinking on the subject of Travel, our conclusions, our postulates, our hypotheses. I described my fellow brothers, one by one, in the greatest detail.

All of this took quite a long time, and much Jack Daniel's. "It sounds like Heaven!" he cried at one point, and I answered, "It *is* Heaven!" and looking at him I saw he was in tears. Well, and so was I.

He questioned me as I went along. More detail, and more, more. And more Jack Daniel's, and more, and more. I had souvenir empties for our entire Brotherhood, and then some. I described our traditional Christmas dinner, I described our attic, I described our courtyard and our grapes and our cemetery and our chapel and our undercroft.

And finally, I described our present predicament. The bulldozers, the real estate developers, the coming Wanderings in the desert. "Oh, no!" he cried. "It must not happen!"

"All hope is gone," I told him. And then, being full of Jack Daniel's, I frowned at him, wondering if perhaps God had not sent this man at the last moment—machina ex Deus?—with that one unsuspected salvation that would make the difference.

No. I saw him shake his head, and knew that he too was mortal. "It's a crime," he said.

"Absolutely," I agreed, and took some time to struggle with the cap of the next Jack Daniels bottle. They were getting trickier for some reason.

"But you'll move somewhere else, won't you?"

"Oh, yes, of course. We won't disband."

"And you're not priests, you say. A man could walk in off the streets and be accepted among you. Like that Brother Eli you told be about, the whittler."

"Absolutely," I said again. I suddenly had discovered it to be a word I was fond of saying aloud. I did it again: "Absolutely."

Mr. Schumacher was silent for a while, and when I looked at him he was deep in thought, chewing on his lower lip. I let him do his thinking in peace, and at last he muttered (to himself, not to me), "I never see my family anyway. They'll never notice the difference."

I considered saying "absolutely," but refrained. I had not been addressed, after all, nor was I entirely certain "absolutely" was the right response to what had been said.

Mr. Schumacher continued to ponder, though without verbalizing any more of his thoughts, and I finished my last little bottle of Jack Daniel's. Looking up, hoping to catch the stewardess' eye for a refill, I saw her making her way down the aisle in my direction, pausing to say something to each passenger along the way. When she reached us she said it again: "Please fasten your seatbelts, we'll be landing in a moment."

"No more Jack Daniel's?"

She smiled at me and shook her head. "I'm sorry, Father," she said.

"Brother," I said, but she had gone on.

✝

233

I clinked as I walked. Many little Jack Daniels were stowed about my person, and they tinkled together with my movements as though I were some sort of living wind chime.

We had landed, sailing down the late afternoon sky to New York and coming at last to rest. The airplane door had opened, to reveal a corridor on the other side of it—could that corridor have flown all the way from Puerto Rico with us?—and Mr. Schumacher and I had joined the other deplaning passengers in deplaning. I was carrying my vinyl overnight bag, packed with my new razor and my new alarm clock and Brother Quillon's socks, and Mr. Schumacher was carrying a battered canvas bag festooned with zippers.

He had remained silent through our descent, and didn't speak at all until we had passed through the mysterious corridor and found ourselves in the terminal building. Then he said, "You got luggage?"

I held up the overnight bag. "This."

"No, more than that. To pick up." He gestured toward a sign saying *baggage,* with an arrow.

"Oh, no," I said. "This is all I have."

"Smart," he commented. "Travel light." Then he lowered his brows and looked thunderous and said, "If you're going to Travel at all."

"I'm not," I said. "Never again."

"Good man," he said. "Well, then, let's go."

"Go?"

He was impatient with my bewilderment. "What did you think? I'm coming with you. Travel, goodbye!"

✠

We did Travel, though, by cab, from the airport to Manhattan. And while sitting together in that back seat I tried gently to suggest that this sudden urge of his was a mere passing fancy, a transitory whim brought on by Jack Daniel's and Traveler's fatigue.

But he'd have none of it. "I know what I'm talking about," he said. "You described to me a place I've been dreaming of all my life. Do you think I *wanted* to get into this business? A grandson of Otto Schumacher, what chance did I have? Travel Travel Travel, it was pounded into me from the day I first learned to walk. A day, by the way, that I've cursed ever since."

"But your family. Haven't you a wife, children?"

"The children are grown," he told me. "My wife sees me about two days a month, when I bring her the laundry. She says, 'How was the trip,' and I say, 'Fine.' Then she says, 'Have a nice trip,' and I say, 'I will.' If she misses all of that, I can phone in my part."

"Your business?"

"Let my brothers handle it. And my cousins and my uncles. Neither of my sons would follow in my footsteps—a dreadful phrase, that—so I leave the world with a clear conscience."

"But not with a clear head," I told him. "I know *I'm* feeling the effects of all that alcohol."

"If I change my mind tomorrow," he told me, "I can always leave, can't I? You people won't chain me to a ring in the wall, will you?"

"Absolutely not!" I said, finding another use for my favorite word.

"Well, then." And he faced forward, smiling cheerfully and expectantly and—I thought—a bit madly.

✛

The building was there, where I'd left it, but its future could now be counted in days, perhaps hours. At midnight it would begin to fade, like Cinderella's coach. Mr. Schumacher, his cheek against the cab's side window, said, "Is that it?"

"That's it."

"It's beautiful."

He paid the fare and we clambered out to the sidewalk, freeing the cab to surge back into the melee. I was certainly no more drunk than when I'd left the plane, but for some reason I felt less steady on my feet, and apparently Mr. Schumacher was much the same. We leaned on one another for support, each of us grasping our luggage, and we paused for a moment on the sidewalk to gaze at the nearly featureless stone wall—the dull facade—that the monastery presented to the transient world. It was after five by now, evening was nearing, and in the fading light that stone wall seemed somehow more real, more substantial, than the glass and steel and chrome erections thrusting themselves skyward all around us. They in time would fall of themselves, but this stone wall would have to be murdered.

"It's beautiful," Mr. Schumacher said again.

"Beautiful," I agreed. "And doomed."

"Oh, it must not be," he said.

Passersby were pausing to look at us, not sure whether to frown or laugh. I said, "Why don't we go inside?"

"Absolutely," he said, having picked up my favorite word.

The door to the courtyard was locked—*there* was a case of locking the barn after the horse has gone—so we staggered instead to the scriptorium door, which was also locked. Thundering on it, however, via my fist and Mr. Schumacher's shoe, produced a startled-looking Brother Thaddeus, who gaped first at Mr. Schumacher and then at me. "Oh! Brother Benedict!"

"Brother Thaddeus," I said, stumbling on the step, "may I present Mr. Schumacher."

"Thaddeus," said Mr. Schumacher. He gripped Brother Thaddeus' hand and peered intently into his face. "The Merchant Mariner," he said, "safe at port. The sailor, home from the sea."

"Well," said Brother Thaddeus, blinking and looking bewildered. "Well, yes. That's right."

I managed to enter the building and close the door behind me. "I met him in my Travels," I explained.

"I want to join you," Mr. Schumacher told him.

"Ah," said Brother Thaddeus. "That's very nice." For some reason, I had the impression he was humoring the both of us.

I said, "Where's Brother Oliver, do you know?"

"In the chapel," he said. "They're all there, a vigil, prayers for a last-minute reprieve." Hope entered his eyes and he said, "Do you bring us good news, Brother Benedict?"

"I'm sorry," I said, and I knew I'd be seeing that crushed look another fourteen times before this day was over. "I failed," I said.

"Don't say that. You did your best," he assured me. "Of course you did your best."

"It *must* not happen," Mr. Schumacher announced. He was now glaring around at the scriptorium's woodwork, his expression an odd combination of defiance and pride of ownership.

I said, "Come along, Mr. Schumacher. We'll go see Brother Oliver."

"Precisely," he said.

We left our luggage with Brother Thaddeus and walked through the building to the chapel. Mr. Schumacher loved everything he saw along the way, from the doorframes to the Madonnae and Children. "Wonderful," he said. "Precisely."

The chapel was silent when we entered it, but not for long. Faces turned, robes and sandals rustled as the brothers rose from their pews, and at first the question was asked in whispers: "What news?" "Did you have success, Brother?" "Are we saved?"

"No," I said. "No." I shook my head, and the faces fell, and they clustered around Mr. Schumacher and me at the rear of the chapel to hear the worst.

When Brother Oliver approached I introduced Mr. Schumacher. "He wants to join us," I said, feeling very much like the small-boy-with-puppy ("He followed me home. Can I keep him?"), and added, "He's a Travel agent."

"No longer," said Mr. Schumacher. "I'll Travel no longer. I've come home, Brothers, if you'll have me. May I be one of you? May I?"

Everyone seemed a bit taken aback by Mr. Schumacher's intensity, and also, perhaps, by the fact that both Mr. Schumacher and I were staggering just slightly. I myself didn't *feel* drunk any more, but my footing and tongue were both still less than certain.

However, Brother Oliver handled the situation, I thought, very well, saying to Mr. Schumacher, "Well, certainly you can stay as long as you like. After you've been here a day or so, we can talk about your future."

"Precisely," said Mr. Schumacher. Apparently that was *his* favorite word.

Brother Flavian suddenly burst out, "But what of *our* future? Are we going to *lose*?"

"We've done our best," Brother Oliver told him, and I noticed that no one was looking directly toward me. "If it's God's will that we leave this place, then there must—"

"But it *isn't* God's will!" Flavian insisted. "It's *Dimp's* will!"

Brother Clemence said, "Flavian, there comes a time when it's pointless to rail against fate."

"Never!"

Brother Leo said, "I agree with Flavian. We should have been more determined from the outset. We should have been more belligerent."

Several Brothers responded to that, pro or con, and it looked as though some rather heated discussions were about to take place when Brother Oliver loudly said, "In the *chapel*?" Looking around, he said, "There's simply nothing else to be done, that's all. It's all over, and there's nothing to be gained by arguing among ourselves. Particularly in the chapel."

"Precisely," said Mr. Schumacher.

There was a little silence after that, with everyone looking sad or bitter and with Mr. Schumacher shaking his head as though annoyed with *himself* for not somehow rescuing us. And then I took a deep breath and said, "Once more."

They all looked at me. Brother Oliver said, "Once more what, Brother Benedict?"

"One last try," I said. "We have till midnight, this day isn't over yet. I'm going to go talk with Dan Flattery."

"Flattery?" Brother Oliver spread his hands. "What good can *that* do? We've already tried to reason with the man."

"I've had dealings with him," I said, "of a sort, in the last few days. I don't know if there's anything I can do or not, but I have to try. I have to. I'm going out there now."

Brother Flavian said, "I'm coming with you."

"No, I—"

"And me," said Brother Mallory.

"*And* me," said Brother Leo.

"And *me*," said Brother Silas.

238

Brother Clemence said, "I think it's time I saw this Flattery demon for myself."

"We'll all go," said Brother Peregrine. "Every last one of us."

Brother Oliver looked around at us in dismay. "Travel? The entire community?"

"Yes!" cried Brothers Dexter and Hilarius and Quillon.

"But—but how?" Brother Oliver seemed to reel under the complexity of it. "All of us? On the train?"

"Wait!" said Mr. Schumacher, and we turned to see him standing very upright, one finger pointing up in the air. "*I* am the hand of Fate," he announced. "What has my life prepared me for, if not this moment? Sixteen—seventeen, with myself. Transportation for seventeen, New York to— Where?"

"Sayville," I said, in a hushed voice. "Long Island."

"Sayville," he repeated. "Was that a phone I saw, where we came in?"

"Yes."

"Precisely," he said, and marched off, the rest of us in his wake.

✠

In the hall, as we moved in a cluster toward the scriptorium, Brother Quillon moved to my side and said softly, "I saved you some pie."

"*Thank* you," I said, touched and delighted. "Thank you, Brother."

"Your friend," he said, nodding ahead toward Mr. Schumacher navigating the turns of the hall, "seems a bit unusual."

"I have to tell you," I said, "he's been drinking."

Brother Hilarius, on my other side, said, "Brother Benedict, I have to tell you *you've* been drinking."

"On the airplane," I said, as though that excused it. "It was something of a depressing return."

"No doubt," he said.

Behind me, Brother Valerian said, "Brother Benedict, excuse me, but aren't you clinking?"

Clinking. "Oh, yes," I said, remembering my souvenirs. All at once, the notion of distributing empty whiskey bottles as

239

mementos of my Journey seemed a less than felicitous idea. Apt, perhaps, but not quite fitting. "It's just some bottles," I said, and from then on walked with my arms against my sides, to muffle the music.

Brother Thaddeus watched in astonishment as we all trooped into the scriptorium. While several Brothers explained to him what was going on, Mr. Schumacher went to the phone and dialed a number from memory. We stood and watched and listened, knowing we were participating in what was for us an alien rite.

Mr. Schumacher whistled softly between his teeth. He tapped his fingernails on the surface of the desk. He seemed less drunk and more efficient, and all at once he said, "Hello. This is Irwin Schumacher of Schumacher and Sons. Is Harry there?" He listened, his mouth twisting in annoyance, and then he said, "*I* know it's New Year's Eve. Do you think I can be in the business I'm in and not know when it's New Year's Eve? Let me talk to Harry." Another pause, with more tuneless whistling between his teeth, and then, "Harry? Irwin Shumacher. — Fine, and how are you? — Terrific. Listen, Harry, I need a bus. — Right now, round trip tonight, New York to Long Island. — No, sir, none of that at all, it's a religious order. — Harry, have you ever known me to have a sense of humor? — Right. It's a pickup at the monastery, Park Avenue and 51st. Going to Sayville, Long Island. — Tonight. — Precisely. Charge it to the firm, Harry. — Right. Oh, by the way, Harry, this is my last call. I'm retiring. — Yeah, I guess you could call it a New Year's resolution. I'm through with Travel, Harry — That's right, pal." Holding the phone to mouth and ear, he looked around at the rest of us and this room with a big beaming smile on his face. "I've found my home at last," he said. "So long, Harry."

SIXTEEN

I T WAS A REAL BUS, with a real driver in a real uniform. Mr. Schumacher signed some papers on the driver's clipboard, Brother Oliver gave the Flatterys' address, and we all climbed aboard for our Journey.

It was now nearly seven o'clock. In the interim, I'd washed off the Travel grime, emptied my pockets of all those little empty bottles, eaten several pieces of Brother Quillon's pie, and drunk enough coffee to make me both reasonably sober and totally jittery.

Although I suppose I would have been jittery anyway, all things considered. When I'd made my decision, back in the chapel, to try Dan Flattery one last time, I'd visualized the two of us in private confrontation and I'd thought it just possible that somewhere in our reluctant relationship I could find a handle I could grasp to turn the man around. But that intention had become lost almost at once, and now with seventeen of us on our merry way I had no idea what we hoped to do or how we hoped to do it.

We were not the only Travelers abroad tonight. Our bus flowed like a whale through schools of passenger cars, moving in endless lines along the Long Island Expressway. My fellow passengers, new to Travel (as I had been until a scant four weeks ago), gaped and gawped out the windows, not even trying to look disinterested or unimpressed. I remembered behaving the same way on that first railroad Journey, and how far had I come since then, both in miles and attitude!

This bus was very comfortable, with reclining seats and a spacious central aisle and a smooth commanding feel to the ride. The driver had a black cloth draped behind himself to eliminate distracting reflections, so we could have lights on and we could visit back and forth from one seat to another. I myself stayed in one place, next to Brother Oliver—who had beaten me to the window seat—but many of the others were apparently too keyed-up to sit still and there was a lot of milling about in the aisle as a result.

Several Brothers came by to chat with me, or with Brother Oliver. The first was Brother Mallory, who sat on the armrest of the seat across the aisle and spoke casually of this and that for a minute before coming to the point: "Brother Benedict," he said, "when we get there, would you point out this fellow Frank Flattery?"

Brother Oliver leaned past me to say, in a shocked voice, "Brother Mallory! You aren't thinking of *fighting* the man?"

"No no," Mallory said. "I just want to see him, that's all, see what he looks like."

"We're peaceful men," Brother Oliver reminded him.

"Of course," said Mallory, but somehow the glint in his eye didn't look all that peaceful to me, so I said, "Brother Mallory, it won't help us if we do a lot of brawling there."

"The farthest thought from my mind," Mallory insisted, and went away before we could lecture him further.

"Hmmmm," I said, watching his broad back move down the aisle.

Brother Oliver cleared his throat. "Father Banzolini, were he

242

here," he suggested, "might agree that a lie under the circumstances would be a very very minor sin."

"I'll fail to find Frank Flattery," I agreed.

Brother Silas came by next, perched on the same armrest, and began to talk to us casually about the Flattery household. He seemed fascinated by architectural details, the layout of the rooms and so on, and I didn't catch his drift until he asked, still casually, "You didn't see anything that looked like a wall safe, did you?"

Brother Oliver lunged forward across me again; he seemed to be spending much of this trip in my lap. "Brother Silas," he said sternly, "we do not intend to *steal* the lease."

Silas gave us that glare of outraged guilt with which he used often to face policemen, judges, wardens and other authority figures. "What do you mean, steal? They stole it from *us*. Getting it back, getting our own property back, isn't stealing."

"That's sophistry, Brother Silas," Brother Oliver told him.

"It's common sense, is what it is," Silas grumbled.

I said, "We didn't see a wall safe. Besides, they probably keep leases and things like that in a safe deposit box in some bank anyway. Most people do, don't they?"

Silas nodded, reluctantly. "Yeah," he said. "Mostly what you get in a house is personal jewelry."

Brother Oliver said, "I hope you aren't going to suggest bank robbery next."

Silas glanced at the other brothers all around us. "Not with this string," he said, and went away.

Brother Oliver frowned after him. "What did *that* mean?"

"I'm not sure," I said.

Brother Flavian was next. "I think we ought to call the media," he said.

While Brother Oliver was saying, "What?" I was saying, "I really don't think so, Brother. Reporters and cameras and things like that just don't lend themselves to reasonable discussion."

"Reasonable discussion? We're talking about *pressure*. Maybe Dwarfmann and Snopes don't mind public pressure, but Flattery has to go on living in his community."

243

Brother Oliver returned to my lap, apparently having caught up with the conversation. "Absolutely not," he said. "We are not performing penguins, we are a Monastic Order and we have to behave like it."

"Even if we lose the monastery?"

"Capering for television cameras," Brother Oliver told him, "is not going to solve anything."

"It ended the war in Vietnam," Flavian told us.

"Oh, hardly," I said.

"It sounds unlikely," Brother Oliver said. "But even if it did, ending a war is not the same as renewing a lease."

"Even if the media showed up," I said, "which is unlikely, and even if they took us seriously, which is unlikely, and even if they took our side—"

"Which is *likely!*" Flavian insisted, and shook his ever-present fist.

"Even so," I said, "our deadline is midnight tonight, and our message wouldn't *get* into the media until tomorrow at the earliest."

"It's the *threat,*" Flavian told us. "What do you think this man Flattery would do if he looked out his front window and saw his lawn full of television cameras?"

"From what I've seen of him so far," I said, "I think he'd reach for a shotgun."

Brother Oliver nodded and said, "I couldn't agree more. We know this man, Brother Flavian, and I must say he's very nearly as hot-tempered and stiff-necked as you are yourself."

"I believe in justice!"

"You certainly do," Brother Oliver said.

Flavian switched gears all at once, saying to me, "What do you intend to say to this man Flattery?"

"I have no idea," I admitted.

"Do you mind if *I* talk to him?"

That brought Brother Oliver back into my lap lickety-split. "*I* do," he said. "I absolutely forbid it."

I said, "Brother Oliver, all I ask is to talk to him first. If I fail, anybody can talk to him who wants to, as far as I'm concerned."

"Fine," said Brother Oliver.

"Fine," said Brother Flavian, and *he* went away.

Mr. Schumacher was next. A kind of dazed but beatific smile seemed to have fixed itself permanently to his face, and I couldn't help contrasting this euphoric look with that pinched cranky expression he'd worn when I'd first met him. Sitting where all the others had perched, he leaned across the aisle and spoke past me to Brother Oliver. "Abbot," he said, "when I join up with you people, do I get to pick my own name?"

"Of course," Brother Oliver said. "Just as long as it's the name of a saint. Or if it's Biblical in some other way."

"Oh, it's Biblical all right," he said.

"You know the name you want?"

"That I do." His smile turning a little sheepish, he shrugged and said, "I suppose it's the result of all those Bibles I've read over the years in all those hotel rooms, but if nobody objects I think I want to be known from now on as Brother Gideon."

✛

There was a party going on at the Flatterys' house, the only center of commotion in an otherwise darkened neighborhood. The driveway was full of parked cars and the air was full of accordion music. Light gleamed into the night from every window in the house, upstairs and down, and boisterous party noises bubbled and frothed amid the accordion chords.

"Oh, dear," said Brother Oliver, looking out the bus window.

"A party," I said.

"Why a party?" he asked plaintively. "Tonight, of all nights."

"Uh, Brother," I said. "It's New Year's Eve."

"Oh, yes."

Brother Peregrine, moving past toward the front of the bus, said, "Accordion music was one of the things that drove me away from the world in the first place."

I asked him, "What is that tune, do you know?"

"I'm afraid it's 'Danny Boy,' " he said. "In polka time." He moved on.

The driver had turned the bus in among the parked cars, had

245

pressed forward as far as he dared to go, and had now come to a stop, with a great sneezing of air brakes. Looking around the edge of his dark cloth drape, he called, "Here we are, Mr. Schumacher."

Mr. Schumacher—the potential Brother Gideon—was still seated across the aisle from me, and now he turned in my direction to say, "Well, what next?"

"We can't very well come back another time," I said, "so I guess the only thing to do is join the party."

✛

So that's what we did, and for some time nothing at all happened. Flattery must have invited all of his relatives *and* all of his friends *and* all of his neighbors *and* all of his business acquaintances *and* everybody not covered under a previous heading, and they'd all come, and the result was that sixteen robed and cowled monks (plus one semimonk in mufti) were swallowed up in the incredible crush of people like a water buffalo in quicksand, causing not the slightest ripple of excitement or even attention. And a second result was that I couldn't seem to find my host.

One of my troubles, of course, was that Dan Flattery was so thoroughly a type rather than a person, as I'd noticed when he and two of his look-alikes had emerged from that boat of his at our first meeting. Buffeted by the throng, I kept haring off in the wake of one thick neck after another, none of them turning out to belong to the man I was looking for.

Brother Mallory fought his way to my side at one point, saying, "Did you see him? The son, I mean, Frank."

"I haven't even found the father," I told him. Then, noticing how fixed his jaw and eyes looked, I said, "Brother Mallory, you promised. No pugilism."

"I just want to look at him," he said, and ducked away from me again. Worried about him, but with more urgent problems to concern me, I went back to my search.

With all of this scrambling about, I was picking up stray bits of conversation along the way, and gradually I was coming to realize that *this* was the society whose iceberg tip I'd met down

246

in Puerto Rico. All the people who had been so thoroughly character-assassinated by that group down there were now here, the parents and cousins and schoolmates, the dishonest uncles and frigid aunts and round-heeled older sisters, and of course *these* people were merrily dishing that absentee bunch down south.

All of which was well and good, but where was Dan Flattery? Not in the living room, with its buffet-style table of food surrounded by stocky patrons. Nor in any of the rooms behind it as far back as the enclosed porch where we'd all had lunch that first day I'd ever met Eileen Flattery Bone. And not in the kitchen full of liquor and drunks, not in the dining room full of hoppity dancers and the accordionist (a shriveled old man accompanied by a machine that made drum sounds), not in the line for either bathroom, not in any of the second-floor bedrooms with their beds under mounds of coats and their populations of two or three or four people in serious tête-à-tête, and finally not in the library.

Wait! In the library. I'd just given up on that room and was about to press on to the outside world—there seemed to be more partygoers doing something or other in the icy dark cold of the back yard—when I spied the man himself, leaning against his shelves of self-improvement and talking with fierce red face to two identikit replicas of himself.

How white that face went when he saw me, without losing any of its fierceness. Shock, in fact, seemed only to emphasize Dan Flattery's patriarchal air of bulldog determination. Without a word to his companions, he pushed his way through the intervening partygoers, thrust his face toward mine, and yelled, "I thought you were going to stay away from her!"

"I want to talk to you!" I yelled back. (Whatever other reason *he* may have had for yelling, it was the only way under the circumstances for either of us to make himself heard.)

"You've done e—" he started, and then blinked, looking past me, and yelled, "Who's *that*?"

I turned. "Brother Quillon," I said. "And Brother Leo." The former was deep in conversation with a pair of beaming buxom maidens, and the latter was disapprovingly browsing among the sets of Dickens.

"You brought them *with* you?" He couldn't believe it.

"We want to talk with you about the lease," I yelled, and then the first thing he'd said finally triggered itself in my head and I double-yelled, "WHAT?"

"I didn't say anything!"

"*What* did you say?"

"I didn't say *anything*!"

"*Before* that! The first thing you said to me!"

"I said—" Then he paused, and frowned at me; apparently a similar triggering event had just taken place inside his own head. "You're here to talk about the *lease*?"

"What did you mean, 'stay away from her?' I *am* away from her."

"You—" he looked at his watch. (Nothing like Dwarfmann and his skittish red numbers, this was a monstrous old turnip of a pocket watch with *roman numerals*.) "Come with me," he announced, put the turnip away, grasped my elbow in a nongentle grip, and started hacking his way through the wall of human flesh, pulling me along like a canoe behind him.

We crossed the central hall and waded into the living room, where Flattery suddenly stopped, pointed the hand that wasn't welded to me, and cried, "*More* of you?"

I followed his pointing finger and saw Brother Flavian in haranguing dialogue with half a dozen college-age youths. They all seemed to be enjoying themselves tremendously. Beyond them, Brothers Clemence and Dexter, cocktails in hand, were in civilized discourse with several ur-Flatterys.

Flattery shook my arm, crying, "How many *are* you?"

"We're all here," I told him. "Sixteen of us."

"Christ on a crutch!"

And he towed me onward, through the living room and into the dining room—Brother Peregrine was fox-trotting to *How Much Is that Doggy in the Window?* with a suspiciously-blonde blonde, while Brother Eli was managing to do the monkey to the same music with a girl who looked like all folksingers—and across the dining room to a door I already knew was locked because I'd tried it earlier in my search. Flattery, however, had a key, and without releasing my arm (my hand was beginning to suffer from lack of blood) he unlocked the door and pushed it open by shoving me into it.

An office, small and compact and horridly messy. It reminded me of field engineer's offices in mobile trailers, with its charts and blueprints and scale drawings thumbtacked over one another on the walls, its leaning stacks of flimsy papers on the desk, its looseleaf manuals crammed every which way into the narrow tall bookcase, and even its outsize air-conditioner jutting so far into the room that anybody sitting at the desk would have to lean slightly to the left at all times or else remove his head.

Flattery closed and relocked the door behind us, and now we were in privacy and comparative quiet. The rattle and roar of the party could still be heard, but at least we wouldn't have to yell at one another to be heard.

Flattery yelled anyway: "What the *hell* do you think you're up to *now*, you son of a bitch?"

"You don't have to yell," I told him. "I can hear you."

"It isn't enough," he yelled, "you steal my daughter away from me, now you want to blacken my name with my family and friends!"

"Not at all," I said. "We had no idea you were having a—"

"Well, I don't care, do you understand me? Bad-mouth me all you want, those goddam freeloaders out there bad-mouth me all the time anyway, what do I care about that?"

"Nobody wants to—"

"But when it comes to my Eileen," he said, shaking a fist close enough to my face for me to admire every orange hair and orange freckle and knee-shaped knuckle, "it's about time you started to watch yourself."

"I don't have anything to do with Eileen," I said. "We said goodbye to one another."

"That's what she told me," he said. "She called me and told me." The fist became a pointing finger. "But you didn't fulfill the deal," he said, "so don't come around as though you did. You left her to believe her own father's a two-faced liar and a crook."

"Her own father *is* a two-faced liar and a crook."

"And what about you? You break my poor girl's heart, you

leave her forever, and the same goddam day you're *back* again."

"What do you mean, back? She's in Puerto Rico."

He peered at me, as though trying to read small printing in dim light. "Are you on the level?"

"What is it?" A suspicion had entered my mind, and I very much wanted to be wrong. "She isn't *here*, is she? How could she be, she's still in Puerto Rico."

"No, she isn't here," he said, and I breathed with relief (and regret). But then he looked at his watch and said, "But she will be, in less than half an hour."

I couldn't even speak. I backed up to a chair littered with papers and books and sat down on them all and just looked up at Dan Flattery's heavy face.

The printing had become much larger and the light much better; he could read me now. "Goddam it, look at you," he said. "You *do* want to make more trouble."

"I'm back in the monastery," I said.

"And you'd damn well better stay there."

"But why's she coming here?"

"She got upset," he said. "When you left, you bastard. So she booked on the next flight out. Alfred Broyle's meeting her at Kennedy, he's probably picked her up already by now."

Alfred Broyle. Was that the future I'd left her to? "Oh, I'd better get out of here before she arrives," I said.

"You'd better get out of here now. You and all your buddies."

"With the lease," I said.

"No! Goddamit, I told you on the phone the situation I'm—"

"That's all right," I said. Suddenly stronger, suddenly sure of myself, I rose from the chair and approached him saying, "You're smart with money, you've got other businesses, you know you'll work it out. And you're going to give us the lease. Not because of Eileen or anything my friends are saying to your friends or any of that other stuff. You're going to give me the lease because it's *right* to give it to me and it would be *wrong* not to."

"Bullshit," he said.

I didn't say anything. I stood looking at him, and he stood looking at me. I had no idea if I was right or wrong, but we were down to the final moment and this was all I had left. I said nothing more because there was nothing more to say.

So Flattery had to break the silence himself, which he finally did by saying, a bit more softly than before, "You'd better get out of here. Eileen's going to show up."

"Eileen has nothing to do with this," I said, astonished to realize I was telling the truth. "It's you and me and the lease and that's *all* it is."

That made him frown. "*You*? Why you in goddam particular? What's so special about you?"

"I'm in your hair," I said.

"You can say that again."

"Anybody can cheat an anonymous group," I told him. "It's like bombing civilians, it's easy. But now it's two people, it's you and me, and we're facing each other, and you have to tell me what you're going to do."

He thought about that for a long time, while various emotions crossed his face, some of them of an apparently violent nature, others less so. Suddenly, abruptly, he turned away from me and wriggled around his desk to sit in the chair—he automatically, I noticed, tilted his head to the left. Pulling a pad of white paper toward himself he said, "I don't have the lease here, it's in my safe deposit box."

"I thought it probably was."

"I'll give you a handwritten promise now," he said, "to deliver the lease to you as soon as practical tomorrow. No, tomorrow's a holiday. Friday."

"And will you acknowledge in this letter that we have an exclusive renewal option?"

He frowned at me. "I hate you," he said.

"But you will."

"Yes, you son of a bitch, I will."

He bent his head to write, and a sudden pounding started at the door. *It's Eileen*, I thought, and my legs grew weak. Flattery, looking up in irritation from his writing, pointed the back of his pen at the door and said, "See who the hell that is."

"All right."

251

I unlocked the door and it was not Eileen but her mother, who came bustling worriedly into the room, saying "Dan, some fellow in a long robe just punched Frank."

He gave her a look of such extreme exasperation that she recoiled a step. *"What?"*

"A robe like this gen—" She gave me a closer look. "Oh, you're that Brother."

"Hello, again."

"Oh," she said, remembering even more about me, "you're *that* Brother."

"I'm afraid so," I said.

"Margaret, get the hell out of here," Flattery said. "Let Frank fight his own fights."

Giving me several bewildered and mistrustful—yet curious—glances, Mrs. Flattery retired again, I relocked the door, and Dan Flattery went on with his writing.

It didn't take him much longer, and then he extended the paper across the desk to me, saying, "I suppose you want to read it."

"I might as well," I said.

It was exactly as Flattery had described it. "Thank you," I said.

He rose from behind the desk, managing without apparent effort not to remove his right shoulder on the air-conditioner. "Let me tell you something," he said.

"Yes?"

"I don't want you to get the wrong idea about me," he said. "I didn't give you that on moral grounds. I'm a pragmatic man with responsibilities and you can go shove morals up your ass. I'm turning over the lease because I *want* that monastery standing, I want it right where it is with its wall around it and you inside it and I want it to *stay* that way. Because if I ever see you on the street I swear by that cross you carry I'll run you down."

"Um," I said.

"Good-bye," he said.

✛

It was not at all easy to turn fifteen monks and Mr. Schumacher from partygoers into Travelers again. They were all of them

252

happy right where they were. I had to explain to Brother Oliver about Eileen being on her way here, and then he added his own authority and sense of urgency to my panic, and the brown robes began at last to separate themselves from the party.

I went outside and stood by the bus, trying not to look toward the road. What would I do if a car came down that dark street, slowing to make the turn into this driveway? I should get into the bus, that's what I should do, and stay there in the dark, not even looking out the window. That's what I should do. That's what I *should* do.

The Brothers trailed out of the house, one at a time, every one of them combining reluctance to leave the party with joy at our success. The monastery was saved! Wasn't that supposed to be the point of all this?

It was for the others. "Wonderful," they told me. "Congratulations. I don't know how you did it," and things of that sort. They patted my arm, they shook my hand, they smiled at me. They loved me, and I kept looking toward the road, and no car came.

Brother Mallory came out of the house, smiling, licking a skinned knuckle. "What a night," he said. "I'll never forget you, Brother Benedict."

Brother Oliver and Mr. Schumacher came out last, arm in arm. They came smiling and beaming over to me, and Brother Oliver stood with me while Mr. Schumacher got into the bus. I looked out at the road.

Brother Oliver said, "It isn't a prison. You can leave if you want."

"I know that. I don't want. It's just— Alfred Broyle, that's all."

There was no way he could understand what I meant, so he simply patted my arm and murmured some nonsense. I said to him, "If there was any way it could work, I'd stay here right now. Any way at all. But I'm no good for her, and after a while she wouldn't be any good for me, and after we were done with one another we'd both be spoiled for *any* kind of life. I'm just sorry to be leaving her to—without things worked out for *her.*"

"But what does this mean for your vocation, Brother? Your beliefs?"

"Brother Oliver," I said, "to be honest with you I don't know

253

any more *what* I believe. I don't know if I believe in God or just in peace and quiet. All I know for sure is, whatever I believe in, it isn't out here. The only place I've ever found it is in that monastery."

The bus driver honked his horn at us. He was grumpy, having expected us all to stay until after midnight and having been found just now doing the twist in the dining room. Having honked our attention, he called out the open door to us, "You two coming or not?"

"We're coming," I said. "Come on, Brother Oliver."

✠

We were half a block from the house when a car passed us going the other way. I stood and craned my neck to watch out the bus's rear window. The car turned in at that driveway, where the party was still going on.

✠

Saturday, nine P.M. I sat in my pew in the chapel, waiting to see Father Banzolini for the first time since I'd gone away to Puerto Rico, and what a lot of sins I had to confess. I should have been rehearsing those sins in fear and contrition right now, but I wasn't; instead, I was smiling around at my familiar surroundings with relief and delight.

Home. I was home, and to stay. I wouldn't even be Traveling for the Sunday *Times* any more, having cheerfully abdicated that function to Brother Flavian. (Let *him* worry about censorship from now on!) The outside world was already receding from my mind and I was becoming again what I had always been. (Before Brothers Clemence, Silas, Thaddeus had become monks they had been lawyer, thief, mariner. Before I had become a monk, I had been a monk who didn't know he was a monk.)

The Confessional curtain rustled and out came Brother Gideon, in his stiff new robe and his soft new smile. I took his place in the dark booth, next to Father Banzolini's ear, and began belatedly to organize my thoughts. "Bless me, Father," I said, "for it's a long story."